PRAISE FOR THE NOVELS OF DEBORAH BEDFORD

WHEN YOU BELIEVE

"The joy of this contemporary novel of faith lies in Bedford's calm, competent voice. . . . This is a well-told tale."
—*Publishers Weekly*

"This story of trust and forgiveness will appeal to many, especially those who live with hidden pain."
—*CBA Marketplace*

"*When You Believe* gently explores the hearts of two women—one younger, one older—and the desperate secrets they keep hidden inside. . . . Deborah Bedford takes us on a journey inside those hurting hearts, plumbing their depths, seeking answers to questions we've all asked."
—Liz Curtis Higgs, author of *Thorn in My Heart*

"Deborah Bedford spins another stirring tale. . . . Give this one to any person who has lived in silence with secret pain."
—Patricia Hickman, author of *Fallen Angels* and *Sandpebbles*

"Faith and love gleam like twin jewels in *When You Believe*. A heartrending story of redemption and hope."
—Angela E. Hunt, author of *The Shadow Women*

"Compelling. . . . With realistic characters and problems, this finely woven tale reminds us to put our trust in the One with the real answers."
—Melody Carlson, author of *Looking for Cassandra Jane*

A MORNING LIKE THIS

"The writing is solid, the pacing steady, and the description satisfying."
—*Publishers Weekly*

"A compelling read that will appeal to readers of all kinds, but particularly of Christian books." —*Southern Pines Pilot* (NC)

"I finished *A Morning Like This* with tears in my eyes and hope in my heart. Deborah Bedford reminds us that nothing is too hard for God, no heartache is beyond the reach of His comforting, healing hand." —Deborah Raney, author of *Beneath a Southern Sky*

"Real problems . . . real faith . . . and a God who gives songs in the night. *A Morning Like This* reminds us all that we can do more than just 'grin and bear it.' We can overwhelmingly conquer."
—Stephanie Grace Whitson, author of *Heart of the Sandhills*

A ROSE BY THE DOOR

"A story of relinquishment, reconciliation, and grace . . . grabs the reader by the heart and doesn't let go."
—Debbie Macomber, author of *Ready for Love*

"A compelling page-turner and a surefire winner from Deborah Bedford." —Karen Kingsbury, author of *Sarah's Song*

If I Had You

DEBORAH BEDFORD

WARNER®
Faith

NEW YORK   BOSTON   NASHVILLE

Scriptures are taken from the HOLY BIBLE: NEW INTERNATIONAL
VERSION®. Copyright © 1973, 1978, 1984 by International Bible Society. Used by
permission of Zondervan Publishing House.
All rights reserved.

Warner Faith
Time Warner Book Group
1271 Avenue of the Americas, New York, NY 10020

The Warner Faith name and logo are registered
trademarks of Warner Books.

Printed in the United States of America

ISBN 0-7394-4463-8

To those of us who thought we could forget,

who thought that it might not really matter.

ACKNOWLEDGMENTS

I would like to thank Jack and Bonnie West and Tad and
Judy Fyock for arranging a safe writing haven when I
needed it most, Sherrie Lord for standing behind my work in
prayer and friendship, and Louise Kiessling for her beautiful
stories about her boys, her prayers, her flowers for Mollie, and
so much more.

I thank Janet Wood, OB-GYN nurse at St. John's Hospital,
for all her enthusiasm and her patient help with research. I
thank Ted Tilbury for his help with the Grumman Ag-Cat
scenes. I thank Kathryn Helmers, Agent 007, for her wisdom,
her passion, her belief, her friendship, and her faith.

Much gratitude to my talented editor and friend, Leslie
Peterson, whose guidance and partnership meant so much
during this project. A salute and laughter to Claire and Nanny,
too, for being willing to let me use the Chuck E. Cheese's
scene. The entire Warner Faith team has encouraged me in the
name of the Father and it means so much to serve the Lord
with them, side by side.

I thank my family at Jackson Hole Christian Center, and
Kate Halsey for allowing the Father's love and ministry to work

through her, in my life, and in so many others. I know that what the Father has called you to do has been frightening. Yet with every phone call you've made and every hug you've given, you are being faithful. The thankfulness I offer goes to the Father, because He orchestrated everything. This book has been written because of your obedience, Kate. Press on to take hold of that for which Christ Jesus took hold of you (Phil. 3:12)!

Finally, words of gratitude are not enough to Pam Micca, who agreed to one last reading of this manuscript to make sure everything was in its proper place. May the Father bless your life the same way that your friendship has blessed mine.

And so they argued before the king.

The king said, "This one says, 'My son is alive and your son is dead,' while that one says, 'No! Your son is dead and mine is alive.'"

Then the king said, "Bring me a sword." So they brought a sword for the king. He then gave an order: "Cut the living child in two and give half to one and half to the other."

The woman whose son was alive was filled with compassion for her son and said to the king, "Please, my lord, give her the living baby! Don't kill him!"

But the other said, "Neither I nor you shall have him. Cut him in two!"

Then the king gave his ruling: "Give the living baby to the first woman. Do not kill him; she is his mother."

1 KINGS 3:22–27

∞

A mother who is really a mother is never free.

HONORE' DE BALZAC

If I Had You

PROLOGUE

———— ⌗ ————

S he had that crawly bad feeling—the one you get when
you know you're being followed.

Seven-year-old Tansy Crabtree scuffed her way along the
sidewalk between the school-bus stop and home, sending black
pill bugs and chunks of cement skittering with her footsteps,
her backpack bouncing a pleasant rhythm against her back.

Her thoughts had been sailing off in as many directions as
the bugs and stones she sent flying with her feet. She'd been
thinking how she might get to go out and play after she finished her reading-packet worksheet. She'd been thinking how
she liked it best when her nana used these purple hair ties to
fasten the top and bottom of her braided pigtail, because then
it stayed tight and felt like thick rope. She'd been thinking how
Dennis Lund had kept slurping from the water fountain the
whole time they'd counted one-Mississippi two-Mississippi,
and they'd gotten all the way to nineteen before he stopped to
breathe.

Tansy had gotten off the bus the way she always did, her
arms swinging loose and wide with her steps, walking heavy

on her heels, slapping the pavement happily with her white-and-pink Payless sneakers. She plopped a crumpled baseball cap sideways on her head, flicked her pigtail over her shoulder, and headed toward the corner.

The bus had driven away and Erin Hamm, her best friend of years, had turned the corner on Meriweather Road four houses back.

Then, a few steps later, Tansy noticed the car and began to feel afraid. The person driving seemed to be going slow now that Tansy was alone. Tansy hurried a little, and the car sped up. She walked slower, and the car didn't pass. Out of the corner of her eye, even though she didn't dare turn and look, she could see a tire and a gray fender with rusty dents the shape of fingernail moons.

Her mouth had a taste in it like dry straw. She didn't know if she should run away or scream or hide. So she kept going forward without stopping, fighting to breathe, her book pack growing heavier each time it slapped her taut spine.

At the edge of the street, the car came so close behind her that she could hear its wheels crackling over gravel. Someone started turning down a window.

"Hello."

And, for one fearful moment, Tansy allowed herself to glance up across the seat at the man's pointed features, his scraggly brown hair, his shiny forehead. He bent over the passenger seat to look at her.

"What's your name?"

Not telling.

Up ahead, she could see that Mr. and Mrs. Lester had left their green trash barrel sitting square in the middle of the sidewalk beside their driveway. Today was trash day, and the Lesters had their bin sitting out. The lawn had just been mown; she could tell by the sweet, grassy smell, the paperlace wheel-tracks along the pavement.

"You *do* have a name, don't you?"

She didn't like the man's tangled hair pulled back in a pony-tail, his dark beard that pointed down from his chin like an arrow. His lips were very red, and wet.

He swigged some water out of a bottle. She could see the white pearl snaps on his Western cuffs. "Tansy. That's your name, isn't it? Purple Tansy, like the weed."

She missed a step.

"You are Tansy, aren't you?"

She shook her head, no. She kept going, walking straight toward the trash bin, until she reached it. She put the bin between herself and the curb and felt a moment of safety for it.

"Will you talk to me?"

Tansy twisted her wrinkled ball cap from the side to front-and-center. This time, she said it aloud. "No."

"You won't talk? But you just did."

The turn-off to her street was just ahead. A tall cedar that poked into the sky like an exclamation point marked the jut-ting corner of the pink brick house that belonged to the Simms. If she could just make it that far, she could drop every-thing and run to the back window where Lavinia Simms was always sitting this time of day, working on her crossword puzzles. Tansy knew she could make it that far for help before someone jumped out and grabbed her.

Then again, she hadn't realized there was anyone else in the car. The woman must have been leaning over or rummaging on the floor or stooping down to hide. Suddenly there she was in the frame of the open window, white-faced and large-eyed, clutching at the chrome from inside the car. Her yellow-white hair was cut in sharp, thin layers, and her violet eyes, smudged with mascara, were as big around as teacups.

"Tansy, honey. Wait a minute. I got you a present."

"I don't know who you are."

"Look here." The woman plucked something out of a blue-and-yellow bag from Wal-Mart. And up into view popped a stuffed purple bunny, loose limbed and huge, with visionless eyes that gave it a cartoonish look. The woman held it by the neck and made it move its head. "Hi, Tansy. I'm your mommy. Do you want to come with me?"

Tansy stutter-stepped, the rubber toe of her sneaker catching the pavement. Her pack slipped off her arm and thudded into the grass. She didn't even realize she'd let it go.

"Now, see. I didn't mean to make you drop that. Is it heavy? Do you get a lot of homework?"

She shook her head. *No.*

"You didn't know you had a mommy?"

That made her stop walking altogether. *Yes, but I've never seen her.*

The bunny pushed farther out the window. "Do you like this? Here. You can have it. I bought it for you."

Tansy reached out tentatively to touch one long, fuzzy paw.

"Go ahead. Take it."

Tansy pointed toward the driver. "Who's he?"

"He's Jimmy Ray. My . . . friend."

"There's a code word." Tansy eyed Jimmy Ray with distrust. "I'm not supposed to go with anybody I don't know unless they know the code word."

"Who told you that?"

4

"Nana Nora." A pause. "My grandma."

"My my. You have a very smart grandma. But it's okay, can't you see? I just want to get to know you a little better."

"Do you know the code word? It's Nana's rule."

The rabbit pulled out of Tansy's grasp, and its head started moving again. This time, the lady made it speak with a stupid, childish voice that Tansy didn't like. The stuffed animal's head moved back and forth with the voice. "Nope, I don't know the password. But that's okay, isn't it? For someone that's your mom?"

"Tess." Jimmy Ray smacked the wheel of the car. "*Mira.* Quit fooling around. Just grab the kid and let's go."

"Shut up, Jimmy," The woman said crossly. "I don't want to scare her." Then, back out the window, "Your nana hasn't showed you pictures of me, or anything?"

Tansy shook her head. *No.*

"She didn't tell you anything about me?"

She shook her head again. *No.* But this time it was a big lie. Her nana had told her *some* things about her mother. She'd answered a lot of questions, but it hadn't been anything Tansy liked or had been able to understand.

The Simmses' outdoor gaslight had a rudely twisted fork of coat-hanger wire on top of it, put there to dissuade any bird from alighting. *This is my mockingbird discourager,* Mr. Simms had announced once when he'd seen Tansy walking by and staring at it. *Just let any mockingbird try to terrorize my Sullivan.* He'd lifted his cat from the ground and made a croaking motion with his hand against his throat. But a mockingbird stood atop Mr. Simms's discourager just now, oblivious to the twisted wire it perched on, its head lifted high toward its song.

"Are you scared?"

This time, a nod. *Yes.*

"You don't have to be, you know. I wouldn't hurt you."

That didn't convince Tansy at all.

What happened next came almost too fast to understand. First, the bunny fell. It tumbled out of the window in a mad purple flurry of arms and legs and ears. It smacked against the curb, facedown.

Tansy dove to grab it. Smudge-eye Girl glanced around briefly at the same time Tansy moved. No one was watching. No one.

The car door flew open. With just one stumbling step, two, the woman raked Tansy onto the front seat. The door slammed and locked.

Jimmy Ray reached across their laps to crank up the window. Tansy stared at the dusty dashboard in terror.

"There, baby. There, baby," the large-eyed lady was crooning to Tansy. "Everything's going to be okay now, can't you see?"

"I want to go home," Tansy begged. "Please, take me home."

"Your home's gonna be with us. Me and Jimmy Ray. That'll be okay, won't it? The way it was meant to be."

Even though the lady was clutching her around the belly, Tansy squirmed until she could see into the lady's eyes. Those eyes—they were the same violet blue as her own, with brighter flecks of gold in their centers. As her heart thudded, Tansy tried hard but couldn't understand what she was seeing. She felt as if she were staring into a mirror, staring into those other eyes.

The bunny had gotten stuck in the car door. They had to tug and yank to rescue its arm. As the car started to roll forward, Tansy began to wail.

The lady named Tess didn't even take the hair ribbons out or unfasten her plait before she pulled out scissors and began to cut Tansy's hair.

Tansy's last view of her own street was of the Simmses' house . . . and she could see her backpack lying in a heap in the yard.

∽

NORA SNIPPED THE PYRACANTHA SHRUBS with her shears, hoping to end up with the shape of a turkey's tail.

Tansy ought to be home by now.

Bus must be late again.

She stepped away, surveyed her handiwork from the opposite angle, and moved in to snip-snip-*snip* when she saw Lavinia Simms strolling up along the sidewalk.

"Hallooo." Lavinia waved.

"What do you think?" Nora pointed to the shrub. "Is it even? Or do you think I ought to take some off the left side?"

Lavinia stopped and squinted through her bifocals. "Oh, heavens. Don't ask me. You ought to see what I did to Claude's hair last week."

Nora held the shears toward her.

"He wanted me to shave a little off the neckline. Now I catch him every morning, checking to see if it's growing out."

Nora pushed her bangs out of her face with a garden-gloved hand. "I'll ask Tansy when she gets home. She likes giving her opinion."

"Oh. Here you go." Lavinia held out Tansy's backpack. "That's why I came over."

"Why?"

"Thought I'd better bring this back. Tansy left it in our yard."

Nora didn't take it right away. She stared at it as if she'd never seen it before.

Lavinia gave it a little shake. "Her backpack. She forgot it on the sidewalk over there. Claude picked it up when he went out to chase off the mockingbird."

"When did she forget it, Lavinia? This morning?"

"Now he thinks that crazy mockingbird is building a nest in the mulberry tree. Can you believe it? Those birds, they've given him nothing but trouble."

"When did she leave her backpack, Lavinia? This morning?"

"Just a few minutes ago, I think. You know how kids can be. I'm sure she just laid it down, got distracted by something while she was walking home."

A mourning dove hooted in the distance. Then, with no warning, the weekly garbage truck came lurching around the corner, ready to grab trash with its gigantic green claw. Nora took the pack from Lavinia as she watched the approaching truck. "Walking home? Isn't the school bus late?"

"No. I don't think so."

"Tansy is not home yet."

"Well, I could be wrong about the bus. I didn't see it. Claude found her backpack and I just assumed."

"She'll be in trouble with Ben again if she's gone off to play with Erin. We've told her she has to check in with us before she does that." Nora took her cell phone out of her jacket and called the Hamm house. Her voice tinged with disapproval, she asked: "May I speak with Tansy? . . . Well, is Erin there?"

Then, as worry began to seep in, "How long ago did you say? . . . You haven't seen Tansy at all?" The sanitation truck roared forward, its airbrakes bringing the vehicle to a huge, squealing halt at the curb next door.

How stupid to be anxious like this.

Nora punched in the number to Stitch 'N Time, the fabric shop where she worked. "Babs? Did Tansy call over there after I left? Or did her teacher call?"

"I don't think so. But let me check around."

Nora could hear Babs Stanton's voice asking, "Anybody call for Nora?" A long, lingering silence, then muffled noises as she came back.

"Nope."

This feeling, on the edge of concern. Nora kept reminding herself of the times she hadn't needed to worry. She kept reminding herself of times when Tansy had just stopped to play in someone's yard.

With a hurried good-bye to Lavinia, she began to walk the neighborhood, checking yards, swing sets, fences. Any minute now and she'd hear shrieking children playing, dogs barking, birds rustling up out of the hedges.

How odd, the silence. How odd that the wind didn't blow. Nothing moved. She stopped, listening, wondering if this neighborhood had ever seemed so deserted before.

Across the way she could see Cubbyhole Creek doing what Texas creeks did in October, sitting orange-stagnant, floating leaves as still as moored boats on Caddo Lake. Even the mallards had gone. Nora stopped on the sidewalk corner and with small, wise eyes peered in both directions. She waited with her hand on top of her head, as if she needed to hold her thoughts in.

There can be no accounting for the passing of time. How it rushes when a person wishes it would stand still. How it stops when someone wishes it would move along.

"When did you come and tell me? How long has it been?" Nora asked Lavinia when she passed her in her own yard.

Lavinia checked her watch. "Only about ten minutes or so."

It seemed like hours.

"Nora? You want us to help you look for her? Are you that worried about this whole thing?"

"Tansy?" Nora began to walk faster. *"Tansy?"* In another place besides Texas, Nora might have gotten an echo, some sound bouncing back to prove that it had gone out at all. But in this flat grassland place where a person could see the freight trains curve off toward Oklahoma in the distance, her calls filtered to nothingness, in the same direction as the tracks. That was all the answer Lavinia needed; she ran to find Claude and call other neighbors.

Nora began to think about taking the car, lecturing herself. *Oh, I've just missed her. That's all. She's waiting at the house, wondering where I am.* And with one last false start of confidence, Nora backtracked to 125 Virginia Street, traipsed through the rooms, found them empty. Her heart began to pound when somebody banged on the front door. "Tansy Aster?" But it was only another neighbor asking, "Have you found her?"

Nora shook her head, ignoring the feeling, the adrenaline tingle in her limbs, the distant uncertainty. *She's okay. She wouldn't be missing. Of course, I ought to pray*

But that wouldn't come, either. No words. Only pounding numbness. Only the rush of impossibility through her ears.

She wasn't sure whether minutes or hours had gone by

before Ben drove up in his truck. "Ben," she called, running out into the street and stopping him, grabbing hold of the open window. "We can't find Tansy." Then the rain began, a breeze came up, wind chimes clanged from porches, and the edge of a storm moved in.

PART ONE

Tess

Eight years earlier

CHAPTER ONE

———— ⌇ ————

If Nora Crabtree had expected her life to change, it
wouldn't have been because she sent her husband to Bargain Food Basket for the groceries. That's exactly where it all
began, though. On Aisle 8 beneath the sign marked *Condi-
ments, Salad Dressings, and Sandwich Spreads,* Ben told her later,
right there beside the ranks of ketchup bottles, Spanish olives,
and pickle jars.

Nora heard Ben call her name, "Nora? *No-o-ora?*" as he
jostled in through the front door with arms full of grocery
sacks. She turned off the faucet, lifted her chin, and called, "In
the kitchen, honey!" She propped a pan in the dish drainer and
reached for a flowered dish towel to dry her hands. "Did you
remember the orange juice?"

"No."

"Oh, Ben. Juice is what we needed from the store in the first
place."

"I know that."

"Then, wh—"

She turned and saw his expression, and decided that something must have happened. She saw it in the sharp motions of his hands, his face gone as colorless as the limestone road-dust that coated everything in Gilford County. The towel stopped moving in her palms. "What is it?"

He dropped the grocery bags on the counter beside her. A cluster of carrots, lacy tops still intact, tumbled out. Two grapefruits thumped into each other and rolled in opposite directions like billiard balls. "You have to come outside."

"What's wrong?"

"Have to come outside . . ."

"But . . . Ben . . . what is it?" she asked. "What's wrong?"

Ben had left the front door open and, without another word, he propelled Nora toward it. He pulled her through the living room, past the aging lamp that cast its low, comforting light into the shadowy corner, past the cheap chest of drawers where Nora stored magazines. And, for one insane moment, as he hurried further ahead of her, she wondered with some odd, futile hope, if this was going to be like one of those absurd television commercials where the husband leads the wife to the driveway to show her some expensive sports car with a red bow.

Ivy lined the brick wall beside the door and the pyracantha obstructed the view from the porch, but she could see the entire expanse of lawn; there wasn't anything parked in the yard except for their twelve-year-old Chevrolet Lumina. Nora gripped Ben's elbow and glanced a question at him.

He only narrowed his brows in the direction of the Lumina. "She doesn't have a car anymore. She was hitchhiking. She ended up . . ." That's when Nora noticed the girl climbing out of their car. Even though she gasped, no air went into her lungs.

Nora gripped Ben with her other fist as the ground began to buck and pitch beneath her. Everything around her, everything that she had thought was steady and solid and fixed, began to spin out of control. Her mouth went dry.

Ben coughed into a curled fist, as if he were trying to steady his voice. But he couldn't do it. "It's Tess," he said, his voice catching over her name.

Tess.

"I was just shopping," he said. "Looking for those pickles you like on your hamburgers, Nora. I looked up from the basket and there she was, standing in front of me, waiting."

"Waiting for what?"

"Waiting for me to recognize her, I guess."

Nora stared. True, she was barely recognizable. This wasn't her daughter. Not this girl, who looked older than her young years, already beaten and worn down by life. Not this girl, who did not resemble in the least the little child who had once watched Ben assemble her first bicycle, who had asked with innocent blue eyes and her hands outspread as if she had just finished a magic trick, "Why didn't you read the *destructions?*"

They jumped at her voice now, both of them, when she spoke. "Well, don't get all freaked out or anything."

So, that was it? After two years of not knowing whether she was alive or dead, or whether she was still hooked on cocaine after they had forced her into rehab up in Dallas. After the day she'd tried to run away from them, and the Oklahoma Highway Patrol had picked her up near Tecumseh. And the day she'd made it as far as Bartlesville, only to spend the night in the Washington County Jail because it took hours for Ben to drive that far north to pick her up. After the six thousand dollars she'd spent, using a credit card she'd stolen from her father's top bureau drawer.

Just, *Don't get all freaked out or anything.*

Nora had always imagined what this moment would be like, with her little girl finally come home, running into her arms, holding on. *Mama,* Tess would whisper in a tone reminiscent of when she'd been three and had needed Nora to save the world. *Mama, I'm home.*

This was far different. They did not embrace, nor did they come close to each other. Nora couldn't welcome her daughter with open arms. She and Tess had been estranged too long. It hurt far too much. This strange girl yanked off a filthy bandana and shook free all that white-blonde hair that everybody from fifteen miles around would recognize.

The dirty bandana twisting, untwisting between Tess's fingers, and already it seemed that she was trying to get away from them.

"I'm not staying."

Three people moving around each other as if they were locked in a cage together. Three people, each afraid of what might be lost if they made a wrong move or said the wrong thing. The father stood tallest, closer to fifty than forty, his shoulders and jaw square, his hair going to grey, his skin ruddy from days supervising his highway crew. Beside him, his daughter's frame seemed slight and fragile, her skin as pale as candle wax, her violet-blue eyes desperate. The mother was barely the shortest of the three, with lines around her mouth and eyes, a sharp chin; her hair could be seen as blonde even though it had faded.

I should welcome her, Lord, Nora thought. *I ought to be able to forget all the times she's left us and all the times she's pushed us away and all the times she made choices that broke my heart.*

In mute disapproval, mother and daughter stared at each other. Nora finally said, her voice as dry as dust, "It's a surprise, seeing you."

"Yeah, I guess."

"Honey," Ben said again, his voice firmer now, and Nora knew that he was trying to step in and save them. "Tess, why don't you come on in the house? All those groceries I just bought at the store. There's Chips Ahoy."

"Maybe I shouldn't come in. Mom doesn't look very glad to see me."

"Don't be ridiculous." And, as he said it, Nora felt Ben's hand tighten over her shoulder. As Tess walked toward them, everything around Nora became indistinct; the lawn blurred into dabs of color. She stood, watching, ready to follow her daughter into the house, her heart as empty and impassive as sand. All the years of bleakness had left her bereft of feeling, too frightened even to hope.

"Sit down on the sofa," Ben said when they got inside. Tess turned away from them and began stalking around the family room as if she were looking to buy the place. "I'll get the cookies." And he dug out the blue Chips Ahoy bag from the other packages, tore it open so fast that the seal broke and crumbs flew everywhere.

Tess said, "I don't want anything to eat."

"Nothing to eat?" Ben stood holding the bag as if he'd been destroyed, his wide shoulders slumped. "But you were just at the grocery store." Cookies had been the only thing he had known to offer.

"I'm not hungry. That's just where I got dropped off. I was buying—" A pause. "—something else."

They stood staring at each other beside the broad couch in the family room, with the thick Texas sun seeping in through the open blinds and casting perforated shadows on the polished wood floor. "You want me to bring your duffel bag inside?" Ben asked. "It's still out in the car."

For a moment, Tess shot a glance at her father that reminded them both of the way she'd looked at him when she'd been eight, when he had been able and willing to do anything for her. But her expression hardened then, and she said, "Yeah, it's out there. But no big deal, okay? I can carry it in myself, if I decide I want to."

You wanted to get away from us, Nora ached to say. *Why have you come back now?*

"Don't you want to stay awhile, honey?" Ben asked in a pleading voice that showed he was just as doubtful of where he stood with her as Nora. "Were you here because you had other plans? Did you come to see friends instead of us?"

Tess gave them both a narrow-eyed look that was a touch uncertain. "Okay, so I came back for a day or two. It isn't such a shocking thing. Kids come home all the time."

"But you weren't even at the house. You were at the grocery store."

Nora thought, *I can't help it, Lord; I don't trust her. I don't want to be suspicious. I don't want to expect the worst, but I do.* She felt ashamed, above all. No matter how badly a mother's been hurt, she ought never to feel such horrible dislike for her own daughter. She couldn't help herself; the words just erupted out of her. "Why would you just show up like this?"

"What is it, Mom? You think I wouldn't have come if I didn't need something from you?"

Ben tried to divert them. "Nora—"

"You've spent your life trying to get away from us, Tess. I don't know why anything would be any different now."

"You think, to be here, that I have to have a reason?"

"God help me," Nora said. "But I do."

That's all she needed to say to make Ben stand up and march away. Nora stared after him, debating whether or not she ought to feel guilty for being honest. She knew he was going to bring in Tess's duffel, even though the girl had said not to bother.

Nora's heart ached for her husband. After all this time, he was still trying. She knew he was thinking, *Give her another chance. Bring her belongings inside. Anything that might make it harder for our daughter to leave us again.*

"Tess," she asked. "Are you stoned?"

A beat. "No."

Nora made a circle around Tess and headed for the groceries that needed unloading. She rifled through the bags, shoved aside bacon, and picked up the butter, already forming sweat on the carton because it was warm. The cold things would be ruined if they sat out any longer. Nora pushed the half gallon of Rocky Road into the freezer and closed the door with a pop. She placed the bottle of Tabasco in the pantry with a hard little thump. She skated the milk across a wire refrigerator shelf, taking pleasure in the hard *thrum* it made, like a pianist rolling a fist over the keys.

"Daddy," Tess said. "I think I'd like to stay someplace else. I know when I'm not welcome." And the minute she called him *Daddy* in that wounded tone, Nora felt coerced. Tess was trying to turn them against each other again, the way she'd done so many times before. It was a miracle their marriage had been able to survive their daughter.

With her bedraggled green overnight case dangling at his

side, Ben accused Nora with his eyes. He grabbed the screen and held it shut. "No, Tess. Please."

"You can't keep me here," she said with a slight, hard smile. "Not if I don't want to stay."

"But I think you do. I'll put this in the—"

He stopped. Nora knew what he'd almost said. *The guest room.* Tess didn't have a room here anymore. Nora had cleaned everything out. She had bought white lamps from Pottery Barn and had painted the walls a sterile yellow. The bed-in-a-bag linens were new and crisp.

Ben didn't finish his sentence. He followed his daughter, who knew where she was going. As Ben carried the bag, Nora saw something drop from one of the pockets. Because the wadded sack said *Bargain Food Basket*, Nora snatched it up, assuming it must be something else he'd brought home from the store. She unwrinkled it and peered inside.

"Hey, this is—"

Tess turned and saw her.

"What are you doing?" She grabbed it away. "That's mine."

Nora had seen enough to make her curious. The narrow pink box had lain sideways and Nora hadn't seen the label. She'd glimpsed *Can be used as early as*— And *This kit contains everyth*—

Just as Tess had grabbed it out of her hand, she was able to read these baffling words:

THE MOST CERTAINTY IN A TIME OF UNCERTAINTY.

Nora pressed her bottom lip with her teeth. "It fell on the floor. I was just picking it up. Why did you rip it out of my hand?"

"Because it's none of your business."

Goodness, Nora thought. *When had it gotten so hot in this house?* She fanned her T-shirt at her neck. Out the window in the side yard she could see the sun bearing down through the gaps in the high wooden fence.

What could that little box mean?

The answer to her unspoken question came suddenly, grave and warm. *She's pregnant.* It had to be; why else would Tess grab the bag that way? *Well, of course that's why she's come home. Of course, that's why. She wouldn't have come if she didn't need something from us. She needs us to help her because she's pregnant.*

They reached the guest bedroom and Tess stared. Over the months of no visitors, Nora had used the room for sewing. Yards of gingham and polyester were draped over the dresser. Both chair arms were swathed in challis, one arm green, the other one blue.

"Where did you put all my things? This isn't my room anymore," Tess demanded.

Ben set the bag on the barren bed while Tess turned all the way around. "Well, sure it is, honey. We just painted."

"Tess?" Nora asked. "It's a pregnancy test, isn't it? That's what you were buying at the store."

Tess lowered herself to the edge of the bed that wasn't hers anymore and they knew what she was going to say, even before she said it.

"What if I were pregnant?" she asked. "How would that be?"

That would be awful, Nora thought. But she didn't answer Tess's question out loud.

Tess's hands stretched over the coverlet, as if she needed all ten fingers to balance. "I was going to do the test before anyone knew I was here. But Caroline Rakes knows about it. You might as well know, too."

Caroline Rakes had been running the register at the Food Basket this afternoon when Tess had brought the box to the counter. "Hi, Tess," Caroline had said, running the little carton across the scanner as if she hadn't really looked at it, as if she had absolutely no idea what it was for. Then she handed over the small bag and gave the cash drawer a sharp little shove. "What brings you back to town?"

As if that isn't obvious, Tess had thought with a self-righteous *humph. Buying a pregnancy test; that's exactly what I'm doing. You don't even have to ask, and fifteen other people will know before tomorrow.*

Ben spoke up. "If you are pregnant . . . you know who the baby's father is, don't you?"

Tess's brown eyes filled with irony. "What does that matter? I'm going to get rid of it. You know there'd be something wrong with it anyway, if it came."

"You don't have to rush into this." Ben hefted her bag off the bed and stood it on the floor. "You can stay here for a while. Think this over before you do anything."

"There isn't anything to think about," Tess snapped.

Ben wouldn't be sidetracked. "Why would something be wrong with it? Are you still on drugs?"

The father's eyes locked onto his daughter's. Outside the window a cardinal hopped through the pyracantha and let off a string of loud, rapid whistles—*cheer cheer cheer.* Tess said only, "You know me."

Her confession was so unexpected that at first her parents thought they hadn't heard her.

"No," Nora said, her words almost inaudible. But then the emotion began low in her chest; her lungs felt as if they were weighted with stone. "We don't know you at all."

Tess met her mother's eyes head on, with pride. "I just need money to take care of it."

CHAPTER TWO

The little town where Nora Crabtree first planted her pyracantha hedges and listened to cardinals singing, the town where her daughter had been born, was called Butlers Bend. It huddled on the land about seventy miles from Fort Worth in the direction of the Oklahoma state line and about seven years behind Fort Worth when it came to the fashions in the window of Noelle's Chasing Skirts Boutique.

Or so anybody under the age of forty would tell you.

The vista was endless. The morning sun ran like a river in this place and the soil—as dark brown and rich as blackstrap molasses—curved on forever toward the vast expanse of sky. Only the proud thrust of Harlan Lane's three gleaming grain silos broke the endless view; in the distance, their downspouts angled high over the Texas and Pacific train tracks like spouts on vintage coffee percolators.

The owner at Stitch 'N Time—the fabric shop where Nora worked measuring lengths of gingham and chintz and satin, the place where she arranged bolts of cloth in rainbow displays—didn't often schedule her for Saturdays. Today, though, with Tess prowling their home, and Ben out in the grass flaying the edge of the pavement with the weed eater as if he wanted to flay Nora for not opening her heart, all Nora wanted to do was escape.

Earlier, when she'd headed toward the laundry room, a washload of Ben's dark T-shirts hugged against her chest, Tess was pacing back and forth, her hands shoved inside the pockets of her ragged denim shorts as if she were reining herself in from taking flight. Then, when Nora sat at her desk paying bills, Tess circled her, her heels dragging on the carpet, the scuffles saying, *You write checks for all those other people. You could write a check and help me.*

If Nora held any hope that she'd been wrong about her daughter, that Tess might be sorry or humbled or afraid, Tess's actions dashed those hopes. Tess never met her mother's eyes. She never settled. Instead she moved in and out of rooms, heavy footed and sour faced, like a housefly that wouldn't alight.

When Nora heard the hose running she fled outside to find Ben. "I'm going out to mail these bills," she told him, her eyes never leaving the lawn stubble that covered his shoes. "Then I'm headed over to the Stitch."

"Why would you do that? You don't work on Saturdays."

"I want to get out."

"Those bills can wait until Monday."

"I know, Ben. I'm sorry. I just . . . can't be here right now."

"Why not?"

"You know why not." Nora felt like she'd been tiptoeing around her own house for hours. "I just can't . . . I just can't *breathe* when she's around."

When Nora stepped into the shop, the air conditioner hummed out cool air. Nora caught the sharp scent of dye, crisp cotton, sewing-machine oil. Babs Stanton looked quizzically at her as Nora came behind the counter. "I had a few extra hours," Nora lied. "Thought I'd finish cutting those sales remnants before Monday. I didn't want you to get behind." Nora slid her sewing glasses onto her nose and that was that.

Once Nora finished her sorting and cutting, a surge of customers kept the cash register busy until almost suppertime. Fran Coover purchased green chintz to make into curtains. Dolores Jones brought in six shiny, stiff cards of ladybug buttons and asked for an exchange. Meg Lang sought her advice on the newest Butterick patterns. Babs Stanton regaled her with stories about Bab's recent fabric-buying trip to New York. "It's a shame you're so afraid to fly, Nora. Some year, I'd love for you to go with me."

Only when Jo Ellen Wort carried up three bolts of pastel flannel and let them topple over onto the table did Nora falter. "Three yards of each, please," Jo Ellen said as Nora narrowed her brows at the cloudlike outlines of yellow bunnies, green clowns, pink bears. "Just feel how soft these are. Perfect for baby blankets, don't you think?"

Nora unfolded, marked the three-yard measure with her thumb, brandished the shears, and began to snip. "Perfect."

"I'm going to crochet around the edges with embroidery floss. It makes such a nice finish. Like lace."

Nora felt the cloth texture through the scissor handles, through the slight vibration of blade against Formica. "Who's having the baby?"

"Paige Lee. My middle girl. Due in February."

Nora began to fold the yardage. She shook out every wrinkle, paying scrupulous attention as the flannel fell into smaller and smaller squares.

Tess, my little girl. Due in God-knows-when.

She measured out the second length of fabric and, while she cut that one, her mind began to calculate dates. Jo Ellen's daughter, with six months to go. Add another three months for Tess, perhaps.

An April or May baby.

A child born to a child.

"That's great for Paige Lee."

Nora punched the price and quantity buttons on the cash register. She crunched the paper sack closed with both fists and handed it over. She closed the cash drawer with a sharp little shove of her thumbs and said the thing they'd all been trained to recite: "Come Stitch another Time."

"Thanks, Nora."

What was beginning to horrify Nora the most about herself was that she wasn't at all disturbed by the idea of Tess getting rid of a baby. She *wanted* her to get rid of it. With the horror came memories of sermons she had heard from the pulpit. The pictures she'd seen of tiny, perfect little feet that the Gilford County Right-To-Life ran in the *Butlers Bridge Echo-Bulletin* every Wednesday. Even when she heard the word *fetus,* she cringed.

She knew as a Christian she ought to urge her daughter, *Have the baby, honey. Give it a life the way God intended.*

Only she didn't really believe that was the answer for everybody.

Did she?

I can't do this. It's too much to expect from us.

During the months after Tess had disappeared, Ben and Nora had paid for a counselor, trying to make some sense out of everything they'd lost when their sixteen-year-old daughter left them for the Dallas streets. They'd sat as straight as two clothespins in an office almost as small as a broom closet, Ben's fingers curled lightly over hers, bookends on either side of the sofa. They'd paid a detached young man with smooth skin and a smoother voice to tell them, "You mustn't think it was because you were bad parents. She's made her own choices. You mustn't blame yourselves."

Nora didn't let herself ask the questions anymore, because they hurt too much. She didn't let herself wonder what she had to make Tess run away and stay away. Had she and Ben smothered their daughter? Had they ruined her self-esteem? Had they been too strict? Too lenient?

She remembered Tess at the bathroom mirror once, styling her hair with a curling iron. "I heard you," Nora had said as the anger in their similar blue-violet eyes reflected back at each other from the glass. "I know what time you climbed back in the window."

"You can't tell me what to do, Mom," in a tone that had made Nora want to slap her.

"Yes, I can tell you what to do. I'm your mother. You are my child, my responsibility. We have to talk about this."

"There isn't anything to talk about."

"It was almost four in the morning when you came back."

"So—?"

"You don't think your dad and I have a right to be upset about that?"

"It isn't any of your business anymore."

"You're only sixteen years old. What do you mean, it isn't any of our business? As long as you live under our roof, it's our business."

Tess clamped the steaming curling iron around a handful of

hair and pulled it straight from the crown of her head, ignoring her mother.

"Your Diversion curfew is eleven o'clock. You certainly broke that last night."

"I know how to tell time, Mom."

"You don't have another chance to get it right, Tess. The officers set it up this way to keep you under control."

"I don't need anyone to keep me under control. I'm fine. Leave me alone."

"What if I called the officer and reported you? I have every right to do that. Your father and I aren't as helpless as you seem to think we are."

Nora felt heat on her wrist from the curling iron before she saw it being shoved at her like a sword. She heard Tess say, "Why would you narc on me to my Diversion officer? You're supposed to help me. Nothing I've ever done is good enough for you."

"Stop it." Nora grabbed the appliance by the barrel, trying to get it away from her arm. The pain made tears come to her eyes. "Forget it. Just forget it. I give up, Tess. I can't deal with you anymore." Nora fumbled with the faucets in shock, trying to run cold water over her smarting forearm, the sting sinking deep. But the shame she was feeling stung deeper. "Why are you always so much trouble? Nothing I've ever done will change you."

"I've tried to make you happy," Tess sobbed. "But no matter what, even when I was a little girl, nothing I ever did was good enough for you."

Nora couldn't deal with the rising sense of guilt and shame. She had tried to build a comfortable, protective wall around

31

herself and her husband. Anger and resentment had helped her do that.

And now Tess was home, bringing more trouble.

Forgive me, Father. Can't you see?

It would be better for any unwanted child not to be born than to be raised by a mother as angry and uncontrollable and dangerous as her own daughter.

෨

THAT NIGHT, as a breeze fretted with the Dutch lace curtain above their heads, Ben lay with his head imbedded in his pillow, his nose a sharp silhouette, his arms rigid against his sides.

Nora lay on her left hipbone, her pillow bunched into a knot beneath her ear, staring at the shadow that was the hollow of his throat, the heft of his chest. She watched his ribcage rise, fall, rise, fall before she touched the crook of his arm.

He moved it away from her.

"Ben," she said. "I need you."

The sheets rustled. She saw his head turn slightly. But he didn't reach for her and draw her close the way she'd expected. Instead, "I can't stop thinking about Tess."

Silence.

"She's hurting, Nora."

"I can't help the way I feel."

"This could be our chance. The thing we prayed for all those years ago."

"She's had all the chances in the world."

The darkness surrounding them. Over his head, powder-blue wallpaper dotted with cottage daisies, awash in the frail moonlight.

"Maybe she's not pregnant after all. Maybe she just thinks she is. You're being too hard."

"Am I, Ben? Am I, really, when you think about it?"

"She's our daughter."

"Don't you think I know that? Don't you think that hurts me the worst of all?"

"You could back down, Nora. You could offer to forgive her."

"And what about me?" A sharp retort, said with quiet desperation in her voice. But something Ben had to remember if he meant to stand beside her.

The mattress sagged beneath his weight. She felt him reach for her at last, the brush of his knuckles against her jaw, the rush of sensation as he cupped her skull with one rough hand. Her body responded to the simple motion much quicker than her mind. This one thing could draw them together when nothing else would, uniting them. Their marriage bed.

He said, "We could help her together."

When she closed her eyes, the pain began behind her eye sockets. Even so, she kissed her husband fervently, following his lead. "Oh, Ben," she whispered against his mouth.

"I love you," he said. And his words, though she knew they were spoken by rote, reassured her.

"I love you, too."

His arms tightened around her.

Tess. In the bedroom down the hall. Saying she didn't need them.

That thought changed everything suddenly. Locked in Ben's kiss and desperate for air, Nora felt as if she were smothering. She gave a frantic gasp and he pulled away. *No, Lord.* She felt the blood hammering in her ears and realized she could hear her own heart. *You've got to help me. He's my husband.*

33

But there wasn't anything she could do. Her panic was as sure and powerful as any swift weapon. With open eyes now, the pain behind her skull wouldn't go away. Her tongue became a wood slat in her mouth. Her shoulders flattened the pillow. *Breathe,* she told herself. *Just breathe.* Only, she couldn't.

"Nora?"

"I don't care anymore," she said, rocked by her own stiffness, tired of trying to explain it, even to herself. "I can't do this anymore."

"You've turned yourself off."

"I can't help it."

"It's like there's something of you that isn't there."

"I haven't done this to myself, Ben."

Yes, you have, beloved.

For one long, horrid silence, he stared at her. The mattress slumped as he lolled to one side, his head propped on one hand, his face looking down at her, chiseled with disapproval.

She struggled harder. "It's the best thing for Tess, too, to handle this herself."

"Is it?"

"You remember what the counselor said. It's the loving thing. Letting her face her own consequences."

"To a point."

"It's healthy for us to have our own boundaries with her."

"You could care," he said. "You could try and look at things differently."

"Ben."

"If we let her go through with this, we're letting Tess do something that she might regret for the rest of her life. You believe abortion is wrong, don't you? You would never want her to do anything like that, would you?"

"The last thing I need," she said, "is for you to heap that on my head."

She turned to rustle the sheets, to yank them across her hip as she flopped toward the wall.

CHAPTER THREE

B utlers Bend Baptist Church sat directly beside the town's
namesake, a broad leftward yaw in the road that came
about because of Miles Butler's improper Model T handling.
Stories had it that, back around the turn of the century, Miles
had been demonstrating how much easier it was to steer an
automobile than a horse. When he hit a rock and went out of
control, the cotton farmers walked away, shaking their heads.
But Miles stood up and shouted, "Why are you laughing at
me? I started this town. Of course I'm driving where the road
is supposed to go!"

This stark left-handed turn in Texoma Road, which was
otherwise a hundred-mile, straight-as-a-board drive, had been
talked about since 1911 and would not (as long as the elders of
the town had anything to say about it) ever be changed. Beside
it stood a sign that read, "This is God's Country. Don't Drive
Through It Like Hell."

The ochre frame church building was bedecked with planter
boxes overflowing with marigolds. The walk and the steps, edged
with limestone laid in 1921, now stood half hidden between

Bargain Food Basket and Milton Hubbs's used-car lot, Kick-A-Tire Trade-Ins. Like Johnson grass, the progress of Butlers Bend had sprung up to surround it. There were those who said that Kick-A-Tire had been a special blessing to the Baptists, because numbers in Sunday school had started swelling again and Hubbs's few empty spaces made a handy parking lot.

"No Money Down! No Payment Until November!" announced the windshield of a Taurus beside her when Nora turned in. She tucked her Bible and purse beneath the crook of one arm and locked her doors. Her eyes focused on the church and her steps full of purpose, Nora joined the Sunday-morning worship crowd with the desperate intent of a football quarterback who needed a first down.

She sat alone in her regular spot, tense with concentration, unruffled in appearance, her outfit as neat as a pin. The collar of her yellow summer jacket turned up jauntily at the nape of her neck and her earrings clamped onto her earlobes like two miniature gold suns. No one could have known, as she closed the tissue-thin pages of her hymnal and slid it, *thunk,* into its proper padded shelf, that she wasn't thinking about heavenly things at all.

She'd emptied the guest-bathroom trash early this morning and had found exactly what you'd expect to find in a young woman's bathroom—rosettes of toilet paper, an empty travel bottle of Pantene shampoo, an over-large wad of purple gum. At first, when the white plastic wand toppled out, she was confused. One side had a deep, round circle, the other a little square; Nora could see the vertical pink line inside the square opening. And beside that, the label read:

|		O
Pregnant		Not Pregnant

The line in the window matched perfectly.

It's really true, she'd thought. Until now, she hadn't realized how badly she'd wanted Tess to be wrong about being pregnant. As she'd dressed for church, her heart vaulted between despair and anger. *I'm not going to let her upset our lives again!* Nora decided. *There's only one way to deal with this.*

Now she balanced on the edge of the pew with her hands folded into each other as if the only thing she had to hold onto was herself. Her stockinged knees, which she kept crossed, and her skirt, which she kept tugged down, provided the perfect perch for her clasped fingers. Her lips were set in an unreadable slash of Revlon *Moulin Rouge* red.

Pregnant, the line had indicated. *Of course.*

As she stared straight at Pastor Franklin in the pulpit, not hearing a word he said, her mind was a battlefield.

I can't believe this has happened. She's made another mess for us to clean up.

It isn't the end of the world, you know. This is just another problem for me to fix.

So why do I feel like my world is falling apart?

She shouldn't have come to church. Here she sat, pretending to be in the presence of the Lord. And no one could have known that the ideas she cast off so lightly last night hung around her neck this morning like heavy pearls.

Folks said the black soil in Butlers Bend—God's gift for growing cotton and winter wheat and grain sorghum—could suck the tires off a pickup truck when it was wet just as sure as it could swallow up a man in one of its cracks when the dirt dried out. Everything that Nora wasn't, everything she knew she couldn't be, welled up within her like that black Texas clay. Nora felt riddled with cracks, dry-broken, rock-hard.

She tried to concentrate on the service. Pastor Franklin was saying, ". . . so important to make choices to do things God's way . . ."

What would they think down at the Gilford County Right-To-Life if they knew what I'm thinking of?

". . . even when it's difficult in our lives . . ."

Who cares what they think? This is my private business. I refuse to condemn myself.

". . . there are always those choices."

It's Tess's sin, not mine, she spoke to the thing that swelled and ached inside her. *Tess has done so many things wrong already, what is one more mistake going to matter?*

Later, Nora would tell herself she didn't understand what made the church stained-glass window begin to glow that moment. A cloud must have been blocking the sun and, at that moment, moved away.

The window, located directly behind the pulpit over the pastor's head, depicted Jesus Christ standing upon a mountain, his arms outstretched, offering a loaf of bread and a golden chalice. The first stained-glass window in all of North Central Texas, some said. It may even have been designed by Louis Comfort Tiffany himself. When the 1953 tornado had hit Butlers Bend full bore, every window in the church had been shattered. Every window, except for that one. Mavis Halloran still kept pictures at the Gilford County Museum of the destroyed windows beside this perfectly whole pane.

The window grew jewel blue, amber golden, ruby red, the light so strong that colors streamed in slabs onto the floor. The pastor's head shone red from the radiance of Jesus' cloak. Nora glanced at her lap and saw her fingers shining red, too.

I will have blood on my hands if I let Tess do this.

Even though it was warm in the room, Nora began to shiver. Pastor Franklin's head turned as he spoke to worshipers in the side pews. The sun spilled through the glass behind him; his silhouette stood like a pinprick against the light.

Nora felt as if she was being drawn further and further away from him. His voice droned on while her ears buzzed. The sea of heads began to stretch out in front of Nora, growing larger. The words that penetrated from the pulpit were: ". . . choosing God's way even though there may be difficult consequences on earthly terms."

Don't dwell on the past, beloved. I will carry you through this.

Nora placed a hand over the dead weight in her chest.

"Jane," she asked her neighbor in a hoarse whisper, "is anything funny about that window right now?"

"Heavens, no," Jane Ruckmann said, narrowing her eyes at it.

The church smelled of candle wax and flame, bruised carnations, someone's strong aftershave. Nora massaged her temples. She had the beginning of a headache. Pastor Franklin was still speaking monotonously, still far away.

No one really knows when life begins. It's just a cluster of cells right now.

In the choir loft the sopranos were getting antsy. Nora saw Frieda Storm touching up her lipstick, Fran Coover straightening the stole on her robe. Any minute now, their director would rise and instruct them to stand to their feet. If Nora made it out the door before the end of the hymn, she'd beat the rush of hugging. She'd beat everybody clapping backs, discussing Pete's message, and getting a group together for lunch at Leslie's Chicken Shack.

She couldn't bear to talk to anybody.

Just as she'd known it would, the choir rose and the organ began to play. Nora waited until the third verse of *I Stand Amazed in the Presence* before she collected her Bible and made her getaway. She exited the side door, thinking she'd gotten away clean. But when she rounded the corner, there stood one of Milton Hubbs's used-car customers shining her left front fender with the rear of his jeans. He bent to inspect what he could see of her dashboard.

"I got here first." He switched his frayed toothpick from one corner of his mouth to the other. "This here's a beauty. My dad's always been a Chevrolet man."

"Pardon me?"

"How many miles she got on 'er?"

"What? That's my car."

"Yeah, but how many miles?" He squinted through the window glare. "That what I think I see? Sixty-eight thousand?" He took the toothpick out of his mouth and pointed with it. "That's pretty good." He tried the handle on the Lumina and found it locked. "Got any idea what Hubbs wants for 'er?"

"Excuse me." Nora slipped right in front of him and used her key, smooth as butter. "No, I don't." She bumped into him while she climbed into the driver's seat. The upholstery was hot as Hades. She bit her lower lip as the seat seared the underside of her legs. She ignored that, though, and hit the ignition. "This is not for sale."

CHAPTER FOUR

———— ✑ ————

M ost people who knew about kicking cocaine said the craving only got worse. Tess lay in the crisp bed that had never belonged to her, the guestroom blanket wadded against her jaw as her need for a hit grew into a physical pain.

Of course, she'd brought her stash with her. A lid or two of pot and enough coke to keep her going. But that had run out over two days ago; she'd never intended to be here this long.

The slant of the sun through the blinds told Tess it must be late in the day. When she wasn't craving, she wanted to sleep. Underneath everything else, her stomach roiled. She felt like throwing up. She thought, *Maybe it's not because of withdrawal that I feel this way. Maybe it's because of—*

She tried to stop herself. She didn't want to think about this part.

—the baby.

And then the great, crippling, pulsing need started all over again.

Even though she'd buried her head beneath the sheet, light burned her eyes. Her ears throbbed. She lurched from the bed, yanked shut the blinds, and scrabbled through the pack on the floor. She shoved aside clothing, a hairbrush, a square of rolling papers. Maybe she'd brought more blast with her than she'd thought. But nothing. Wishful thinking. She raked the plastic bottom with her fingers two, three times before she gave up.

She couldn't bear the sound of her mother's sewing machine in the next room. "Couldn't you just—?" she called in a fierce voice, her heart roaring in her ears. And then she submitted, nauseated again.

I just want to go. I just want to get out of here.

She slammed open her door, ran for the bathroom. For a long time as she clamped herself around the toilet bowl and retched, she could hear the Singer speeding up, slowing down. Her hair stuck to her neck with the sweat.

Tess felt incapable and dirty. She hugged herself with her shaking arms and the thrumming bursts of her mother's sewing surging forward, holding back, surging forward, seemed to take her where she'd never wanted to go. The cold on the tile floor soaked through her pajama shorts.

She didn't hear the sewing machine stop. Her mother called, "Tess?"

Silence. Just staring at the tile on the bathroom counter, remembering when she'd barely been tall enough to prop her chin there.

"Tess?"

"I heard you the first time."

"Are you okay?"

She grunted some incomprehensible answer.

"Do you need something to eat?"

"No." Then, "I-I couldn't eat anything."

"You've got the door locked. Tess, are you sick?"

"Yes."

"Do you need help in there?"

"No."

Their words to each other sounded as brittle and crisp as a hornet's nest.

"I just keep thinking—" came her mother's voice.

Mom, Tess wanted to say sarcastically as she clenched her teeth, *thinking is so hard. Don't hurt yourself.*

It was the last thing her mother said for a very long time. The house went quiet. Tess's left arm had gone to sleep. Her hands were so cold. There were times she thought she might have moaned, only she wasn't certain she heard herself. Her ears felt disconnected from her head.

Tess had no idea how much time had passed before she unfolded her stiff legs, pulled herself up, and turned on the shower. In the middle of August the air was breathless with record-breaking heat, and yet she felt so cold that she ran hot water until the room filled with steam. She let the water pound her head, her shoulders, and her belly until the water heater began to run low. Still shivering, she turned off the faucet, stepped out of the shower, and wrapped herself into two thick towels. She closed her eyes, smelled the laundry-fragrance of the terrycloth, and would have thought it nice if she hadn't felt so bad.

There was another knock at the bathroom door. "You took a shower, didn't you? You can borrow one of my robes. If you'll unlock the door, I'll hand it to you."

Tess wanted warm wrapped around her so badly that she opened the door. "Your father and I want to talk to you when you come out," Nora said.

Tess took the robe from her mother, then closed the door and locked it again.

❧

SHE FOUND HER PARENTS sitting stiffly on the sofa, side by side. When she saw them waiting for her that way, she knew exactly what it meant. "You aren't going to help me, are you?" she accused.

Tess's father did all the talking. "It depends," he said.

"On what?"

"You can't raise a baby, Tess," he told her, "not with the life you lead."

"I know that, Dad."

"It isn't our responsibility to fix your mistakes, Tess."

"I know that, too."

"My only responsibility is to tell you what I think is right."

"So." She stood before them, crossed her arms over breasts that had begun to ache. "Tell away."

"You can stay here until you give birth and put the baby up for adoption," her father said. "We will help you any way we can if you agree to do this. It's the right thing to do."

"I don't want to have this baby. I want an abortion."

"We will not help you financially or any other way to get an abortion," he said.

Tess glanced pointedly from her mother to her father, then back to her mother again. For a long time, she stared at her mother. Then she rubbed the underside of her wrist with her fingers and issued this challenge. "Mom, you don't agree with Daddy. I can see it."

Her mother started. "Don't."

Tess stood twenty seconds or so, her arms wrapped around her own ribcage, considering something. "That's what you want, isn't it?" She saw her mother go pale. "For this baby to go away?"

"Tess, listen—"

"Daddy, Mom feels the same as I do. She wants me to get an abortion."

"You don't know what I'm thinking." Oh, but she did. By the darkening of Nora's eyes, Tess could tell her mother was lying. "Don't you dare speak for me."

"I don't want to have a baby. If I have a baby, a person related to me would exist somewhere. Someone I would have to wonder about. Someone I would have to think of."

"Right now, in this town, *right now,*" her father argued, "I'll bet there are houses with a room all ready, decorated into a nursery. These are solid homes, with fenced-in yards and two parents. Good for a baby."

"I just want this to be over," Tess said. "I just want it to end."

She leveled her eyes on her mother's face. She had struck a nerve when she changed her tack; she could see it.

"I know you want it to end, too. I know you don't want me here." She had some distant view of her mother shifting her weight on the sofa. Tess thought with pleasure, *Good.* Because a long time ago in this family, it had become the thing to do, to wound each other. Then, in the midst of her insight came something so overpowering, so true, that it burst from her mouth before she could prevent it.

"I'm afraid to have a baby."

Not afraid of stealing CDs from Walgreen's that she could sell, or shoplifting underwear or fried chicken; not afraid of sleeping in a house where the Ambrose Deuce gang threatened to break down walls and shoot them if Cootie dealt anywhere close to Kiest Park. But this she recognized breathlessly: "I'm scared to have a baby because I might love it."

Those words hung in the air, shocking. Tess's ears began to clamor again. But before she had time to consider what such a statement meant, her father interrupted her. "Somebody else out there loves your child right now. Somebody's arms are aching. Somebody who doesn't know where it's coming from, and yet already cares for it."

"It's always been this way, don't you see, Daddy? All those times you tried to make me accept help from you. Now that I really need something, you aren't going to give it to me."

"Listen to yourself."

"It's always the way *you* want to help, never the way I need to *be* helped. Everything from you comes with strings attached."

Tess stopped, fists clenched at her sides, her eyes flashing defiance. She waited to see what they would throw at her next.

Only they didn't say a word.

Her parents sat elbow to elbow on the sofa, their knees aligned. Her mother did not rise from her seat in tears or fling accusations at her. Her father did not begin another tirade about babies and the thousands of strangers who wanted them.

"Well?" she asked, baiting them. "Well?"

They only gave her one answer, and she didn't know what it meant.

She saw her mother place fingers over her father's hand.

∽

NORA WAS NOT going to let this divide her and Ben. "I want to stop talking about this, Tess," she told her daughter firmly. "I want you to just stop."

"What?"

"I want you to listen to me."

"I'm sick of listening."

Late Sunday-afternoon sounds filled the neighborhood outside, sparrows roosting and warbling in the side-yard tree, a neighbor parking his speed boat after a trip to Lake Texoma. Tess watched her mother's eyes close, as if in prayer. Then, in warm certainty, the words came. "You need to hear me—" There was no indictment in Nora's voice, only a tone as gentle as the rustling of the birds in the trees outside. "—telling you that you are right."

Tess's fists, which had been clenched in bitterness, opened at her hips. She straightened her shoulders as if she were bearing the weight of Nora's words.

To her daughter Nora offered the one thing she would never have expected. "You're right about me."

Tess's chin jerked up. "What?"

"You heard me."

Tess took one step forward. "What am I right about?"

"The way I feel. The conflicts I have. Seeing you here. Thinking it's impossible to start over."

Tess stared at the ground, tracing a seam in the linoleum with one big toe. Ben shifted his weight awkwardly from one hip to another. Not one of them knew what was going to come next.

Then, "I am choosing to stand beside your father in what he thinks is right."

"I see."

"You are right. I want you to have an abortion. But that would be wrong."

Tess's chin jerked up in disbelief. She stared at her mother with piercing blue eyes. "How can you tell me to do something that you don't even want me to do? Why are you making this decision based on what *you* think is right? What about me? What about how this will affect me? How I feel? What I need?"

"Tess, it's like I just said. I am *choosing* to do what is right," Nora said with a sudden, tremulous smile. "And I was wrong; I am not doing this to stand by your father. I'm choosing to stand on what's right because it is what God wants me to do."

CHAPTER FIVE

T ess zipped her jeans with trembling fingers.

Well, of course they wouldn't do it.

Although the sick had subsided, her head felt like it was going to detonate. She tugged her white tank top over her head and worked it down around her middle. When she smoothed the shirt over her stomach, her hands paused a beat there, feeling the blood pulse in her fingers, the warmth of her own skin. She had to try hard to imagine anything besides herself being there. Cootie's baby, beneath her own flesh.

Down the hallway, the sewing machine had started surging again. Tess knew perfectly well what that meant. Her mother used the sewing machine to hide behind. When her mother didn't want more discussion, she shut the study door behind her, snapped down the presser foot, and let the thread fly.

Tess had watched her mother stitch her way through enough craft-bazaar orange dog bandanas to festoon every hunting dog in Gilford County, a quilt to be auctioned for a new lighted bike path across Texoma Road, and seven fleece jackets for elderly friends who complained that someone kept the air conditioner too cold in the senior center.

Tess peered both directions in the hallway, wanting to avoid her father.

I never needed them anyway.

Satisfied that she wouldn't be seen, Tess pitched the few items she'd brought with her into her duffel bag. She zipped the bag and velcroed both handles together in one determined motion. Only then did she stop and peer out the window for a moment, as if something she could see there would give her guidance. A fly's wings beat a sharp sizzle against the glass. The limb of the maple tree stretched toward her like a partner beckoning her to dance.

Her mother probably kept her jewelry in the dresser.

Tess checked the hallway again. The coast was still clear. Maybe there wasn't anything worth pawning in her mother's collection. Or maybe there was. She walked to her parents' room and soundlessly slid open her mother's top drawer.

It was all here, everything she remembered, in a dusty red velvet tray that smelled of Estée Lauder *Youth Dew* and powder. Tess did not rifle through the tray like someone who had never seen these pieces before. Instead she lifted one gold-link chain with ginger fingers and examined the three items beneath it— a brooch with blue stones, a pair of pearl earrings, her mother's diamond Hamilton watch.

Tess remembered stories about the watch. Her dad had given it to her mother in the hospital the day Tess had been born. It must be worth something. Her mom didn't wear it often because she was afraid she might lose it.

Tess shoved the watch into her pocket. She thought a minute before she pocketed the pearl earrings and the neckace, too. Then she returned to the room where she'd been sleeping and made her final plan. Her parents' car keys would be hanging on the brass hanger beside the cupboard.

Oh, she knew her father well enough! He wouldn't like to report to the Butlers Bend law that his daughter had stolen his car. She'd have plenty of time to ditch the Lumina before he ever phoned the police.

Leaving her bed unmade, Tess thrust the jewelry inside her bag. The sewing machine ebbed for a moment and she straightened with fear. Out the window toward the side yard, she heard her father comparing lawn fertilizer with Claude Simms. In the other room, her mother began stitching again. Tess shouldered her bag, strolled with purpose toward the family room, and swiped the keys.

The heat burned her cheeks when she stepped into the sun. Though she tried to go silently, her sandals slapped the pavement. One step. Two. Three. She wouldn't look back, and she wouldn't look forward. She unlocked the Lumina and pitched in her bag. She meant to put the car in gear but started the windshield wipers instead. While she fumbled to find the gearshift, she glanced at the door, expecting to see her mother come running out, trying to stop her.

But her mother didn't do any such thing. The black rectangle of porch stood empty, a gaping wound. As Tess eased the car out of the driveway, her arms leaden from the irreversibility of her action, a ragged breath burst from her chest.

I'll pawn this stuff and pay for my own abortion.

I'll get myself a line in Dallas, and everything will be okay.

She swiped her face with the back of her hand and realized she was crying. She didn't accelerate until she passed the third driveway down the street.

~

WHEN A PERSON is in an empty house, the air settles. Quiet seeps in and the house sings a familiar noise. Nora glanced up from sewing the zigzag hem, listened for a moment, and knew she was alone.

"Tess?" Nora could hear the refrigerator humming. The clock beside the study door ticked evenly, the second hand springing forward with each new beat. "Ben?"

Nora heard a door slam. The blue denim she'd been working on pooled on the floor when Nora stood to check the window. If Ben was going off somewhere, he hadn't told her.

Light flashed across the front seat as someone reached for the gearshift handle. She yanked off her sewing glasses, which she always used for close work. Nora recognized her daughter's silhouette in the car.

Tess.

Nora raced to the guestroom and threw open the door to make sure. She took stock of the empty room, the bed linens in a heap, the indentation on the chair where Tess's bag had been. Even though she already knew, she shoved the tumble of sheets aside and found the bed empty.

"Tess, wait!" Nora headed toward the front of the house. "Don't—"

Nora had gotten as far as the entryway and had grabbed the door handle before something stopped her. She stood alone, her chest heaving, not knowing whether to feel relief or despair. She had been getting used to the idea that Tess might stay.

This is what I wanted, isn't it? For everything to go away?

As pebbles crackled beneath tires and the Lumina left the driveway, Nora called out, "Ben, Tess is stealing the car!" In spite of the Texas heat, the glass window where she laid her forehead felt like ice. She wouldn't go after her daughter.

I'm a failure as a mother, Lord. I'm so tired.

∽

Tess didn't cast a backward glance as she drove away. She kept her eyes forward, did not notice the yeasty sweet smell when she passed Congdon's Bakery or the late-afternoon laughter and splashes coming from the turquoise-tiled city pool. She kept her eye on the road, one hand on the steering wheel, the other tap-tap-tapping her jeans with nerves.

The white dashes on Texoma Road came at her in succession. When the car rounded the curve that had become the town's namesake, she was driving fast. Three gold caution lights loomed in the front windshield.

Tess accelerated into the turn, letting the sensation of speed drown out her frustration. Only she hadn't counted on these stones in the road. She felt the car lose traction on the gravel and, as she stepped on the brakes, she already knew she'd made the wrong choice. In slow motion, the car veered and began to skid.

It was odd how the loose coins in the front console went flying, the CD holder fell off the visor, the glove compartment gaped open, and all Tess could hear was silence. The seatbelt cinched her belly as she slammed forward. The Lumina fishtailed into the oncoming lane and then spun off the edge of the shoulder. Dust billowed in a blinding cloud as the car jerked to a stop.

Tess scrubbed grit from her eyes with the back of a shaking fist. She had almost lost it. *Now that was a stupid thing to do.*

She had to drive off like nothing had happened. That was the only way to keep someone from pulling off to check if she'd been hurt. She reversed and steered the dusty Chevrolet onto the blacktop again. In frustration, she threw a little more tire dust. *Good-bye, Butlers Bend! Good-bye to everything.*

But by the time she'd made it through one stoplight and had almost run the second, she realized her hands were still trembling. She couldn't focus on Texoma Road. The skid had frightened her more than she'd thought it had.

Tess turned into the first available driveway and found herself in the parking lot of the Gilford County Library. She let the engine idle and took deep breaths, trying to compose herself.

In the broad lawn that skirted the building, an eighty-year-old windmill turned in the wind, the last vestiges of Miles Butler's cattle land that had long since been deeded to the county. Each time the blades made their rattling circle, water arced into a trough that had been transformed into the community fountain. A carved granite stone at the base of the windmill declared, *"A great part of the information I have was acquired by looking something up and finding something else along the way."—Franklin P. Adams.*

Tess had planned to stop only until her nerves settled and her wave of nausea subsided. She couldn't leave the engine running. She needed every iota of the fuel in the tank to get to Dallas. But the car became an oven the minute she turned off the engine. The library would be cool and quiet; she wouldn't stay long. Tess held the stolen keys between two fingers for an instant before she tucked them inside her pocket and hopped out. For a moment she wavered, weak in the heat. She held onto the side of the car and steadied herself. When she opened the broad glass door, blessed air conditioning drew her inside.

Her eyes took precious seconds to adjust to the florescent lighting after being in the sun. She stood in the foyer squinting, smelling book glue and old paper, before she ducked behind a row of geography and history books. She rested her palms against the tattered spines and willed her pulse to slow. Not until someone removed a volume from the shelving behind hers, leaving a hole for her to peep through, did she give a start.

It couldn't be Creede Franklin sitting at the conference table over there, could it? After all these years, he still looked the same. Tess shifted to the biography and travel section for a better view.

There could be no mistaking him with his wide shoulders and his leather flight jacket and his sandy curls cropped close around his ears. If she had any doubts, those were erased when he glanced up with his familiar brown eyes.

She darted behind the stacks so he wouldn't see her, felt her pulse start to pound again.

The preacher's son.

Tess didn't recognize the man sitting across the table from Creede. This uniformed gentleman had only slightly more hair than a bowling ball, buzzed close in the way that made you want to rub against the grain and say something funny. He couldn't have been much older than Creede himself, yet he looked so official with a laptop computer and a stack of forms to be filled out waiting in front of him.

"Any injuries?" he was asking Creede. "Any medication?" And when Creede shook his head no, the stranger's fingers tapped the keyboard in sharp jolts.

"Any history of medical problems?"

Creede shook his head again.

Tess moved a little closer, trying to figure out why they'd be talking about such things. From the *General Works* shelf, she picked up the latest edition of the *Echo-Bulletin* and shook it open, just looking for something to hide behind. As luck would have it, the paper opened to the classifieds—the *Personals* section. "A loving choice." "Free confidential support services." "A gift that keeps on giving." "Help a child for a lifetime."

She folded that particular classified section into fourths, eighths, until it was very small. She shoved it toward the rear of the shelf.

"Have you ever had asthma?"

Creede said, "When I was a little kid, once."

"When was that?"

"On a Cub Scouts camping trip. I was running through stinging nettle and I fell and I—"

"If you say you've had asthma, they won't take you. And it's been so long ago."

"Really?"

The recruiter nodded, his fingers poised expectantly over the keys.

"They wouldn't take me in the Air Force just because of that?"

A nod.

Creede, leaving Butlers Bend? Joining the Air Force? He'd never told her he was thinking of that.

Tess remembered how, when other Butlers Bend boys raced along Texoma Road, squealing their brakes around the midtown curve marked by caution lights, Creede Franklin had taken his daring to the sky. While other kids learned to parallel park between orange cones in the high school parking lot, Creede managed to perform a ground loop. When everyone else had been learning how to speed up and merge onto the highway, Creede had been learning how to pull up short so the green-and-yellow Grumman wouldn't hopscotch into his grandfather's cotton field.

The high school girls had all gone mad for him then. On any given afternoon, three or four of them would be waiting out by the farm-to-market road, giggling and twittering, trying to convince him to give them rides in that old plane.

Only it hadn't been like that for Tess. Oh, no.

Tess had been in love with Creede Franklin since the second-grade Christmas pageant.

Every year at Butlers Bend Baptist, Creede played Joseph because he was the pastor's son. Beautiful, blonde Paige Lee Wort always nabbed the role of Mary. And Tess, who often fought against going to Sunday school because she didn't like wearing itchy tights, ended up being an extra sheep because she wasn't in attendance when Mrs. Storm doled out halos and assigned the angel parts.

That Sunday before Christmas, the telephone rang just as Tess and her mother headed out the door. When her mother answered it, Mrs. Storm began talking so loud Tess could hear every word. "Oh, thank heavens you're still home. Nora, can we borrow Tess's doll to be Jesus? Paige Lee brought hers this morning and, well . . . it's a Cabbage Patch doll. I *like* Cabbage Patch dolls, mind you, but somehow it just doesn't seem right, that big round plastic head with that little tuft of yarn. It just doesn't seem like Jesus. I was hoping to find something more *traditional*."

Even though her father didn't attend church, he watched their time schedule. He was always proud of her mom for doing the right thing. He pointed at his watch. "Nora, you're going to be late."

Her mother covered the mouthpiece with her hand. "Tess? Can you run and find Pink Baby? Do you know where she is?"

Tess nodded. "She's in my toy box. Right on top."

"Go grab her. They want us to bring her along. They want her to be Jesus."

Even though Tess stood in the periphery that day, with her sheep costume tight enough around her belly that it gave her a stomachache and the black velvet ears on her furry hood folding forward when they were supposed to hang to the side, the pageant felt better than it had ever felt before. Something of Tess had been placed in front today, highlighted in center stage. Phoebe Rakes stepped forward to say her only line, "Do not be afraid. I bring you good news of great joy that shall be for all the people. Today in the town of David a Savior has been born to you; he is Christ the Lord. This will be a sign to you: You will find a baby wrapped in cloths and lying in a manger."

Tess couldn't stand still any longer. The baby in cloths, lying in the manger, was *hers*.

She stepped out, jostling the wings of several angels, and making Daniel Staves, the camel, move aside. She climbed over two strategically placed bales of hay and worked her way past Maddy Fox, who wore her mother's satin robe and carried a polished wooden box so she looked rich and smart, like one of the wise men. Just as Adam Davis released the rope from the choir loft and lowered the gold spray-painted star, Paige Lee grabbed her by the wrist and said with a violent whisper,

"What do you think you're doing, Tess Crab-Apple-Tree?" Paige Lee elbowed her away. "Sheep aren't supposed to come this close."

Creede Franklin was two years older; he had no reason to even know who she was. Just by looking at him, you could tell who he belonged to. All that golden curly hair, and the long nose, and great elbows that jutted out like the handles of fence-cutters. And suddenly he reached out his hand and drew her forward. "She can be up here if she wants to."

"This isn't what it's supposed to look like!" Paige Lee hissed through clenched teeth.

"How do you know what it was supposed to look like, Paige Lee?" he shot back.

At that moment, Laura Clark said her line, "And all who heard it were amazed at what the shepherds said to them. But Mary treasured up all these things and pondered them in her heart." On cue, the three of them leaned over and peered into the manger, into the face of Pink Baby, Mary (Paige Lee) and Joseph (Creede), with Tess between them. Even though she wore sheep's clothing as thick as a bathmat, Tess had felt Paige Lee and Creede crowding against her. If Creede hadn't been standing up for her, shielding her with his arms, Paige Lee would have crowded her all the way out.

Seven years later, Creede Franklin was the first boy she ever kissed, the one who sat hip-to-hip with her on the front steps of Butlers Bend Baptist after evening service and pointed out the stars that made Pegasus and Orion, the perfect line of Orion's belt, the upside down neck of the horse, the bright point of Orion's long sword. Even now, remembering what it felt like to follow the sight of Creede's gesture toward the sky, her cheek resting against the rough cloth of his sleeve, brought a longing to her heart.

The Air Force recruiter in the library was asking him, "Why don't you go ahead and answer the question, Creede. Have you ever had asthma?"

"Nope."

The recruiter typed that, squinted and double-checked the screen. "That ought to work."

Tess started to step forward. But when Creede spoke again, she stopped. "What are the chances of me getting Carswell after boot camp? Any idea?"

"You're not color-blind, are you? They won't take you if you're color-blind."

"No. I'm not."

"Any broken teeth? Crowns? That sort of thing?"

Creede opened his mouth to show his teeth, pulling his lips away from his gums. He might as well have been showing horse teeth instead of his own. He pointed. "*Righ ere.*"

"Can't guarantee whether you'll get Carswell. Can't guarantee whether you'll get Ramstein or the North Pole. Or New Jersey. There's always that possibility, too."

Tess just stood there, her hand resting on the ancient copies of *Texas Highways* and *Texas Monthly*. She didn't know whether this yearning she felt was the deep need to be high again, or for something she'd left behind and couldn't go back to.

"Can I ask you why you've decided to sign up with us? Why you've waited three years since you graduated from high school to proceed with your future?"

With his pointer finger, Creede explored the cusps of three more molars before he clasped knuckles together on the tabletop.

"I don't feel like I've missed out on anything, if that's what you mean. I fly my dad's Grumman."

"One of those old Ag-Cats. Great little planes. I went up in a Kaydet once."

"I've seen those."

"Friend rebuilt it. His grandfather bought it at a surplus store for $250 right after the war."

"I'd like a shot at flying the big birds."

"That's why I did it, too."

"I'll come back eventually. With more of my own identity, I think. More of my own faith."

"That's honorable."

"Reason I asked about Carswell is that I'm getting married. We've talked about all this, and my girl would like to know where we'll end up."

The recruiter grinned. "She's going to end up alone, that's where she'll end up. Other than when you're off on leave. Then you'll be together."

What felt like fine slivers of metal prickled inside Tess's ears. Creede was getting married?

"Give me the girl's name. I'll put it in the record, let them know you're going to have someone to come home to."

"Her name's Candice Murfree."

And so the consonants and vowels were entered into the document, each letter one succinct punch. C. A. N. D. I. C. E. Space. M. U. R. F. R. E. E.

"And how did that incident occur to your upper left bicuspid? Do you remember?"

"I was on a Cub Scouts camping trip." A long drawn-out explanation about falling over a downed pecan limb and being trampled by a stampede of other cub scouts. While Tess thought, *Candice. Candice. I don't know any Candice.*

Tess started thinking about what it would be like to be marrying Creede. She thought about Cootie, how he'd said, "You aren't coming back here as long as you think you're pregnant. I don't want to hear anything about that."

"Any distinguishing body markings?" the recruiter asked him. "We need to know that, too."

"What?"

"This is the last question, I promise. No more. I need distinguishing markings."

"You mean, like scars? Birthmarks?"

"Or tattoos. Do you have any of those?"

The last question was the first one to make Creede balk. "Why do you need to know that?"

"You know. In case something should happen. To *identify* you."

"Oh. I see." Creede stared at the light fixture high overhead. He examined his thumbnail from three different angles. He rubbed a pencil marking off the table with his pointer finger. Then he met the recruiter's gaze. "Well, yes. I do."

"Where? What are they?"

"A birthmark on my left hip. A large mole."

"What shape?"

"Round."

"Protruding?"

"Yes."

"Dark? Or light?"

"Light."

He typed that into the computer.

"And I have a tattoo."

"Describe it, please. And describe its location."

"My father wouldn't want anyone to know."

"That's all right, Creede. This is between you and me. Strictly confidential."

"It's this design. Here." To indicate its position on the outside of his thin T-shirt, he placed his big farm-worn hand over his heart. There they sat, in the middle of the Gilford County Library, and Creede began to roll up the shirt.

"Hm-mmm." The recruiter smiled slightly and tilted his shorn head. "I hadn't expected anything like that."

"Well, here it is."

The thing was beautiful—if tattoos could be beautiful—and much larger than anyone would expect. Two intertwined, interlocking knots, woven into each other with a number of carefully drawn strands. In the small center of the knots stood four filigree letters, intricate and interlacing.

T and E and S and S.

"You know how it is with tattoos," Creede said. "I got this a long time ago."

But it was too late for Tess to hear that part of the story. The queasiness took over again and conquered her. She had just enough time to think, *This is what it feels like to faint. This is fainting. I'm fainting.*

At the slight sound she made, Creede glanced in the direction of the periodicals. "Tess." He yanked his shirt down. "What are you doing here?"

Her ears buzzed and the room spun. She heard him, but couldn't answer. The pile of magazines flittered like birds onto the library carpet when she fell. And Tess lay on the floor, as curved and helpless as the letters she'd seen spell her name.

CHAPTER SIX

Tess felt arms lifting her up, heard voices murmuring around her. Someone touched a cloth to her forehead. It felt cool. Someone was easing something off her arm.

"Can I get you to take your coat off for me?"

"I don't—" She didn't remember wearing a coat. But then she remembered she'd been leaving her parents' house, carrying everything. She'd shoved her arms into her jacket on the way out the door.

"The blood-pressure cuff is going on. It could get a little tight."

"I'm fine. I don't need—" She felt alone and disoriented. She didn't know what she'd been about to say. She heard the hum, felt the cuff constricting her bicep. Her blood rose within her, pulsed against it.

"Do you feel pain? On a scale of one to ten, can you tell me if you feel pain?"

She shook her head. Her cheek scraped against the carpet. They began to talk louder, as if she couldn't hear. "The same scale, one to ten. How is the pain in your head?"

"No, I—"

Creede. Where was Creede?

Mrs. Paris Bramlit, who had been the librarian so long that Tess couldn't remember anything about books without her, began to gather the issues of *Texas Highways* that littered the floor. "Honey, the EMTs are here. You passed out in a public place. We can't just let you get up and walk away."

∽

THE GILFORD COUNTY Day-and-Night Clinic had a helicopter pad with an orange windsock so the critical patients could be transported to ER at the big hospitals in either Dallas, Fort Worth, or Oklahoma City. All others fell under the jurisdiction of Dr. Levi Strouth, who clearly enjoyed pursing his mouth while he examined his patients. This he did with regularity as he pressed the cold stethoscope against Tess's chest to hear her deep breathing, and as he used the otoscope and its pinprick of light to peer inside the caverns of each ear. Next he directed the thin light into her throat where he used a tongue compressor and asked her to say "ahh." A lab technician pricked her finger for a blood sample. Tess followed directions to the lavatory and peed in a cup.

"Well, I think you're going to be fine, young lady. But that's a nasty cut you've got above your eyebrow. I'm going to want to stitch it up. And your blood pressure's low. When you begin to feel faint, you need to sit down."

"I'll try to remember that."

"You get these spells often?" he asked. "Dizziness? Fainting?"

She shook her head.

"Any idea why you went weak like that? Why you would feel squeamish?"

She said nothing. She slouched, her fingers splayed around the front of her tummy, a firm barrier. With his mouth thrust sideways toward his left ear, Dr. Strouth warned her that this might pinch and gave her a shot of anesthetic to deaden her forehead. Then she watched as the doctor threaded the needle, making ready for the sutures, jabbing the strand of fine filament through the tiny eye. She thought of the times she'd watched her mother handle a needle, the deft movement of her fingers as she tied the knot, pierced the fabric, drew a stitch through. "I've got something I can put over your face so you don't have to watch this," Dr. Strouth told her.

She shook her head. "I'll be fine without it." She bit her lower lip and closed her eyes so she couldn't see.

As she felt the sutures tugging at her skin, he said, "I'll bet you hit a bookshelf when you fell."

Her voice muffled, as she bit her lower lip against the unpleasant sensation. "It's -ard not to do that in a -ibrary."

He finished at last and was just jotting notes inside a manila folder when a nurse brought in results of the tests he'd ordered. The nurse motioned at something without speaking. The doctor read something there, snapped the folder shut, and, with a large amount of kindness in his voice, said to his nurse, "Why don't you stay in here? I think we need to do a pelvic."

Well, here we go, then. Tess lay down as instructed on the examining table and kept her eyes on the odd landscapes in the ceiling. It didn't take long for the doctor's voice to become serious.

"Do you know this, Tess? That you're pregnant?"

The ceiling, brushed into shapes, long faces, jutting trees.

"How far along are you?"

She didn't answer.

He prodded further. "With the baby?"

"Not very."

"Which means—"

She raised herself up on her elbows and looked at him.

"—you probably don't know."

She bit her bottom lip again and nodded.

"Are you seeing anyone about this? Getting prenatal care?"

"No."

"And, do you want to?"

She stared at him, didn't say a word.

"Tess?"

"Maybe." And as he waited for her to say more, she hated herself because she began to cry again. "I'm s-sorry. I-I don't know. There are so many choices, and I—"

"Are you married?"

She shook her head.

"Are you willing to do this? Do you have family that's willing to help?"

And then she said it very slowly. "They've told me they will."

"There's a class with the public health nurse. You can take that."

Silence.

"Are you experiencing morning sickness? Do you know the date of your last period?"

No. Tess shook her head. And again. *No. No.*

As the activity began around her, Tess felt trapped. Things appeared before her and she had no choice but to take them. An enormous bottle of prenatal vitamins. A brochure titled "Bonding and Beyond: How to Massage Your Baby." A thick reference book called *The Complete Guide to Pregnancy and Birth,* which promptly fell open to a page: "This week your baby is the size of a telephone receiver."

Once she had those goodies in hand, they herded her into a different room. "We're going to check this out," Dr. Strouth said, "see what we can see." The nurse squirted clear goop on a probe ("This is called a trans-vaginal ultrasound," the woman explained. "We'll be able to see a lot even though the baby is small.") and inserted it. Dr. Strouth took hold of it in rubber-gloved hands, making satisfied *humphs* as globs of black and white slid past on a screen beside Tess's head.

"Nice picture. I'd say you're seven weeks along. Let's measure this right here." He tried a different angle and clicked. "And this, here." He clicked again, narrowed his eyes and smiled. "I'm going to say late April, early May."

"What?"

"This makes it easy to figure dates. Look, you can see the backbone. Right here. And a heart beating. Here. Everything looks great."

"No. What did you say about April?"

"April 29. That's the due date for this little guy."

A tiny spot to the right of her breast bone, a vacant place, suddenly touched something bright.

A date on a calendar was all it was, a landmark by which to measure time passing. "April 29," she said, repeating it, trying it on for size. "In the spring."

"Yes. And I'd like to see—"

She wasn't listening. She used every ounce of energy to try to fathom this. All of the months she'd carried everything she owned in a shopping bag from Dillard's and spent everything she could on another line of coke. All of the nights she'd gritted her teeth and reined in her heart and given Cootie what she thought she owed him. And now, here Tess was, swimming deep, seeking the surface, her lungs bursting for air.

She had a date. April 29. And that one square on a calendar held more sway than anything her mother or father could say.

"You know the most important thing is taking care of you and taking care of your baby, don't you? No matter what happens, we want the two of you to stay healthy."

Tess nodded.

"Oh, don't leave without this," the nurse said after Tess had dressed and hung the examination gown over a chair. She handed Tess a reminder card for her next appointment and a complimentary diaper bag with green bunnies. The bag was still swinging from her shoulder when she stepped into the Day-And-Night Clinic lobby and saw her mother.

"Tess." The leather straps to her mother's purse pretzeled around her knuckles. "Honey. You decided not to let us help you? Why were you trying to leave?"

Well, don't get all freaked out or anything. Tess almost blurted it out again in self-defense. But the words didn't come. Her mouth felt too dry to speak.

"When the clinic called, I borrowed Lavinia's car," Nora said. "That's how I got here. You look awful."

"April 29." Tess stuffed the reminder card inside her jeans pocket. "That's when the baby's due."

"What happened to your forehead?"

Tess touched the bandage. "I got stitches."

"Why?"

"I fell. Cut my head."

Nora's fingers worrying the leather.

"You talked to the doctor about your head? Or did you talk to him about the baby?"

"Both."

"You did?"

"Yes."

Although Nora didn't ask this at first, Tess knew the question was waiting for them, hanging between them, so important that neither of them would speak it. Tess realized that all her thoughts these past hours, about Creede, about Cootie, about herself, about a date on the calendar, all boiled down to the question that her mother would now speak aloud.

"You're going to have it, aren't you?"

Tess felt like she was jumping off a cliff when she answered. One meager nod; that was all.

"Yeah. I guess I will."

CHAPTER SEVEN

⸺ ❧ ⸺

Four Months Later

The Best Beginnings Prenatal Class was held in a brown room at the clinic with a circle of chairs, a dry-erase board, a pull-down screen, and a poster titled THE HUMAN PLACENTA hanging on the front wall. The layers of the placenta were marked in glow-in-the-dark colors—fuchsia, teal, chartreuse. "We know you aren't keeping the baby," the nurse at Dr. Strouth's office had told Tess, "but we recommend this class to everybody. You'll need to take it earlier in your pregnancy than some of the others; we want to make sure you aren't struggling with anything. You'll need to bring a support person." And the teacher, Mrs. Janet Whitsitt, had phoned Tess to acknowledge that she would be there.

Mrs. Whitsitt, who looked like a baby gift herself, dressed for the winter in a pink turtleneck and a matching strand of pearls, began with a pep talk on how smart it was to be attending this class. She listed newborn complications related to mothers who didn't take care of their own health, which resulted in preterm birth. "To prevent this," Mrs. Whitsitt said, "stop any smoking or intake of drugs and alcohol, and eat balanced, nutritious meals so you can gain the appropriate weight.

"If you feel like your labor is beginning early, empty your bladder, lie down on your left side. It's better for your circulation if you're on your left side. Drink three to four glasses of fluid while you're resting, and stay down for an hour."

There they sat, an entire roomful of women with growing tummies, slouching in their chairs, hands with perfectly painted fingernails embracing their girths. Every time one of them would come back from the bathroom, another one would jump up and go.

Someone mentioned snacks and they leapt from their chairs at once while their labor partners cast knowing glances. Everyone began filling tiny paper plates with crackers and caramel dip and sliced apple.

As Tess heaped snacks on her plate, she tried to convince herself she was the same as the other women in this class. But she wasn't, and Tess knew it. She'd made it through drug cravings, which had intensified, by sheer will and by the grace that there wasn't any illegal substance available from anyone she knew. Even now, a craving might still hit her. But day by day, she survived. She found it impossible not to look at these man-and-woman couples together, how the men helped their wives out of their chairs, how they stood together at the snack table and the men placed their hands against their women's backbones in a show of strength and support. The couples carried notebooks and pens, looking official and ready. The men helped the women off with their jackets. Everything about their lives seemed so *planned*.

After what seemed like an hour of details, everyone brought

out their assortment of bed pillows—plaids and cabbage roses and bright stripes—to begin prenatal exercises on the floor. They shucked their socks and shoes to reveal painted toenails, too.

"As your pregnancy progresses, your blood volume will also increase." It seemed absurd how many frightening details Mrs. Whitsitt was giving them at once. "Most of that extra blood collects in the pelvic area and legs. These ankle circles will help your circulation."

A dozen feet extended into the air. "One-two-three!" Someone counted aloud. A dozen ankles began popping and twisting, gyrating like the waterweed that grew in the shallows of Cubbyhole Creek. They giggled. "Next foot!" They switched, giggled more.

"Could you speak a little bit about getting the babies on a regular cycle?" asked a girl with blue-and-pink retro daisies on her pillow. Obviously she was more talented than the rest of them because she could both talk and flail her ankle at the same time. "You know, about getting them to sleep through the night?"

"You don't even know what type of baby you'll *have*," Mrs. Whitsitt assured them. "Some babies are mild-mannered babies. Other babies have fiery tempers; these are more spirited babies. It's difficult to know what to do with them until you know who they are."

That opened a floodgate of questions. One by one, ankles went down.

"Why do babies look cross-eyed at the beginning?"

"One of my breasts is bigger than the other one. Will I still be able to nurse?"

"How soon do we have to name the baby? It's a huge thing, a name."

"They'll put a note on the form and let you go home without a name," Mrs. Whitsitt said. "They'll give you five days."

And Tess asked, "Can I name my baby if I'm giving it away?"

The room fell silent. The person who had insisted he come along to be her birth partner leaned forward and took her hand. "I'm Ben Crabtree, her dad," he said, all hearty, filling the quiet. "I'm her labor support." And when the murmur started, they knew everyone in the room was impressed by how they were handling it.

"I'm sure she can name the baby. But I can't promise the adoptive parents will keep the same one. They'll probably want their own, you know." Mrs. Whitsitt began fumbling at a pile of papers cradled in her arm. She went on to explain how to take advantage of the baby's quiet-alert state, how to watch for jaundice, and how to prevent cradle cap. "Now, I want all of you to be careful driving home." She handed out a sheet of paper to everyone. "Here are the items you are going to need."

From Best Beginnings Clinic, Janet Whitsitt, R.N.
What to Pack in Your Hospital Bag

The average hospital stay for an uncomplicated vaginal delivery is 24 to 48 hours; for a cesarean delivery, 3 to 4 days. The mother will need:

- one or two nightgowns
- underwear
- toothpaste and toothbrush
- slippers
- robe
- nursing bra
- hard candy

- lip moisturizer
- hairbrush/comb
- shampoo
- camera
- personal items
- phone numbers of those to call
- clothes for the mother to go home in
- clothes for the baby to go home in (according to the weather)

It took a while for everyone to read over the list.

"Of course, your items won't be exactly the same." Mrs. Whitsett wrapped a light arm around Tess. "You won't bring a nursing bra. You won't bring clothes for the baby to come home in because someone else will be bringing those."

∽

At Stitch 'N Time, Nora aligned bolts of fabric and arranged spools of ribbon. She sorted the buttons according to color and restocked the threads. Whenever Babs Stanton called her to the cash register to ring up a sale, she cringed. Every time she measured and cut lengths of cloth or rang up piles of buttons and patterns and threads, she couldn't dodge the questions and condolences. They came at her as fast as bullets.

"Oh, Nora. I'm so sorry she's gotten herself into trouble again."

"You know the Hendersons are looking for a baby, don't you? They're paying some lawyer a fortune down in Fort Worth to find them one."

"You've got to let us know what we can do."

"I'm so sorry."

Nora felt whipped every time she couldn't answer.

It's in your hands, Lord, not mine. If she doesn't cost me my heart this time, I can survive it.

"I heard they're hiring at the Bootlegger. If she stays with you this long, why doesn't she get a job?"

"There's a state-wide adoption registry you ought to look into. It would be a good way to find the baby a decent home."

"Is she seeing Dr. Strouth?"

"Does she need to borrow maternity clothes?"

"Is your daughter still an addict?"

"I'm praying for all three of you, Nora. Heaven knows, you aren't taking the easy way out."

She steeled herself, knowing that no matter how she measured her words, no matter how she tried to say the right thing to people, she would end up sounding wrong.

That night after Ben had taken Tess to her first childbirth class, Nora had as many questions to ask as the others had asked her.

Had they found out if a mother could be a birth partner?

Did anyone teach Tess deep-breathing techniques, which had been the thing to help Nora get through labor?

Could they expect the adoptive parents to pay any of the bills?

Nora knew that the moment she opened her mouth, Tess would close up as tight as a zipper. So she said nothing at all. Nora kept quiet while Ben checked the window thermometer, shook the folds out of his leather jacket and hung it on a peg. She didn't say a word while Tess plopped on the sofa, worked her sandals off her heels, propped her feet on the coffee table, and pointed the remote at the TV. She asked no questions as Ben sifted through the mail and sent an assortment of bills sliding across the tabletop. She said nothing while Tess chose a digital music channel that pelted them with hip-hop, yanked a comb out of her pocket, and examined the split ends of her hair the same way she'd examine a dog for fleas. And all the while Tess stayed silent, Nora's heart kept yearning, *Please tell me what you're thinking, now that we're doing this. Please don't cut me out.*

Finally she couldn't bear it any longer. She said the words very meekly: "So, what did you do there?"

"Where?" Ben asked.

"At childbirth class."

Tess's head sank into the couch pillow and Ben punched something on the remote, overriding the hip-hop channel. Ben said, "We had snacks."

Nora glanced at Tess right then. By the way Tess suddenly stopped and placed her hand on her belly, Nora knew that Tess must have gone a month or two by now, feeling the baby move.

That feeling, as if a butterfly had lifted its wings inside of your middle, a thumping and kicking that grew until you couldn't sleep at night. How Nora longed to be invited to share her own experiences, too. "Tess," she said with a hopeful smile, "what do you think?"

Tess lifted her chin in defiance. "About what?"

"That's something you and I can share, you know. I understand what it's like to feel a baby move. I remember how I enjoyed feeling *you*."

Maybe the retort came because Tess wanted to protect her own territory. Maybe it came because the teenager was terrified that her mother could read her feelings so well.

"I don't want to talk about this," Tess cut her off. "It's bad enough that I'm here. Just don't *watch* me all the time."

"I'm not watching you," Nora lied, and she felt unfathomable sorrow, as predictable and sure as the windmill turning, as the water that ran into Miles Butler's old cattle trough.

CHAPTER EIGHT

⸎

The house on Bunyan Street in South Dallas had seen better days. For one thing, no one had seen fit to give it a decent paint job in at least two dozen years. The clapboards had cured to a flat grey. For another, the grass hadn't been watered or weeded in so long that it had died away, to be replaced by vicious Johnson grass and sunflowers and burrs.

For a third thing—and a big deal this third thing—Cootie had changed his truck tires last winter; some friend of his had traded him a massive set of monster treads for a sweet little Mazda he'd managed to hotwire out of a 7-11 parking lot. He'd ditched all four of the old, slick tires right there. Nobody made it to the front door without having to step around one of them.

Neighbors had phoned the police often during the past three years, complaining that they lived next door to a drug house. But the police couldn't prove anything except that a bunch of kids used the place to chill. Nobody remembered who owned it anymore; somebody's father who'd divorced and run off to Minnesota held the title. It served its purpose, the officers explained to the neighbors, kept these homeless kids—a few whites and Latinos, mostly—with a roof over their heads and off the streets.

"You know," Cootie said as he leaned forward and brushed wood shavings from the carving he'd been working on from his knees. "I never thought she'd do it."

"What?"

"Leave this place and not come back."

"You're the one pushed her to do it," Jimmy Ray said.

Cootie shrugged.

"Thing is, since she's not back, you know what it means, don't you? Means you gonna be a dad."

"Yeah," Cootie humphed. "Right. What makes you think it would be mine?"

"Tess cared plenty about you. You're the one trying to make it seem like nothing."

Cootie spit in the dirt and denied it. "It *is* nothing."

"Sure." Jimmy Ray just kept looking at him, trying to read his mind. "You miss her a lot, huh?"

"Stop poking your nose in my business."

"Not poking my nose, Cootie." Jimmy Ray made a show of pantomiming, his finger folded and hidden on the other side so it made him look like he'd pushed it up his nostril. "*Picking* my nose."

Cootie bent down and chucked a rock at Jimmy Ray. There were plenty of those in the front yard, too. It glanced off Jimmy's left shoulder and Jimmy kicked off a string of curses.

If Cootie had been whittling anything in particular, he gave up on it right then. "Just want to make sure she's okay, is all." He began digging his knife into the wood and thumbing off thin, fragrant curls. He kept going until he had a pile beside his dirty, sandaled toes and a thin stick left in his hand. A sparrow hopped toward him on the sidewalk, cocked her head at him, as if daring him to tell Jimmy Ray the truth. They did have their code of honor, after all. They were the men of this house.

Jimmy Ray was still rubbing his shoulder. He broke into a thread of freestyle rap. "Once that girl left, I felt bereft. Driving down the road with the picture I'd kept—"

"You know as well as I do that a kid wouldn't make it on Bunyan Street."

Cootie stared just over Jimmy's head at the tall spire of Reunion Tower and, in the distance way beyond that, to the Magnolia Building. On the day Cootie's mom had put him on the Greyhound bus a dozen years ago to send him to his grandma's to live, she'd said, "See the red horse on top of that building, Connor? See how it leaps into the air with its red-light wings spread out to fly? Well, that's what Mama's gotta do, too."

"How come I can't go?" he remembered asking, staring at the toe of his sneaker, scrubbing it in the dust. He would have died rather than let her see him cry.

"That's the hard part to understand." She'd laid a heavy hand on his shoulder the last time she touched him, as if she could hold him down to earth. "It's just that, well, there's this guy I met at the Clearwater Club and he's nice, real nice. This is my chance to start over, honey. He don't know about you. You're just gonna stay with Grandma for a while until I see how things turn out. Got to be somebody *different* for him, Connor, or I won't be anybody at all."

She'd walked away from him, just like that. He'd never seen his mother again. He hoped everything had worked out okay for her with that man from the Clearwater Club. He didn't know to this day whether she was alive or dead.

Funny, now, how his grandma hadn't been able to keep him very long after that, how she hadn't even known he was coming, how fast he'd been out on his own. And then he'd found a bed in this house on Bunyan Street. The horse still loomed in the sky; it wasn't on the tallest building anymore. He always had to look to find it, searching for a few minutes like he did when he wanted to find certain stars. And then, always, there it was. His mother's dream, glinting in the sun, prancing as it did now just over Jimmy Ray's left shoulder.

"Maybe Tess don't belong with you, Cootie. She grew up different than we did. She's got family. A reason to get out of this place, not to have to look over her shoulder."

"No." Cootie had left the chair and gotten comfortable squatting, his knees wide, his elbow propped on his thigh. In honor of cooler weather, he'd donned a threadbare red shirt over the tank top. The red shirt flapped open when he rummaged in his pocket. "She doesn't."

"What are you talking about?"

"There's different ways of having your mother leave you. Tess told me all about it."

Jimmy Ray started peeling his thumbnail, working out the day's grime.

"Her mother's ashamed of her."

"Well, hanging out here, maybe I'd be ashamed of her, too."

"It isn't us. Tess says it's been ever since she was a little girl. As long as she can remember. Tess says that every time she catches her mother looking at her, she sees *guilt* in her mother's face. That even when she was a little girl *trying* to do the right thing, everything she did made her mother sad."

Jimmy Ray rifled in his jeans for a cigarette. "Here. Have a smoke."

Cootie ignored the offer. "And you know how that is. People see that you expect the worst out of them and, eventually, they'll give it to you."

He'd told Tess about the red horse once. How it always hung there over his head beckoning him, how there was no way not to look at it. And how, at night when the sun was sinking, the red horse seemed like it had broken free of its wire cables and was surging forward in the sky.

"Its name is Pegasus," she'd told him. "There's a constellation named that, too."

"Smarty pants. I thought you dropped out of school."

"Well." When she shook her head, her hair poked out like porcupine quills around her ears. "There's some things I *do* know."

"My story's very important to me."

"Yeah, Coot." And he remembered how she'd yanked off his tan sweater cap (the one that made everybody tease him and call him Cone Head) and knuckle-scrubbed his dark hair. "I know all about you."

He supposed that's why he couldn't stop thinking about what it had been like when Tess was here. She was the first person who knew all about him, and had said that she would stay.

∽

TESS'S EYES had turned red from reading through Internet sites. When she closed them, her lids felt rough with fatigue.

She'd done every search she could think of during the past eight hours. Adoptionforum.com. Theinfantplanet.com. Rockabye.com. Inyourarms.com. Perfectdecision.com. Just when she thought she'd found all the information there was to find about adoptive families, she'd find even more. Bright, happy photographs with pictures of a man and a woman standing in the middle of a manicured lawn. Beribboned pets. Lavishly designed bedrooms that would rival anything on the pages of *Parenting* magazine. All of this to be shared with a new baby. All of this to be doled out with so much gratitude and love that Tess felt she might die of it. The hopeful mommies and daddies in the pictures were all so beautiful, they didn't look real.

In Tess's mind, the pleading of one voice had turned into the pleading of hundreds. This had been a mistake, seeing so many people at once. As long as she'd been talking only to Mrs. Whitsitt, she hadn't been frightened. But the voices, these faces and beautiful houses and lists of hobbies was too much.

Had anyone told her this would be easy? No. If anyone had, they'd have been telling her one big fat stinking rotten lie.

The whole time she'd sat reading in the chair, the baby had been alive with motion, flipping beneath her bellybutton, and the acrobatics made her laugh. A couple of times she'd gotten so annoyed, she'd pushed it back.

What would Cootie be doing right now? Laughing, too, because she had to pee all the time.

"We love sailing," one of the couples had written in a *Dear Birthmother* letter. What if they let the baby fall off a boat? "We have two little dachshunds," another wrote. What if the baby got a dog bite? "We live in a family-oriented neighborhood in a lovely brick colonial home." "We have a strong faith and a good marriage." "We are nurturing, friendly, hard-working, compassionate, patient, and responsible." It felt so frightening, it was enough to make her want to cry.

Tess sensed the moment someone walked in the room behind her. "You've been on the computer a long time," her mother said. "Aren't you getting tired?"

"They all say the same thing."

"You remember what Mrs. Whitsitt said, that you might get overwhelmed by this. Maybe you ought to turn it off."

"They all say, 'We have a perfect house. We have the perfect life. Our nieces and nephews adore us. We love to read. We want to share our enthusiasm for gardening with our child.' If there were just five or ten of them to pick from, it might be different. But there are *hundreds*. All the same. Like someone's told them what they ought to say to me."

"They *are* all the same." And Tess heard the unbearable melancholy in her mother's voice yet again. "They're desperate. Don't you know that?"

Tess palmed the mouse, moved the arrow to the Start icon, and logged off. The computer took precious seconds before the song rang out and the screen went blank. Both she and her mother stared into the emptiness.

Nora cleared her throat. "I want to make the baby a gift, you know. Something to send along with it, to have from our family."

"I don't want you to do that."

"We have flannel at The Stitch in so many baby colors. Would you pick out something you like? I thought if I made a little receiving blanket—"

"No."

"—it would be like an offering for you to send. So the baby would always know you cared about it."

"There's no need for you to think about things like that. It's not your baby."

But once upon a time, Nora yearned to say this and Tess knew it, *once upon a time, you were.*

CHAPTER NINE

B abies were the last thing on Ben Crabtree's mind as he
watched the Caterpillar bulldozer crush a thick layer of
gravel over the soil roadbed of Highway 37. He had come to
the conclusion that this stretch of road needed resurfacing
more often than any other road in Gilford County. Hadn't it
only been eighteen months since he'd hired a crew to tar
and patch out here? And now he'd had to deal with them
again. Potholes as numerous as moon craters. Last time it had
gotten this bad, Clyde Leonard had sent those hate letters and
copies of his wheel-alignment receipts all the way to the state
capitol in Austin. Ben readjusted his hard hat, pushed his pen
inside his shirt pocket, and began taking long strides along the
roadbed.

As the bulldozer belched past him, exhaust pluming from its
smokestack, he felt as crushed and pressured as the sharp, tiny
pieces of rock beneath his feet. And this wasn't anything he
had done to himself, oh no. *They* were doing it to him. Both of
them, together. Moving around the house and glowering at
each other like two tomcats ready to go at it, ready to shred

each other's fur. Ben found it a whole lot more peaceful out here among the heavy machinery than being at his own house.

It had become clear that Tess would open up to *him,* but not to her mother. Going to weekly childbirth classes with his daughter had actually started to be enjoyable. Yes, it could be scary for a man to hear about contractions and what they actually *did* inside a woman's body. He would take the Army Corps of Engineers most-difficult road plans, a three-ton roller, and a broken-down asphalt paver over *that* any day. But sitting beside Tess, seeing how she listened, watching her face and seeing how she struggled with addiction, seeing her take the hard and the *moral* way out, made him admire her all the more.

He often became sentimental about his daughter. It seemed like only yesterday when he'd sat in the Best Beginnings Clinic with Nora. (Of course, they'd remodeled it twice since then, but it *still* seemed like yesterday.) How proud they had been to welcome this little girl into their lives! And now, look at Tess. So grown up. A few bad choices, but beautiful. Giving birth to a child.

When he looked at Tess, he saw her locking Nora out with the same sureness as someone slamming the lid on a coffin.

Tess, he'd heard his wife ask her, Nora's voice as lilting and hopeful as a love song. *What do you think? I understand what it's like to feel a baby move. I remember the first time I ever felt you.*

I don't want to talk about this to you, Tess had said. *Just don't watch me all the time.* And when she did, Ben wanted to shake Tess by the shoulders and say, "Don't you see what you're doing? Don't you see that this could be a truce?"

But Ben knew his wife, too. He knew that each time she offered this rope of acceptance, she might very well not hang on to the other end. Maybe it seemed disloyal and childish to think this about his wife, but there was a small, real element of truth in it that he couldn't deny. Nora had a way about her with Tess that always seemed to whisper *I look at you and I disapprove of something.* He couldn't help but notice, no matter how much Nora talked about God and wanting to hear His voice and wanting to know His will for her life, Nora was dissatisfied with their daughter. This one thing did not change.

He remembered the day Tess had come home from school with ballpoint pen marks drawn around her fingernails. "That looks dirty," Nora had told Tess with so much conviction that it had made even Ben flinch. "That looks ugly. Go in and wash that off."

"I can't!" Tess had wailed. "I tried at school. It won't *come* off."

And Nora had kept her at the sink for a good thirty minutes scrubbing after that, squirting Goo Gone over her knuckles, until Tess's little nubs of cuticle were worn raw, but the ink was still there.

He remembered the day Tess started work at What-A-Burger, when Nora had said, "Those aprons look cute on everybody else. You've got yours tied wrong or something. It looks ugly, not right at all."

"It's the same as everybody else's, Mom," Tess had said, her voice hard. "What does an apron matter, anyway?"

Or the day Tess had been experimenting with makeup, and Ben had heard Nora say, "You can't carry that off, Tess. It looks cheap. It looks like dirt around your eyes."

Tess had taken to wearing so much mascara and purple eye shadow that she looked like she'd been thrown a good *one-two* punch in the boxing ring.

What had he hoped for when Tess had come home? That it wouldn't be the same between his daughter and his wife? That

Nora might see Tess in a different way? That Tess might *be* different?

Whatever kept them from reaching for each other stayed as set and as rigid as the concrete that the Sorenson road crew was pouring over Highway 37 beside his feet.

Dust imbedded in the nostrils. Ground soil. The stenchy exhaust of passing cars and hot asphalt. Yup, give him earth-moving equipment any day. Front-end loaders and bulldozers and dump trucks might be oily and cumbersome and tricky. But they were predictable. He could handle that better than what was happening at his home.

Ben glanced up and saw Porter McKay sauntering along, heading toward him on the asphalt shoulder, a thermos in one hand, scrubbing off some aforementioned grime from his neck with the other. "Hey," Porter called out as he tossed his hard hat aside. "Got some of Vera Jo's coffee left over. Thought you might want a sip."

"Can't say as I do." Ben cocked his elbow against the front door of a yellow department truck that said PILOT CAR. FOLLOW ME. "That stuff's been sitting since six this morning; it'll probably eat my innards out before it hits bottom. I like Vera Jo, don't get me wrong, but she makes coffee strong enough to choke a horse."

"You insulting my wife's coffee?"

"Nope. Just being honest."

They slapped each other across the shoulder blades in the age-old ritual of understanding each other. Then, just as Ben expected Porter to head on off and offer the coffee even Porter couldn't drink to some other unsuspecting victim, his employee unlatched the tailgate of the pilot car and had a seat instead.

"You got a minute, Ben? There's something I wanted to talk to you about."

"Sure I do. What is it?"

"Well, I . . ." Porter set the thermos squarely on the tailgate and torqued the lid tighter. "There might not be a right way to do this, but Vera Jo's been begging me to try. Got something to ask you."

"About what?"

Porter had pulled a bandana out of his pocket and was wiping sweat off the back of his neck. Then he held the hanky in both hands, wringing and wringing it between his big, dirt-encrusted hands, until he'd twisted it so hard Ben thought he might tear the thing in half.

"You need a loan or something, buddy? You know I'll do what I can."

"No. Oh, no. It isn't that."

"You need time off or something? Are you and Vera Jo trying to get away? I don't see any problem—"

"No. It isn't that." Porter wasn't himself. He kept staring down at the shoelaces of his work boots, examining them as if they were the most interesting shoelaces ever to be strung into a shoe. "Got a question about Tess being in town."

Ben stood a little straighter. "Oh."

"I've been noticing when I've seen her, you know. She's—" He stopped, obviously searching for words. "She's—"

"She's what, Port?"

Apparently Porter had forgotten the dangers of the coffee. He unscrewed the drinking cup and sloshed something that smelled like burned rubber into it. He took one sip and spewed it over the side of the tailgate. "She's either gaining a lot of weight in all the wrong places or else she's having a kid.

Which is it, Ben? Because, you see, I've got a good reason to know."

Ben didn't know what to say. He thumped his hard hat with the heel of his hand. "That's it? That's what you wanted to know? Yeah, she's pregnant all right."

"I was afraid of that. I mean, I heard folks talking in the checkout line over at the Food Basket. Caroline Rakes and all." He broke off. "Gosh, Ben. I'm sorry. That's such a shame. It's such an awful thing to have happen to your little girl."

Ben was taken aback. What was he supposed to say? *I accept your condolences? It isn't all that bad?* "We're getting by," he said, his voice level.

"Reason I said something is this. My boy and his wife, they moved up to Storm Lake, Iowa. You remember him, don't you? Porter Jr.?"

"I do."

"They've been trying to have a little one for a long time. It's been so important to Kelly, that's his wife, and every month she ends up falling apart. It's like something dies every time she . . . well, every time she finds out it didn't take again."

This conversation had started to make Ben uncomfortable. "Porter, I don't think—"

"I can't go home to Vera Jo without at least bringing it up, Ben. Vera Jo's been hounding me every time I go out the door, saying I ought to ask. What's Tess going to do with that baby once she has it? Is she willing to give it away?"

Ben lifted his behind off the truck and began to walk. Porter jumped down and followed him, leaving the thermos behind. "Because, if she is, Porter Jr. and Kelly might like to have it. I mean, they could take real good care of a baby. It would sure perk Kelly up."

"I'm not sure what to tell you, Port."

"Vera Jo thought it would help y'all out, too."

The bulldozer had turned around and was coming toward them again. Thank heavens, something to drown out this conversation. The thought of brokering Tess's baby on the roadside was more than Ben could bear. Porter might be working for years out here. And here Ben would be, listening to stories from Storm Lake, Iowa. The way Porter liked to talk, Ben would be hearing how Porter's grandchild was getting first teeth and taking first steps. He'd hear about the first time it said *Grandpa,* the first day in kindergarten, the first fever, the first haircut.

"You'd better get back to work, Port. You tell Vera Jo to talk to Janet Whitsitt at the clinic. That's what you need to do if you know somebody interested in adopting—" He never could have guessed how hard this would be.

Yes, adopting a baby would be good for Porter Jr. and Kelly McKay. Why should I begrudge them something like that?

Ben couldn't be sure whether his last words to Porter had been drowned out by the roar of frustration in his own ears, or by the roller making a second pass over Texas State Highway 37.

⁓

TESS KNEW THE BIPLANE was winging somewhere in the sun; she could hear its engine droning. A flicker of a cloud and she could see it, its wheels almost skimming the tops of the oak groves as it aligned with the dirt airstrip and flew straight toward her. Just when she thought Creede was headed to land, the plane pulled up again, vapor curling in streams beneath the plane's wings, strewing over the field.

Tess waved. In times past, Creede would have quickly waved back. Instead, this time, he hesitated. With a short, slight cock of his wrist, he circled around to make another pass.

The plane bounced once when he finally brought it down. It alighted, its rotary engine throbbing, its wheels sending up spumes of dust. The heavy sound faded and the propeller slowed. Behind him, the window said AG-CAT. Creede climbed between the wings and jumped out.

"Hi," she said.

Creede didn't speak. He found a massive black dirt clod and chocked it behind a tire.

"I guess you decided that since I passed out when I saw you, you'd better not talk to me or anything. I thought you'd be long gone in the Air Force by now."

"I was making plans with a recruiter, Tess. That's not for a little while down the road."

"And you were talking about getting married. I want to hear about that, too. Nobody will talk about it in front of me."

He searched her face. "I've got to feed Grandpa's horses." He brushed past her with long-legged strides and his words came stringing back to her. "I'm already going to catch it, flying instead of doing my chores."

"I don't know why you won't talk to me about getting married." She trailed him across his grandfather's pasture like a pesky little sister. To keep up, she had to take two steps to each one of Creede's. "Who're you marrying? Who is Candice Murfree?"

Creede had come to a metal gate. He unfastened it, rounded the fence, and began to wrap the thick chain around the post so it stayed secure behind him—whether to keep the horses in or her out, Tess couldn't tell. "I don't know why you'd think it would be any business of yours, who I'm marrying."

Just as soon as Creede had secured the chain, Tess unfastened it again and followed him through. "You said I scared you. Right when they were taking me to the clinic, I heard you. You said, 'Tess, you know how to scare a person.' I heard you."

Creede grunted. "Well, I said it because I was shook up. You fell down in front of me like a tree in a forest." He climbed onto a mountain of bales stacked on the leeward side of the fence and stood with his thumbs hooked through his belt loops, his tattered Six Flags Over Texas T-shirt tight across his broad chest. He stared down at the hay.

She pointed toward the bale beside his left boot heel. "That one right there. That's a good one."

"No. That one's moldy."

As if to spite her, he picked out another instead, pitched it over into the corral as the horses began to nose their way in. He jumped down behind it and, with one tug of his fist, the orange twine snapped. A potpourri of dried alfalfa, meadow grass, and clover tumbled out. She could smell it even where she stood.

The horses began to munch, a lovely sound.

"Don't you think it's time I started getting on with my life?" Creede asked her. "There's other important people out there besides you. What makes you think you can waltz back into town and everybody's going to start caring about you again?"

"I don't think that. I don't think that at all."

He stared at her. "Look at you. Just look at what you've done. I'm mad at you, Tess, and I can't help it."

"How can you throw that at me now? You were the only one I could ever talk to."

That stopped him. He planted his muddy boots wide apart and stared at her growing belly. "Can you still get on a horse?"

"Why wouldn't I?"

"Because of *that*." He nodded toward her middle again.

"I'm pregnant. Not dead."

"If you help get these chores done, we can ride a while."

"What is it, Creede? Every time a person wants to talk to you, she has to ride something."

He scowled at her.

She said, "I'll saddle the horses."

"No you won't. Not with the—" He stared her down. She saw that he wouldn't say the word. "I don't think you ought to lift anything."

"The baby," she said. "It's a baby. You can talk about that with me, too."

He disappeared inside the shed and came out with a thick horse blanket beneath a scuffed leather saddle that was as pungent as an old, sweaty shoe. Something about that leather smell, so sharp and so rich that moment, made Tess feel like she had finally, lavishly come home.

"You can ride Raina. You remember her. You've ridden her before." He clicked his tongue and a huge grey horse bobbed its neck and mane, dragged its hooves through the dust as it started toward them.

Oh yes. Tess remembered Raina. The first time Creede had ever kissed her, they had been riding this horse. Young enough to play games on horseback then, riding bareback and double, they'd been dashing through the pasture toward Grandpa Franklin's cattail pond. Just when Tess thought Creede was going to pull the reins up short and let the horse drink at water's edge, he shouted, "How about a swim?!" and spurred Raina on instead.

The horse crashed into the pond, powerful legs sending up fan-sprays of water. Before Tess knew what was happening, they were in over their heads, bobbing, struggling to stay atop the horse. "Hang on," he kept shouting at her, as Tess clung to the broad wet neck and folds of horseflesh.

Later, with Raina grazing and tethered to a tree, the sun so bright they couldn't open their eyes into it, the warm afternoon baked them dry. Shoulder to shoulder, ankle to ankle, the warm earth soaking up through their shorts and the sun pouring over them like molten brass, Creede raised himself up on one elbow and rolled toward her.

"What?" she asked. "Why are you looking at me like that?"

"Because I like to."

"Why?"

"Because."

She had seen something in his eyes that day that she'd never seen in a boy's eyes before—not one that looked at her. When he had leaned his face toward hers and barely brushed her lips with his, the kiss had been so light, it could have been a gentle wind crossing her mouth.

Today, once Creede had gotten a lead rope on Raina, he tossed the saddle over the horse's back. Tess stood behind him, feeling helpless and ill at ease, watching Creede's biceps knot as he yanked the cinch with more than the usual vigor.

"Can't seem to get away from people who like horses," she commented with false ease, making conversation. "I've got this friend, you know what he likes about horses? That one neon red horse on the roof of that building in Dallas. A city horse. Not a real one."

Maybe he didn't hear. Creede adjusted the stirrups without glancing at her. He had adjusted stirrups for her so many times, he didn't need to measure.

"He's so crazy about that horse, he reads stories about it and talks about it and frames it in his hands when the sun goes down."

"That somebody in Dallas?"

"Yeah."

She didn't accept it when he held out a hand to help her mount. She strode past him and swung herself into the saddle. Creede readied a second horse without speaking.

They set off.

Even in mid-winter the pasture grasses were tinged with green. The breeze and faded light moved through the alfalfa, ruffling it like confetti. They rode in silence for a while until the horses entered a pecan grove, hooves crunching over fallen hulls in the path. Tree limbs intertwined overhead like woven tapestry. Creede's face filled with shadows.

"Now are you going to tell me about her?" Tess let the tail end of the reins drape down over her knee.

"I wouldn't know where to start."

A blue jay cackled in the pecan branches above them. Somewhere in the distance, a crow answered back. The saddles creaked as they swayed with the movement of the horses' withers.

"Start somewhere."

Tess watched him trying to choose the right details. "She's just graduated from North Texas State. She came here to student teach last year; that's how we met each other."

"What's she look like?"

"A little like you." This surprised her, that he would be blunt about that.

"Your parents approve of her, don't they?"

"Yes."

"Your dad, especially."

"Yes."

"That's what I thought."

"What is *that* supposed to mean?"

"I know he talked to you about me. He didn't think I was good enough—"

"Tess." He grabbed her horse's reins and both animals drew up short. "I thought you wanted to find out about Candice, not talk about my dad."

"I'm the wild girl. That's what he said."

"You left. You *left,* Tess. You said you couldn't live with your mother anymore and you took off. It didn't have anything to do with my dad."

She lifted her chin in defiance. "Still, I heard what he was saying. I had come to the church to find you."

He stared pointedly at her belly. "You can't listen to everybody telling you what they think you are. You don't have to *be* what everybody says."

"You were *listening* to him about *me.* You never said a word to tell him that he was *wrong.*"

"I don't argue with my father, Tess. If I think his words have merit, I take them to heart. If I don't, then I discard them. My father taught me how to respect his opinions, even if I don't agree with them. If you had believed in me enough to know that I believed in you, we could have fought off anything anyone said."

Tess wrestled Raina's reins from him. "Yah!" She kicked and the horse bolted, stretching into a hard gallop, crashing through the trees. She gave Raina her head, leaning into the horse's neck, clinging to the animal the same way she'd clung long ago in the pond. After they broke into the open, Tess rode for all she was worth, hearing the thudding of hooves, the hiss of grass, Creede behind her. Not until they'd passed the green-and-yellow biplane did she stop the horse short and let him catch up with her.

"You remember," he said, gasping for breath, "how to ride."

"Of course I do." She was gasping, too. The horses were snorting, sweating. "Riding with you was one of the best things in my life."

He reined his mount in a circle and sat taller in the saddle. In the distance, a squirrel chittered and the cattail pond shone the same color as toffee.

"So," she asked, "do you love Candice Murfree?"

"Yes. I do. More than anyone could ever know."

Tess couldn't think of what else to say. Here they sat, in the middle of the pasture, with horses needing to be ridden home.

"The father of your baby. Is he the one who likes horses? That looks toward the red horse in the sky?"

"Yes."

"I see that red horse plenty when I'm up flying. All the pilots do. All of Dallas glows from the air but, for some reason, that red neon sign stands out from the others." Then, "Are you going to tell me about your baby's father?"

"There isn't much to tell. Maybe life is tough in South Dallas. But I found one person who sees the good in me."

No matter what happened between the two of them, Creede would always feel free to tease her. He'd gotten close enough to tug on a hank of Tess's multi-streaked blonde hair. "You don't watch out, some spider is going to come along and try to make something important out of that."

Tess asked, her heart heavy, "Things could've turned out differently between us, couldn't they have?"

"It seems to me, if you'd found a person to see the good in you, he'd be standing beside you, seeing you now." Creede reined his horse toward the barn and the grass beneath its hooves whispered like voices.

CHAPTER TEN

N ora had taken to going to bed late, waiting until she heard Ben snoring before she turned in for the night. She would peer at him and make sure he was sleeping, his disarrayed limbs making ridges under the blankets like a groundhog burrowing underground, before she would turn back the sheet and slip soundlessly between the covers.

She didn't want him to roll in her direction or take her in his arms. She didn't want to feel his breath or the warmth of his skin. It frightened her, how untouchable she felt. Nora knew this one thing; she didn't want her husband to invade her space. She wanted to stay *separate*.

For what seemed like hours, Nora would lie flat on her back, her arms pressed against her sides, looking back at another day she had lived by rote. She hadn't enjoyed this day or found anything joyous in it. She had merely survived it. Tomorrow, she knew, would be the same way.

Oh, Father.

Nora had no idea how long she'd been there tonight before Ben rolled toward her. It must have been minutes since she'd heard him snore. She held her breath, hoping he'd think she was asleep. He lifted his head and looked at her. "Nora?" he whispered. "You awake?"

Maybe she was wrong not to answer her husband, but she couldn't do it. Behind her closed eyes, she saw only the hopelessness of these past few months. She might as well have been slogging through quicksand, trying to slog through her own life.

Oh, Lord. When I try to reach out to my daughter, nothing comes but stinging blows.

Hot tears squeezed from Nora's eyes. They rolled down the sides of her face into her hair. She didn't dare move. *Let me reach for her through you, beloved.*

She didn't dare wipe the tears away. Her teeth clenched; her chin felt like a stone. Lying beside her husband, she felt utterly alone.

"I don't know," Ben said quietly. "I had a wife once. But I think she's gone."

I can't, Ben. I can only think of Tess and the last thing I want to do is be here for you right now.

"What is hurting you, Nora?" he whispered to nothing. "When Tess was young, why did you find so many things wrong with her?"

I don't know I don't know I don't know.

There he goes again, Lord, accusing me.

Ben waited a long time. Finally she heard him let out a sigh and roll onto his opposite side. She slept then, Ben's face and an awkward guilt looming just beyond where she could see. When she awoke hours later he was snoring again, still beside her, his broad hand splayed atop the blanket. She scooted a little further away from him. He'd fallen asleep reaching in her direction.

∽

THE BUNYAN STREET RITE-AID parking lot glittered with shattered glass, heaps of broken beer bottles. The brick walls on the far corner, the opposite edge of the parking lot from the floodlights, were covered with lewd spray-painted graffiti, the icons and initials scribbled in sharp, disjointed shapes.

Jimmy Ray and Cootie hung out beside the curb, smoking the pack of Winston menthols they'd gone inside to buy. "I got this plan," Cootie said, flicking his spent butt onto the asphalt with his thumb. "I'm thinking about going to see her. Steal a good car and head north."

"You should have sold those tires. Pilsen wanted them. You could have made gas money selling those monster treads."

"Want those for myself. Besides, don't need gas money. Just got to find something with gas in it and take off for a while." Cootie spoke with confidence. "So easy."

"*Mira,* Coot. They'll haul you back to jail faster than a skunk dies on a road, they catch you hotwiring again. They aren't going to let you out so fast next time."

"No reason to look at the bad side."

"My brother taught me. Plenty of reasons. Looking at the bad side keeps you alive, for one thing."

Cootie tapped another cigarette out of the pack. He flamed the lighter and took a drag against it, leaning against a circled red *VL* painted on the graffiti wall. As the tip glowed and he slipped the lighter into his pocket, he became aware of an underlying sound, something building in the distance—an engine rumbling toward them. "Hey, Coot." That cautious, icy sound in Jimmy Ray's voice made Cootie's arm hairs prickle. "Don't look now."

Cootie *did* look. There, threading along the street in front of Rite-Aid, was a decade-old grey Cadillac.

"You know who that is?"

"Sure I do." *Oh, yes. He* did *know.* Alonzo. A rap groove vibrated the windows. Everything had grown quiet along Bunyan Street. Even the crickets had stopped chirring.

"What's he doing this far on the east side?"

"You tell me." Cootie knew his off-handed answer didn't sound convincing. He knew by the way Jimmy Ray shoved up beside him and stared.

"What did you do?"

Cootie shoved his hands inside his pockets. For lack of anything better, he fiddled with his lighter and stared at the moths dancing around the floodlight. "The deal over at Krisik's. I couldn't back out of it, it was too good."

Jimmy Ray gave a thin whistle. "What are you doing, dealing in Ambrose territory?"

"Didn't figure they'd find out."

Alonzo's Cadillac crept along the road. He must have only seen them standing outside the arc of light, their Winstons glowing, their silhouettes dark against the wall, after he passed. Red brake lights glowed and the massive car hung a U and returned. Alonzo cruised into the parking lot, the bass groove on the car speakers so loud Cootie could feel it in his bones. Glass popped beneath the tires.

Jimmy Ray was looking for cover. Cootie could tell by the way he pressed his hands against the wall and his eyes darted. "Don't move," Cootie whispered. "You run and he'll be on you."

"You can't just *stand* here."

"He wants us to run. I'm not doing it."

As the Caddy began to pivot toward them, in that second

before it pinpointed them in its headlights, Cootie thought how the nose of a car could look like a person. The front grille grinned at him with the same leering mouth as a middle-schooler with metal braces. The headlamps glared at him with ill intent. They observed him, unblinkingly *understood* him, as they approached.

Hurt me. I dare you. See if you can take anything away from me that I haven't already lost.

Alonzo eased the Cadillac over the edge of the curb, and Jimmy Ray cursed. They held their ground until you could have bridged the gap between the hood ornament and their jeans buttons with a crescent wrench, and the front bumper nudged their knees. Only when Cootie felt the fear-cold wall pressing his shoulder blades did he realize sweat was pouring out of him. His back felt oiled.

C'mon, Alonzo. Do better than that. Squeeze play. Take us out.

Jimmy Ray arced his lit cigarette somewhere on the asphalt beneath the chassis. It fizzled on the pavement. There they stood in the dusty streams of halogen, crumbled glass at their feet, holding their breaths, unable to hear beyond the growling whine of the engine and the thunder of rap music.

Maybe this is how they would die.

But just as Cootie found Alonzo's face behind the steering wheel, nothing much visible except the whites of his angry eyes and the rim of his green sweater cap and the edge of his teeth, the hydraulics kicked on and the left side of the car began to rise. It fell again, and rose. Fell again, and rose.

Behind the dashboard, he could see Alonzo's eyes narrowing in challenge as he rose and fell, too.

Cootie ached to laugh. He wanted to laugh and laugh until this flood of relief reached every extremity of his body. He wanted to sing with joy when he realized that his best homie, Jimmy Ray, wasn't going to bite the dust in the Rite-Aid parking lot tonight.

"This won't end here," Jimmy Ray said, his breath coming in a nasty rush.

The last thing Cootie saw before the Caddy revved into reverse was a red beaded *A* swaying from the rear-view mirror, the flare of Alonzo's nostrils in hate. "Have a little faith. These guys don't have any guts," he said with false bravado. "They're all show."

Chapter Eleven

Mr. and Mrs. Jack Murfree
request the honor of your presence
at the marriage of their daughter

Candice Jane Murfree
to
Mr. Creede Leonard Franklin

on Saturday March 29
at 3:00 p.m.
The Homestead Bridge
Miles Butler State Park
Butlers Bend, Texas

Reception will immediately follow at the picnic
grounds of Miles Butler State Park

When news of Creede Franklin's marriage to Candice Murfree went around, Butlers Bend felt different, pulsating with excitement and anticipation.

The billboard at A&W Root Beer, right below the pronouncement "Our Strawberry Cheesecake Shake Will Surprise You" read: *Congratulations Candice M. and Creede F.* When Camille Lester strung hearts with big, dull bulbs in her shop window for Valentine's Day, she also posted numbers to count off the days. *Only 45 Shopping Days until The Franklin/Murfree Wedding.* This she kept changing. *Only eight days. Seven days. Six.*

"Is your son going to make his getaway in that Grumman Ag-Cat?" Donny Fraser asked Pete Franklin as the pastor stepped down off the chancel the Sunday before the wedding. "Are we going to have to tie tin cans on the tail of an airplane?"

"I certainly hope not." The pastor shifted his black Bible from one hand to the other. "But with Creede, you never know."

The wedding would be held in a lovely spot, the pulpit placed at the north end of the bridge across the creek, where the bride and groom would be shaded from sun, protected from rain, and standing over a rush of water beneath them. Only the creek wasn't a rush—not anymore. It was an algae pool where minnows nibbled at the banks and leaves floated in circles.

The service trucks Candice Murfree's mother hired to set up the reception rattled along the rutted road like an army battalion occupying new ground, white-panel trucks one after another without any space between. *The Gingerbread House Specialty Catering. Butlers Bend Garden Center. Ranchlander's Linens. TX Sound Systems. Fred's Barbecue. Forevermore Bridal Consultants* (which, Pete Franklin joked, was the logo because the bride's family would be paying bills forevermore).

Guests began arriving not many hours after the trucks did. First came the Butlers Bend Baptist Handbell Choir, members having been told to arrive thirty minutes early to don their robes and figure out where they should stand. Everyone else arrived soon after, from the Heritage House Senior Apartments shuttle van to Pete Franklin's mentor, the chairman of the North Corner State Baptist Association (so-named because some folks thought the top of Texas was as far north as any smart person should go).

Tess and Nora Crabtree entered the gathering the same way everyone else did, stepping smartly through an archway of woven ivy and white sweetheart roses, shoulder to shoulder, chins proudly raised. An usher presented his tuxedoed arm to Nora and she took it, curling her fingers upon his arm. "Bride's side or groom's side?" he asked Nora, smiling, and Tess whispered, "Groom."

They each noticed at the same moment how quiet the crowd became. Not one minute before, everyone had been chattering about the view or the weather or the homemade pink mints molded into the shape of hearts and left in a silver bowl beside the guestbook. Now it seemed those conversations had ceased. A good number of people turned to watch as Nora smiled at the usher and made some off-handed comment about his boutonniere. Why would everyone be staring at them like this? Everyone in Butlers Bend must have known for months already. "What is this?" Nora whispered. "You'd think they'd never seen a pregnant girl before."

Tess's breath caught in her throat. Her mother had never responded this way.

She wants to stand up for me.

That thought was so foreign, so surprising, that Tess wrapped her arms around her shoulders (the only part that was still small enough to wrap her arms around) and gave herself a hug.

Here she was, standing in front of everyone, as big around as the state capitol rotunda in Austin, impossible to ignore. Tess's lower back ached. She touched the yellow bow at the hollow of her throat and remembered that this, too, had been a surprising gift from her mother.

"Here. I've made you something," her mother had said earlier that day as she held the shirt up from the sewing machine and shook out the wrinkles tentatively. "When I was at the end with you, I got so tired of all the old things to wear. I thought you could use something new."

Tess, holding the fresh yellow fabric to her shoulders as if it might tear, measuring to make sure it would fit.

"Here are your seats," the usher said.

"Oh, thank you," her mother said, "but I don't believe we'll sit down just yet. We'll mingle. All these people want to chat with us."

When she had first left home and run away to Dallas, Tess had stolen stuff. Just reached inside cars that had been left unlocked at NorthPark, probably by teenaged girls because any adult would have been too smart. She'd taken lots of things to sell. CDs mostly. Bottles of Clinique *Happy* cologne. And one pair of 14K gold earrings shaped like horses, still posted on a Neiman Marcus card. If she'd sold those, she'd have made money to get high for a week. But a girl who picked her up and gave her a ride to Oak Cliff had liked those and Tess had given them to that girl as thanks instead. The rest of that week, as her craving for coke became something living inside of her, jeering, clawing at her insides, Tess had regretted that choice clear to the roots of her teeth.

That regret seemed only a pinprick compared to her regret today.

When her mother took her by the hand and brought her into the small talk, Tess felt as much on display as the giant yellow Easter egg in the front window of Camille's gift shop. Her biggest "mistake" was here for everyone to see. Beyond that, the bittersweet idea of Creede's marrying someone, the history Tess shared with him—and of course everyone in town knew about that—made this day all the more hollow and jumbled and sad.

Her mother had become involved in a deep conversation about the fabric that had been purchased in Oklahoma City for Candice's bridal gown. As if Tess had conjured him up, Creede came toward her through the crowd, wearing a black tux and a dove-grey shirt with a collar that stood against his throat, secured by one onyx stud. For a moment she jumped and looked around, thinking she shouldn't see him before the wedding. But then she realized: that was only for the bride.

"Hi."

"Hi."

"You doing okay?" she asked.

"A little nervous."

Tess glanced at his face and then glanced down. When she tried to see the ground, she encountered her own robust belly instead. She felt her cheeks flush. She patted her huge middle and tried to make light of it. "I've finally done it. Aren't you proud? I'm bigger around than a cow."

Creede took both of her shoulders in his hands and examined her. "You look good, Tess. You look pretty."

"As long as you don't look any farther south than my shoulders."

"No, I mean it. You're all—" He pushed his hands in his tuxedo pockets and examined her. She looked at his wrists instead of his face. She could see onyx cuff links poking out there. "—bloomy and healthy." He brushed one of her cheeks with his knuckle. "You're pink here. And your hair's shiny again. There's light in your eyes. You ought to be a model for maternity clothes or something. You look like you're, I don't know . . ." He frowned, fumbling for words. "You look like you've got a wonderful secret."

That flustered her all over the place. *Stop noticing his hands.* They stared at each other a minute, her arms feeling extremely small next to the other expanded parts of her body. "Hey," she said. "Congratulations."

"Yeah," he said, as the hand bells began to play. "You, too."

"Don't be sarcastic."

"Whoops, I'm getting the signal from back there. I've got to go."

"Okay." Oh, no. This baby made her a complete, stupid emotional mess. She had the oddest feeling that she was going to cry. *I won't do that today, oh no I won't.* Trying to cover, she said something dumb instead. "Have a good time." *Have a good marriage. Have a good life.*

"Oh, yeah." He turned back to her, gave her a slight grin and a salute with two fingers that made her heart knot as he walked backwards, still grinning at her. "I will."

After he disappeared, Tess wandered across the shaved green

lawn for a few minutes looking for her mother. The acrid smell of Fred's sweet-pickle relish, mesquite-smoked brisket, and hot links stung her nose. Pain tugged at her back and, everywhere she tried to alight, she found herself surrounded by the loud hearing-aid conversations of the elderly residents of Heritage House.

"I know I'm not hearing as well anymore. Used to be, I could eavesdrop without even listening. Now if I want to eavesdrop, I have to really *try.*"

"Dewdrop? Did you say dewdrop? Oh I know, Virginia. I hate not being able to see the dewdrops dry."

"No, not dewdrop. *Eavesdrop!*"

"Does Clara like her new dentures? I wouldn't have them. Too much trouble, taking them out at night."

"What did you say, Judith? Did you say you got into trouble staying out all night?"

"No! Taking my *teeth* out at night."

Just then, one of the elderly ladies noticed *her.* "Oh, dear child. Just look at you!" And she reached to touch Tess's middle without asking, extending parchment hands. Tess suspected that she brought back fond memories of long-ago childbearing years. The little ladies swamped her with questions. Did she have a name picked out? Was she going to breastfeed? Was the baby due soon?

And Tess answered good-naturedly, "It's still a month away."

"What did you say? It's due *today?*"

"You're carrying it so low. You must have already lightened."

"*Frightened,* Eunice? She doesn't look frightened."

"I said she must have already *lightened.*"

A chair opened up and Tess sat down. Their words moved in on her just as their fingers had. Lightened. Frightened. *If I could just bend over and stretch out.* Waves of heat tingled across her back. *If I could ever again find my toes and stop aching.*

The hand bells rang out extended versions of *Ave Maria* and *Jesu, Joy Of Man's Desiring.* Obviously, this was going to be a traditional drawn-out southern ceremony, long on pomp and short on party. Someone had climbed over and tied gigantic white bows on each bridge trestle. And, no. Things weren't beginning just yet. There was a hymn. A flute solo. A soprano rendition of *Love Will Be Our Home* sung by Caroline Rakes who, when she hit a high note, sent an entire flock of sparrows thrashing about and protesting the unaccustomed noise.

"There you are. Oh, good. You saved me a seat. I've been looking for you everywhere."

How odd it seemed, hearing her mother's voice and being somewhat glad. Tess thought again of that protective glare she'd noticed in Nora's eyes. It unnerved her that her mother would act proud when there was so much to be ashamed of. She didn't know how to decipher that. Her entire life had been the other way around—Nora acting ashamed whenever Tess tried to do something, *anything,* to make her mother proud. When Tess leaned toward her mother to whisper, her mother leaned toward her, too. The moment felt so surprising and sweet, Tess was almost afraid.

"I decided something just now."

"What?"

"If the baby's a girl, I'd like to name her."

There was a long moment of silence while Tess expected her mother to claw at her arm in horror and say, "No! You mustn't! Sending this child along with a name you've given it would be like sending it along with your unpleasant, drug-addict past."

115

But Nora didn't say any such thing. She smiled and said, "I think that would be nice. Can you do it?"

Tess's breath came out all in a rush. "I asked at prenatal class. The adoptive parents can change it but I can still do it if I'd like. And they might keep the name I pick."

During all these weeks of talking to Janet Whitsitt, Tess had poured over thick folders with letters and pictures, trying to pick the best parents for her baby. She'd narrowed her choice to three families, and the slick photographs, the emotional pleas in their letters, still danced before her eyes at night when she tried to sleep.

"What name have you picked, Tess?"

"Tansy Aster. Like the flower—the little purple ones, like daisy stars with yellow centers. That's who she'll be."

"Tansy. Tansy Aster," her mother repeated. "That's pretty. I like it."

"Do you?"

"Yes."

"They grow all around here."

"I know. I've seen them."

"I looked it up on the Internet. There's a legend about an angel who loved humans and grieved for them; she loved them so much that, when God made her leave the earth, she looked back and cried. And where her tears fell, starflowers sprang up. Asters."

"Named after a starflower. I do like that."

For a moment Tess thought her mother might touch her. She saw Nora's hand move and pull back, as if she'd thought it through and considered better of it. Pastor Pete Franklin stepped onto the bridge and the moment ended. Behind him, Creede and his groomsmen filed out. The first bridesmaid began stepping lightly across the grass, her hands clutching a bouquet of quivering baby's breath and mauve-colored roses that perfectly matched her dress. Next came another bridesmaid and another and another, until Tess decided that the bride must have more friends than Texas had fire ants. *The Wedding March* began and, as the audience stood, Candice Murfree, as tiny and perfect as a Dresden doll, moved toward the altar on her father's arm.

Tess had never seen a person with a waist so tiny; why, there was nothing to her! And the whirl of jealousy swamped Tess for so many different reasons. To be marrying Creede. To be a person whom everyone approved of. To have a waist like that when Tess felt like she'd always be five miles around! When Candice appeared with the afternoon light slanting across her like sun pouring through a high cathedral window, Tess saw what her *own* life might have been. Beneath the bride's sheer veil, Candice's thick blonde hair was twisted into three fat, entwined knots, resembling a pattern Tess had noticed once in a barbecue bun. Tess had a sudden, idiotic vision of herself, as if she were there in Candice's body stepping toward Pastor Franklin's arms. As if it were *she* who was being blessed. As if it were *she* being welcomed.

Creede stood beside his father, as straight as the San Jacinto monument, with his hands locked in front of his jacket. He had this silly, tender expression on his face that Tess recognized because, when he'd been younger, he had looked at her that way, too.

"Dearly beloved," Pete Franklin started, "we are gathered here today . . ."

At that moment, Tess's heart throbbed with yearning, and her body throbbed, too—so strong and complete that she didn't know where the mental hurt stopped and the physical hurt started. As a man and woman were joined in holy matrimony in front of her, Tess felt like crying again, so she lowered her eyes and stared at the fresh spring grass poking through, struggling to take hold in the dirt beside her mother's feet.

PART TWO

Tansy Aster

Chapter Twelve

─── ⁂ ───

The throbbing had a pattern to it. It tightened, cinched like a strap around her pelvis, became more than cramp and heat. It became pain.

Suddenly, Tess was terrified. What had Mrs. Whitsitt told them to do about preterm labor? Lie down on which side? Right? Left? Drink three or four glasses of something. She looked around for the refreshment table. The only beverages she could see were sweetened iced tea and Dr Pepper. Everywhere she looked, people were eating white-frosted cake.

Tess hadn't worn a watch. She hadn't any way to time these. But when the next pain hit, it came much too soon. It hit much too hard. Tess let out a strange, low cry, which caused a small rustle among the guests around her. "Mama?"

"Oh, my word," Heritage House Eunice whispered. "Oh, my *word*."

"Mama, I need you. I think I'm having the baby."

Evening was coming on. Tess hadn't wanted to have the baby at night. She didn't know why, but it had been a thought that she would give birth in the morning; it would seem like the beginning of something. Not at night, like something hidden.

Nora slipped in beside Tess, put an arm around her and held her up. "Are you having contractions?" she asked.

Tess nodded.

"For how long?"

"I'm not sure. A while." All the strength Tess had used to hold herself together today was suddenly gone. "Let's just go."

"How often are the pains coming?"

"Often enough."

Thank goodness Creede and his new wife had started the dancing, spinning in each other's arms on the makeshift floor. They didn't notice her. On their way out, Tess had to lean against one car in the parking lot and arm the sweat off her forehead, counting and breathing deeply. Her mother walked her to the Lumina and, by the way Nora kept chattering, Tess could tell that she was nervous, too.

"Honey, I'm going to try to get your father."

"That's okay."

"I know he went through all those classes with you. I'm going to find him." Nora punched numbers into the cell phone while she was driving. The Lumina wove a little on the road. "How do you go about phoning someone on this thing if they're out of the area? Do you dial the area code, or do you not?"

"You dial the area code."

Twice her mother tried it, different ways, and must have got a recording both times because she shook the phone and stopped listening.

"Mother, I think you should just *drive*."

"Oh, honey. Oh, honey." They bumped and jarred over the potholes in this narrow, two-laned, neglected road. "Of course, your father would be working overtime repairing roads somewhere *else* in this county!"

Tess leaned hard against the car seat and gripped the armrest for dear life.

"Know what happened when you were born? My water broke and was running down my legs. I called your dad at the highway department and said 'Ben, you have to come home because the water broke.' He thought I was talking about the pipes in the house and told me to call the plumber."

"Mama," Tess said, her voice diminished like someone speaking down a tunnel. "I'm sorry."

"For what?"

"For"—Tess made a circle with her hand.—"all this."

A slight, tentative smile from Nora. "I'm the one who told you that you ought to do it."

No matter how difficult this day, some part of what had happened had begun to bond them. For good or ill, they were in this together.

Once Nora focused on her driving, they made it to the Collin Health Science Center in forty-five minutes.

She sped the entire way.

Once they walked inside the front door, though, and Tess was admitted to a room, Nora felt out of place, like she had nothing left to do. She watched helplessly as a nurse brought ice chips. She helped Tess focus and showed her the little jagged mountains on the monitor that meant she was having another contraction. All the while, she couldn't help wondering, *Just think what this would have been like if it had been a joyous occasion. If Tess had a nursery set up with clothes and toys, and friends to share stories with, and the baby's father had been here.*

The nurse, whose nametag read PATTI, R.N., told Tess it was good her cervix was dilating. She told her she was doing a fine job keeping her breathing steady, because that meant her blood pressure stayed low.

And Nora couldn't help thinking, *I wonder how different it would be, feeling proud of this situation instead of embarrassed.*

The nurse wrapped a cold washcloth behind Tess's neck. She encouraged her to handle one contraction at a time. She inserted an IV port, saying "We're not going to need this, but we do it just the same."

This baby will always be a part of me, too.

And I'm afraid. Please, Father. Help her.

The whole room seemed filled with the fetal monitor once they turned it on—the swishing, insistent heartbeat. "I'll give you a crash course here." Patti filled a Styrofoam cup with more ice chips. "You want to help her breathe?" The phone rang in Nora's hand. She fumbled to answer it.

"Ben?"

"What's going on?"

"Is that you, Ben?"

"Were you trying to get me?"

"We're at the hospital." She ran fingers through her hair. "How fast can you come?"

He groaned. "I'll be there as fast as I can. Maybe thirty minutes or so. It's going to take me a little while."

"Now, you're the one who has to set the mood." Patti squeezed her arm after Nora hung up. "Keep the atmosphere light. Make her give you eye contact, tell her how much faith you have in her. Smile at her a lot. Can you do that?"

Could she do that? Tell her daughter she had faith in her? Nora felt like she was nodding from a thousand miles away.

"Watch how I breathe with her, then I'll expect you to take over. How does that sound?"

Nodding. Nodding.

Tess was watching, her eyes narrowed with purpose.

The vocabulary grew simple as time wore on. *Good job. Perfect. Focus. Here comes one now. Take a good one.* There. *There.*

Right in the middle of a contraction Nora remembered something that ought to be taken care of. She waited until Tess's hand loosened on hers, whispered, "What about the adoptive parents? Wouldn't they want to be a part of this? Shouldn't we call them?"

Patti glanced from Nora to Tess. Then back at Nora again. "What do you think?"

"I haven't settled on anybody yet."

"We could decide it together now, if you'd like. If that would help."

Tess rested her head on the pillow. "I just want to do this right now. I don't want to think about those people. I just want this part to be all *mine.*"

"Here's a contraction again." The nurse directed Nora's attention to the line as it began to climb the scale on the monitor. The whole time Tess worked through the contraction, she kept her eyes narrowed and leveled on her mother, her lips pursed and swollen. When Nora held the Styrofoam cup to her daughter's lips, Tess's jaw was clenched so tight that a shudder ran down Nora's spine.

Patti brushed Tess's hair from her forehead, the exact gesture that Nora longed to make. So easy for a stranger. "You're on the other side of it. That was a hard one. Well done. Are you ready to push? I think you are."

Tess nodded.

"You can't push yet. Your father isn't here." Nora was frantic.

"Yes," Dr. Strouth said from the doorway, "but the doctor is."

Who could have guessed it would go so quickly? Several other medical staff had entered the room, Nora didn't even know when, and suddenly everyone was busy and talking at once, donning blue gowns and paper caps and taking position.

"She's doing a fantastic job."

"Make a C out of your body, Tess. Remember how to do that?"

"I can't do it."

"You're doing well. You're doing really well."

"No, I'm not."

"We're going to do this all natural, young lady. There's no time for an epidural, okay?"

Tess nodded again.

Oh, Father. My little girl. Nora wanted to stand close to Tess through this but she realized, once again, that she was in the way. She hung back a little for a moment, and the only thing she knew to do was pray.

"Here we go. Focus. Pull back on your knees. Keep your chin on your chest."

Tess's entire body arched, her teeth bared, her face red. She fell back on the pillow with a sob, a sigh.

"That's okay. Great. Wonderful."

"I'm so—"

"The baby's going to come quickly and you're having another contraction now, very close. Here it comes. Take a deep breath in."

With the next pain Tess bore down, strained forward, didn't cry out. The nurses pushed flat hands against her belly. Nora shoved in with them, unable to stay removed anymore.

"Push straight down. A little bit at a time. Straight down."

Dr. Strouth with a gloved hand on her knee. "Tess, whatever you did at that last second was very productive." A glance over the towering stomach. "Did you do something different?"

A little sob. "No."

"I saw the baby's head move a little more. Whatever you did, do it again."

"You're doing a fine job, hon."

"Deep breath in. This could be your last one." And, "Straight down," as Tess arched, spread her knees as wide as she could, grunting with effort. "Straight down. Come on come on come on. We've got a head. Lift a little bit. We've got a head. Here come the shoulders, Tess. Here they come."

If we didn't have to be ashamed, this could have been such a joyous occasion.

The baby—all four limbs and the umbilical cord—came straight out, limbs purple and crimped, covered in white smudge.

"Here baby. Here baby," as they cut the cord. "Is it okay? Is it okay?" Tess's weak voice pleaded.

Patti, R.N., crooned, "Look at those big old toes." Dr. Strouth aspirated the mouth, both nostrils, and then the mouth again.

"Mama?" Tess asked so softly that Nora might not even have heard her. "Mama, are you proud of me?"

And all the world seemed filled when Tansy Aster began to cry.

CHAPTER THIRTEEN

N ora met the child's blue eyes and felt the tiny yet sub-
stantial weight of life settle into her arms. Nora hadn't
known it would feel this way, heartbeat against heartbeat, the
baby watching her like they'd already been friends a long time.
That's all it took, and tears constricted Nora's throat.

Oh my goodness, she thought, astounded. *She's a Crabtree.*

What a precious little pink cap she was wearing! And
the mere slip of a bracelet that bore their family name. Such
a face. Such a little face. Uncanny, when Nora saw the resem-
blance. All she could do was blubber, "She looks so much
like me!"

She had not realized that this would seem such a monumen-
tal moment in her own life.

My first grandchild has been born.

She had never expected to feel such instant love for this new,
small person. And with that, Nora felt such relief. Her heart
opened like a child's hand, releasing, each petal finger curling
out, letting go. *Look what Tess has done, everybody!* she wanted to
shout. *This is my daughter's child!*

"I know you don't want to let her go," the nurse said, reaching for the baby again, "but I've got to take her away just one more time. Just to check her heartbeat."

"She's okay, isn't she?" Nora asked, releasing her reluctantly.

"Oh, yes. She's fine." Patti checked her respiration, too, for good measure, and pronounced her fit. "I'll just fill these things in on the chart. Here she is. You can have her back again." And no sooner did Nora have Tansy cuddled back in her arms did she look up and see Tess holding out her arms, too, with a look of wonder on her face.

"You want to hold her, honey? Sure you can." Their arms entangled as they passed six pounds three ounces of Tansy between them. As mother's head bowed over the child, and her grandmother's, too, those blue fathomless eyes seemed to look at them, and understand.

❦

BEN CAME RACING into the room, his hair sticking out like clumps of nutgrass. Nora knew how he riffled his hair whenever he was driving and got stuck in traffic. "Well." He gave thumbs up to the doctor, rubbed his hands together, bent his knees. "Well," he said, and didn't come another step.

"It's okay, Ben." Nora dried her eyes with the back of one hand and backed out so he could come close. "Come have a look at her."

"Her? A girl?"

"Sorry, Daddy. I tried to wait until you got here."

"Good grief, Tess." He laughed as if the joke were on him. "I'm starting to realize you never do things the way they're planned." They had a good laugh together, and then Ben wrapped an arm around Nora. "How's my girl?"

"Tess? She's—"

"No. Not Tess. Here. Come get some fresh air with me." He drew his wife sideways against him and they walked into the hall, out of Tess's earshot, before he said any more. "I was worried about you."

"Oh." Nora glanced quickly at his face. "Oh. I'm *fine*."

"You sure?"

"Yeah."

He kissed the top of her head. "Looks like you came through with flying colors."

It would have been so easy to smile up at her husband and say "Thanks." But this mixture of extreme joy and grief brought on by the baby, coupled with the nudge of guilt, the odd inescapable numbness she'd felt for her husband since this had all begun, wouldn't let her speak. The gravity of all that had happened suddenly hit her. She would have sacrificed this baby's life for her own pride. She might have sacrificed Tansy Aster because it had exhausted her to think of being involved in her daughter's life again, because opening her life to Tess's pregnancy had been so frightening.

She might have snuffed out the life of this lovely little person who seemed to quietly *know* her.

Oh, Father. And, as her husband held her, she felt like a beggar before a holy God. *Oh, Father. What might I have done?*

"Are you okay, really?"

"Oh, Ben." And when she began to falter, the words babbled out like water over stones. "Tess has to make certain she goes to a good family."

"It's going to be okay."

"What if she doesn't? What if she ends up growing up in the back seat of a car?"

"Hang in there, girl." Then, "Tess has that figured out, remember?"

"I thought I'd be good at this kind of thing. Knowing that to love something best is to give it away."

"I don't think anybody ever gets good at that."

As if on cue, Janet Whitsitt from Best Beginnings Clinic appeared down the hall, carrying a thick Filofax beneath her left arm. "I hear it went well."

"Yes, it did. *She* did."

"Do you think she's ready for me?"

"Excuse me?"

"To talk about the adoption. Now that the baby's born, I can't initiate anything anymore, Mrs. Crabtree. Everything has to come from Tess."

"Yes, then. Please. It's time, I know." And Nora thought, *How ridiculous, being free to love something this much, and not being able to make the choices.*

"Do you know if she's made the decision about the birth family? If she'd give us a name, we could call them and bring them in. And there are relinquishment papers; nothing happens without her signing those."

At the mention of "relinquishment papers," Nora closed her eyes, picturing the baby's tiny fist, how it curved against Tess's neck like a cowry shell. How could she be afraid of Tansy being unsafe now? A little girl who had almost been unsafe in her own mother's womb. It was something Nora had almost *encouraged* to happen.

Our first grandchild.

Ben had taken the papers from Janet Whitsitt and was reading over them.

No one could have told me that I was going to feel this way.

↶

THE WEE HOURS of the morning, that time when the sky is at its darkest and the future seems its bleakest—those were the hours that Tess had heard her mother call "the harsh of the night." And, true, to a young woman who couldn't sleep, who had nothing to do with her hours except memorize the face of the child she would never see again and stare out at the severe fluorescent light in the hospital hall beyond her darkened doorway, those hours wounded her heart. She listened to the muted footsteps of the nurses going about their duties and thought, *This time won't ever come again.*

She heard the whirring begin on the automatic blood-pressure cuff, felt it tighten around her arm again and thought, *I will think of this day for the rest of my life.*

Occasionally one of the nurses would step inside her room to check the cuff and ask if she or the baby needed anything. No matter how much juice she drank, Tess stayed thirsty. She couldn't swallow. Her mouth felt as dry as cotton.

I want to remember her face. I want to remember every part of it.

She traced the shape of Tansy's tiny lips with her finger, thinking how when the baby sucked in her sleep, her mouth made the same shape as a Valentine's Day heart. Tansy's face wasn't flawless by any means. Her nose had been bruised when she was born and her head had been squeezed into the shape of a kiwi fruit and there was a red strawberry-shaped stork bite (they had learned about stork bites in childbirth class) beside her left eye.

When her dad had come to visit the second time last night, he had brought the manila folders that Tess had requested. They were lying now on the shelf beside the sink. She didn't have to look at them again to know what each of them contained; she had memorized every name, every detail, every word.

Just before Patti, R.N., ended her twelve-hour shift, she entered with a fresh bottle for the baby. "I came to tell you that I'm leaving, Tess. Marsha will be your new nurse. I thought you might want to try some more water with her, keep getting her used to that sort of nipple."

"Thank you."

"You did a great job today, honey. You are a courageous young lady." A little pat on the shoulder. "Oh, here's Marsha. Marsha, this is Tess."

"Hi."

As the sky began to soften outside the window blinds, Tess made her final decision. She had spent all night thinking about the Laughlins in Fort Worth, the McKay's in Storm Lake, the Smiths in Amarillo. Who can tell if this story might have been different if Tess had not sat in the fifth row at a wedding yesterday afternoon, watching a white-lace version of who she wished she could be.

Who can tell what might have happened if she hadn't thought, *I've watched parts of my life march by these past few hours and nobody will let me have any of it.*

She examined Tansy's face in the first light, thinking, *This is her first real morning.* Tansy lost the rubber nipple and rooted. Tess jiggled the bottle and Tansy found it again.

Let them disapprove of me now.

It's nothing new.

There was no doubt in Tess's mind what she wanted to do.

⁓

MILES BUTLER had often told stories of the beginnings of Butlers Bend, near the turn of the century. He was convinced that his windmill pond could heal wounds.

Documented in the early 1900s, the scrawled ink ledger at the library said: "It is purported that the waters rising from this deep well offer healing properties to those who would bathe in them, much like the recorded properties of the pools at Sulphur Springs." Then other notes followed, of cows dipping their faces in for a drink and their noses, razored by barbwire, coming up whole and pink and wet. And a story of a boy who'd broken his femur when he'd been kicked by the family mule and who had been dipped into the waters and made to walk again.

Now that modern medicine had come, Butlers Bend residents didn't place much stock in those old stories. But they still hung Christmas lights on Butler's old windmill fifty years after the cattle had been auctioned off in the Fort Worth livestock yards and much of the farm acreage had been parceled into lots for homes and the library and the corner Texaco station.

Ben didn't glance in the direction of the legendary pond that morning as they zoomed by. He and Nora had told Tess they'd arrive at the hospital as early as nine, right when visiting hours began. They had to hurry, even though neither of them had the heart. In the distance, as they drove through the trail of small Texas towns toward Collin Health Science Center, Sunday church bells were ringing. Ben drove. Nora sat with her head tilted away from him, her forehead against the glass, the patchwork of houses visible beyond wisps of her hair. There wasn't much traffic. They passed a pickup pulling two muddy dirt bikes on a trailer and a rusty Volkswagen bus with a bumper sticker that read MAY I ALWAYS BE THE KIND OF PERSON MY DOG THINKS I AM.

Ben curled and uncurled his fingers on the steering wheel. "We aren't the first people to go through this, you know, Nora."

"I know."

"I keep trying to think of things to make it easier. It helps, thinking that we aren't the only ones. That there are plenty of others who have gone before." The sky throbbed blue overhead but the brightness wasn't touchable.

"Gone before? You sound like Star Trek."

He grazed her hand with his knee and affected a bad British accent. "Captain Picard."

"You're thinking of the wrong captain, Ben. Captain Kirk is the one who got all the women."

"Before my time," he said, glad to find something to smile about.

"Is not." She popped him on the knee. "You're just as old as I am."

Ben struggled to keep their conversation light until they walked into their daughter's hospital room and saw Janet Whitsitt's face. He hesitated. "What is this?" He could read the distress in the woman's pinched expression. "What's wrong?"

And then Nora asked the unthinkable. "Is Tess okay? Has she hurt herself?"

Janet Whitsitt measured them with her eyes for a long time, a look that made Ben profoundly uneasy. "I can't—" She raised the adoption files at her side, let them fall, like a bird trying to fly with one injured wing.

"Tess?" he asked.

Their daughter waited in a plastic chair, her face turned

toward the glitter of vehicles packed below in the parking lot. She'd set her jaw tightly; there was a hollow beneath it.

"Honey?"

Tess's eyes stayed closed, as if she didn't want to see.

And then, "I'm not signing anything."

"What? What did you say?"

"I said I won't give her away."

Ben drew himself erect, his throat constricting with shock. "Oh." A glance behind him at the others. "Oh, I see."

This idea was so beyond anything they had ever considered that Ben couldn't speak. He kept his eyes on his wife, as if she could give him some answer. She shook her head slightly. *I can't do anything,* she seemed to say, and he turned to their daughter.

"This is what happens," Nora said behind him, and he could hear the helplessness in her voice. "Can't you see that?"

"Yes, Mom. I know."

"You can't make a lifetime decision based on emotion alone. It's too costly. You can't—"

"If Creede and Candice can have good things in their lives, then I can, too."

Nora stepped up beside Ben. "Tess—"

Tansy nestled in Tess's arms, leaning against her so easily that they fit together like pieces of a puzzle. "If I let her go, I'm just one again. I didn't even know her, and she's a part of me. I'm not going to give that away."

Nora pressed harder. "It's different raising a child when you're alone, Tess. You don't have a nurse to tell you everything's all right. You don't have people around to find out if you're okay, or ask if there's anything they can do to help you."

"I know that."

Ben said, "You've got to think of what's right for the baby."

Tess challenged both of them with her chin erect, her chest raised slightly, the posture of someone righteous and indignant. "You don't think I'm good enough to do this, do you?"

One of the nurses brought in a vase of flowers that some other patient must have left behind. No one they knew would be sending congratulatory flowers. Nora picked up the vase and Ben could see her hand shaking. She added water from the sink to them with false calm. "You might look back when you get out of here. You'll see that you could have gone another direction."

Tess asked sadly, "Is that what happened to you when I was born, Mom? You got to your own life and looked at me and wished you had gone a different direction? Because God knows I was never good enough for you."

There it was, the gauntlet laid out between them. The accusation hung between mother and daughter, as tangible and ugly and immoveable as a dead body.

A long, aching moment of silence.

"Tess, I've stood beside you."

"It was Dad who convinced you to try."

All the time they'd been talking, the shock and concern and helplessness had been building up inside Ben Crabtree. Just when he had least expected it, just when he'd steeled everything inside him to tell his granddaughter good-bye, here he was, caught in the middle between his wife and daughter again. He couldn't bear it. His frustration exploded. "Stop it, you two. Just stop it." His voice was so sharp and hard that it made the baby jerk in Tess's arms and begin to cry. "This isn't about the two of you anymore, can't you see? It's about loving someone enough to do what's best for her—"

"I'm keeping her," Tess declared, her voice even louder.

Ben glanced toward Janet Whitsitt and the woman shook her head. "I'm here if Tess should make the decision to give her baby away. But I cannot initiate anything. It must be her choice."

Ben started to say something else, but he couldn't. There was no more strength left in his diaphragm. He met Nora's eyes in absolute stunned, numb acceptance.

Marsha, the new shift nurse, knocked on the door and poked her head in. "I've got papers for you to sign, Tess. You'll need to be checking out of your room."

"That's fine," Tess said, sounding as if she were pleased to be bending everybody's will.

"I *do* have a car seat you can borrow," Mrs. Whitsitt said, her voice sad.

And with that, their future changed.

Chapter Fourteen

⸺ ❧ ⸺

There is a Scripture in the Bible that Nora kept thinking of as she watched Ben slice open the huge cardboard carton and begin to yank out the skeletal pieces of the white baby crib.

"Hm-m-mmm," Ben said as he held two pieces together to see if they would fit. "That looks right, don't you think?"

"I think you should read the instructions."

"There's a plastic bag in here with the nuts and screws. Have you seen anything that looks like that?"

"Be careful, Ben. Don't scratch the paint."

The story Nora kept thinking of was the tale of the widow from the town of Nain who happened to be leaving through the town gate, a large crowd of mourners carrying high the body of her dead son. Nora imagined how, just as the gate swung open to let them out, Jesus and a large crowd of his joyous followers began to come inside.

That's what Nora's heart felt like on this day, those people, those extreme emotions, sorrow and joy jostled together, tight in a small place.

"Maybe this part fits into this piece," Ben said. Then, "Do you remember? Is the end for the head taller than the end for the feet?"

"Honey, you're going to have to look at the picture."

It had been Ben's idea to buy the bed and mattress. Within the hour after they'd gotten Tess settled with the baby, he had suggested they drive to Wal-Mart and pick out something pretty. Although he hadn't said it, Nora knew exactly what he must be thinking. *We'll buy a piece of large furniture. Something permanent. Something that, when it is put together, won't fit through a door or into the back seat of a car.*

In the town of Nain, so the story goes, the people jostling through the gate grew quiet when Jesus said to the woman, "Don't cry." Suddenly, everything stopped. It was a ridiculous thing to say to a mother who had lost her child. *Don't cry.*

Nora had heard this sermon so many times, how Jesus knew the woman's heart. How he never blamed her for giving up, but had compassion because of the grief she felt.

"Many times the first word Jesus speaks to us is not about a physical change but about a heart change. He changes us and not the situation," Pastor Franklin liked to say from the pulpit. "If we don't let His change come into our hearts, then His changes won't ever come to our lives."

How much more changing do I have to do? Nora wanted to know.

Ben had found the bag with the nuts and bolts and screws. He tore it open and began to arrange the hardware beside the list that read: YOU SHOULD HAVE THESE ITEMS. Nora pressed her spine against the closed door. *Of course*, she thought. *We already have our change, don't we, God? She was born yesterday. Healthier than any of us ever dreamed.*

"I'm missing this one wing nut," Ben said, sifting through the pile of hardware. "Have you seen a wing nut? This thing says I'm supposed to have four and I can only find three."

Thank you for the baby's health, Lord. Oh, thank you for that. Thank you thank you.

"Maybe it rolled under your foot or something. Can you look?"

"Ben?" she asked, ignoring the wing nut completely. "What do you think she's going to do? Do you think she is going to stay?"

"I don't know, Nora." Ben's voice had a weary tone. "I honestly don't know."

"She's beating us up with our love for her. Do you know that?" Nora began to cry, muted desperate sounds which she tried to hide behind her hands. She felt unmoored, as if she were floating away from something. Every time she thought the Lord would help her, she lost her grip; her own faith shredded, fraying like old rope, in her hands. "She holds us hostage. No fair, how everything she does makes us change what we're going to do, too."

"I know that." It took Ben a long moment to rise. He had parts of crib spread out from one side of the room to the other, some of them propped against *him*. When he stood up, parts of the baby bed fell inward, propped against each other like a Boy Scout bonfire.

"What if the baby isn't safe?"

"Shhh." He took Nora's shoulders. "She'll hear you."

"I don't care." But Nora crammed the back of her hand against her mouth, trying to muffle her own grief. "I don't understand what God is *doing!*"

"But you're the one who knows God so well."

Nora raised her teary face to her husband's. "I *don't*. Oh, I *don't*. I just keep asking and asking for God to change her—"

"I know I fuss about going to church with you—"

"—and nothing ever happens."

They stood, holding each other up, while Nora untangled her words from his.

"I say the wrong things to Tess. I close myself off from you."

He gave a sharp laugh. "Okay," he said. "Yes. Yes, you do."

As if this discussion made her aware of Ben now, she began to work her way out of her husband's grasp.

"I admire you, Nora. I admire your morality. I admire that you stood beside me and told Tess what you knew was right."

"That thing you lost has to be around here somewhere. What was it? A wing nut?"

Ben said, "You guessed better than I did what the cost would be."

Beloved.

But Nora didn't hear anything.

Beloved, there is something inside you that you can't see. Something that keeps you from freedom, from being everything that you want to be.

"I throw out my prayers and I go through the motions, but there's *nothing there*." She went down on her hands and knees and started searching for baby furniture parts. "We've got to make her stay, Ben. It's the only way that baby is going to be safe. We have to *keep* her safe."

Let Me show you yourself, beloved.

Ben bent beside her on the sewing-room floor and finally opened the instructions.

∽

IN NORA'S DREAM, Tess was leaving. Tess with diapers in her bag, trying to convince someone she could take care of Tansy herself, that a baby wouldn't be too much trouble nor make too much noise. There was always a car waiting outside, loud shouting, a baby crying, slamming doors. She lay there in the dark, not knowing what awakened her. Had it been her jerking movement or the brush of Ben's thumb against her cheek? Her eyes adjusted to the moonlight spilling across the room. The pounding in her heart began to slow. There were dents in her palms where her fingernails had cut into them. She'd been hanging onto her pillow.

The brush of Ben's knuckles, light and wonderful against her skin. He was staring at her through the darkness. "You cried out."

"Did I?"

"Yes."

She squinted, her arm up over her eyes, trying to get her bearings. "I guess I was dreaming."

With Tansy in their house these past three nights, neither of them had slept enough to have dreams. Each time the baby began her faint, urgent crying, they listened for the rustle of Tess's sheets, the padding of her feet across the carpet, the chair creaking, the silence again.

Nora had found Tess crying the first night because her nipples ached and bled as she nursed. "This happens. We'll fix it," Nora had said, and she'd given Tess acetaminophen, a warm, wet cloth, a glass of ice chips, and some of the lanolin cream they'd sent home for Tess from the hospital. Last night Nora had wanted to rock the baby when she wouldn't sleep, when she cried for three frantic hours, but Tess wouldn't let her.

"I'll do this, Mother," Tess had said, so far asleep in the chair that she might have fallen out.

Ben's hand lay close along her hip and the notion of that changed Nora's breathing. She covered his hand with her own, threaded her fingers between his. His shoulder grazed her shoulder. His ear lay beside her ear. She heard the workings of his throat. "Grandma," he whispered, tracing her lips. "Grandma."

"Grandpa."

They were still marveling at the magnitude of this when the bleating noises began in Tess's room. Nora's ears played tricks. Did she hear the bed linens being thrown back? The thump of feet?

The baby was still crying. Nora smiled apologetically at Ben, raised herself with one arm. "Tess? You in there?"

No answer.

"Tess?"

As if in answer a truck passed on the highway in the distance, grew fainter, fainter, until it was gone. Nearby, one cricket *chirru*ped and was joined by a throng.

Nora willed her insides to be still.

Ben sailed covers toward the foot of the bed. "I'll check." His feet hit the floor hard. But before he could get to the bedroom door, they finally heard the guestroom bed creak. There was a thud when Tess must've run into something in the hallway, the kitchen faucet running, and the bleating stopped. Tess, determined to do it herself tonight. Nora didn't know whether to be relieved or sorry.

CHAPTER FIFTEEN

———— ✎ ————

The telephone rang at 4:00 A.M., a shrill, violent awakening that sent Ben staggering to a standing position and Nora sitting up, trying to figure out where she was.

"We're doomed. We're never going to get any more sleep, not as long as we live," Ben said ruefully, looking down at her.

Nora clutched the blankets against her chest. "It's never good when the phone rings in the middle of the night."

"I hope there's nothing wrong with my mother. I ought to have gone to visit this week," Ben said.

"No," Nora argued. "I could have done it, too. But you know how I hate to fly."

Ben felt around the bureau for the ringing phone while Nora fumbled for the lamp switch. "Hello?" she heard him say, and then a long moment of silence while he listened to whoever was talking on the other end. "You don't say."

Their bedroom door slammed open. "Who is that?" Tess asked bleary-eyed, her comforter wrapped around her middle. "Why did the phone ring?"

"I don't know," Nora whispered.

"Tansy didn't wake up. It's a good thing. She'd sleep through a tornado if she wasn't hungry."

"I heard you get up with her." And, if Nora wasn't so frightened for Tansy's safety, if she wasn't so sure Tess had done the selfish thing not letting her be adopted, Nora could have almost said, *Tess, I'm proud of you.* "Honey, I—"

But Ben hung up the phone. Tess stepped toward him. "Who is it, Daddy? What's wrong?"

Ben touched her shoulder. "That was Claude Simms down at the end of the street, our neighbor."

Nora's heart felt like it had stopped beating. "Is Lavinia okay?"

"Lavinia's fine. Claude's got a mockingbird up there that's been chasing his other garden birds away. He was up before dawn trying to find out where it roosts, thinking he could trap it and cart it down to the city park."

"He called us about his *mockingbird?*" Nora asked.

"No, he called us because there's a strange car parked in front of our house. He saw it when he went outside after that bird. There's someone walking around out there."

"Ben!"

"I know. This isn't good. Claude thought we ought to know." He began yanking on his sneakers.

Nora's next thought was of Tansy. "Is the baby safe, Tess? Don't you think you ought to get her?"

"She's fine, Mother. Better to leave her asleep."

"We ought to call Bill Mott or Merrill Horn. Get somebody over here from the sheriff's office." But Nora knew that would be a lost cause. The same way Ben didn't care to ask directions or read instructions, he would handle some prowler in their front yard himself.

Tucked behind the winter coats on his side of the closet,

Nora knew Ben kept his Ruger .22 pistol. He'd bought that gun for $54.95 when he'd been fourteen, using all of his paper-route money. He dug it out now, unzipped its tan plastic case with pride. He rummaged on the closet floor again and came out with an ancient box of .22 cartridges.

Tess darted toward the window. "No." Nora pulled her back by the hand before she could raise the shade. Tess's hand felt cool and bony in her own. "You mustn't look out there. It would give your father away."

It would still be a good hour before the night would begin to lift. The endless black visible between the shades and the sill looked impenetrable as iron. Nora's teeth chattered; she couldn't get warm. The fear sank cold deep into her bones.

"Mama, you get the phone," Tess whispered. "I don't care what Dad says about taking care of himself. We ought to call someone for help."

"You're right. Ben, we ought to call." For a split second, Nora thought about turning on another light. They should have set every light in this place ablaze the moment Claude phoned. That might have frightened their unwanted visitor away. But then they'd have tomorrow night to think of. And the next night. And the next.

One at a time Ben had been loading cartridges into the Ruger. He popped the magazine in, ready for action. "I can handle this," he said in a low, authoritative voice. "You girls wait here."

∞

BEN SNUCK OUT through the back patio door. Beside the patio, there was a huge bank of laurel shrubs growing against the façade of the house. He could hear the shrub rustling as if something were hiding there. Something skittered away from his feet in the grass.

He flattened his spine against bricks that still held the heat of day, his own breath roared in his ears, and he had the odd feeling that everything about to happen in their lives was aiming at him, like a rockslide. At the corner of the house he could see the one square of light from their bedroom, sending a gold shaft onto the lawn. The sharp shadows made his weed-free Bermuda grass look like a bed of razors.

Ben inched away from the wall toward the broad cement step that aproned the spot where, in the evenings after dinner, he and Nora liked to sit out and watch the squirrels and eat bowls of Bluebell ice cream. When his Nikes sank into the turf, he felt like he had stepped away from security. He was a macho character in an action movie. *Skulk around the corners. Let the barrel of the gun lead you.*

The crickets hummed so hard that he could literally feel the pulse in his ears. His tongue felt coated with metal shavings. His eyes had begun to adjust to the light. As he sprang around the corner ready for a show-down, Ben saw a figure poised in the side yard, one arm raised toward the kitchen window, knees locked, both legs together, its head wearing some odd-shaped hat. "Hey! Get away from my kitchen window," he wanted to shout. But the dry metal in his mouth wouldn't let him.

Oh, that he could be like Nora and turn to a higher power at a time like this. What had she taught him about prayer? *Ask and ye shall receive.*

Well, he didn't know if he'd call that his first prayer or not. But no sooner had he thought those words then the paper boy started up the street. When Ben had been a paper boy, he'd ridden his bike the length of ten city blocks every morning before going to school. Nowadays the paper boys' mothers drove them while the boys reclined in comfort on the open tailgate of a Chevy Suburban. Headlights from the Suburban glanced off the figure he'd been about to tackle and Ben saw, instead of the outline of an intruder, the spindly shape of the maple he'd planted and staked up last spring. Nailed in the crook of its branches, almost too large for the fledgling tree, was the arched, head-like birdfeeder Nora had given him for his birthday last fall.

The wave of lightheaded relief hit so hard that he chuckled. *So old Claude must've been seeing things. There can't be anyone prowling in my yard.* But before that thought was out, Ben heard a smattering of stones against the house, the sound of someone diving into the dirt for cover. Three houses down in the Weesners' yard, a dog began barking and jumping against the fence. A sedan of some sort—looked like it had to be a GM—had been stashed curbside.

Ben stopped. His chest was tight. "I know you're there," he shouted, his heart pounding in his chest. No one moved or made a sound. "I've got a gun."

A mosquito whined somewhere close to Ben's ear. When the hum stopped, he knew the mosquito was enjoying a feast on some bare section of his skin. But that was in another world, happening to someone he didn't know. Something bumped the screen in the window behind him, a silky whisper, one of those huge night moths, no doubt. Ben took one more step forward and would have been almost to the center of the yard, almost to the blue-yellow circle given off by the gaslight, except for the fist, wide and hard, that hit him on the side of his face.

Ben lost the Ruger as he went down with a cry of surprised outrage. At the next instant, something struck him on the back of the head and he saw blinding lavender light even in the darkness. He shook his head. It cleared well enough to see the dirty sneakers standing just beyond his nose.

Seek and ye shall find. In a move that would have made the wrestling coach at Butlers Bend High proud, Ben went for the takedown. He clamped his hands around the guy's knees and brought him to the ground hard with a thud—*ugh*. In the split second that gave him, Ben rolled to grab his gun and came down hard. He shoved the Ruger into the knobs of Dirty Sneakers's neck and growled, "Let's get acquainted, son. Who do you think you are?"

When the fellow tried to scramble out from under him, he sounded like an armadillo scratching for bugs. Ben shoved him hard onto his belly again and the air went out of his chest in a sharp guttural *ooof.*

"You're—you're not a cop," the guy said, his chin working against the dirt.

"No, I'm not."

"Wouldn't have hit you if I'd known you're not a cop. Can't get arrested again—"

"You're full of great choices, buddy." Ben had the guy's wrists twisted together now in one hand, his trusty old $54.95 .22 in the other. "You just give me one reason why I shouldn't call the sheriff."

"The car." He had to lift his chin off the ground and turn his face so he could speak. "They'll bust me."

"And they wouldn't bust you for trying to break into my house?"

A brief hesitation. "This is your house?"

"You betcha."

"You going to let me up, mister, or do I have to lie here talking to the worms all night?"

"I haven't decided yet, son. The idea of you talking to worms sounds fine to me."

"C'mon."

The kid tried to wrench his hands free so he could start the armadillo imitation again. But Ben wasn't about to buy it. "You're worrying about getting busted, you tell me why I shouldn't phone the sheriff right now."

"Came here looking for somebody."

"Who'd you come here looking for? Who did you think would be interested in seeing you in the middle of the night?"

"They told me over at the gas station. I asked and they told me she was here."

Fear sliced Ben's gut. *They told me she was here.* Don't tell him this had something to do with his family. He'd gotten slugged in the face; that pain felt warm and alive. It didn't compare to the misgiving that detonated in him now. "Who are you looking for?"

The boy spit. Dirt in his mouth. "You know Tess? Tess Crabtree?"

Ben set the kid's hands free. The minute Dirty Sneakers scrambled up onto his arms, Ben took a fistful of his oily hair and held his head with it. "Are you the one who got her pregnant?"

"Tess staying at your place? She around here somewhere?"

"You didn't answer my question, young man. Let me ask it again. Are you the one who got her pregnant?"

The slightest hesitation. "Well, now. That's anybody's guess."

Ben ached to let the kid up so he could square off with him in hand-to-hand combat. One big uppercut would make him feel much better. Teach that boy a thing or two about how to respect his daughter. But Ben couldn't be certain he'd stop at that; when he finished with this guy, he'd be the one in the sheriff's custody. So hard to resist the urge.

"Stand up." Ben backed off instead, keeping the pistol sighted where it would count the most. "What's your name?"

"Coot—I-I mean, Connor. Connor Banks," he said while he was getting to his feet. "But my friends call me Cootie. My *mother* called me Cootie. I don't go by anything else."

"I'm going to get you inside where you're not going to bolt. I'm going to get you someplace safe so I can decide what to do with you. You hear that?"

"Yes, sir. I do."

"You're not going to make any false moves or hurt any members of my family. You hear that?"

"Yes. I mean, yes, I hear that. I won't hurt nobody." Then, "You gonna call the cops?"

"I'm still thinking about it," Ben said. "We're going to decide what happens with that when we have a conversation with Tess, okay?"

"Sure thing."

Ben prodded Cootie in the vertebra once more and they headed for the house.

❦

IT WAS NORA who noticed Tess's expression when Ben and his capture burst through the front door. Nora had never seen such an explosion of hope, and it terrified her. Tess bounded forward with a frantic cry, "Cootie!" while Ben shouted, "Get back, Tess!" and the boy said calmly, "Hey, Babe. He's out there with a .22, man, thinking he's gonna rescue the world."

"Daddy, it's okay."

With false composure, Nora walked to the refrigerator and began placing ice cubes into a bag. "Ben. You're hurt." She tried to press the ice bag against Ben's swollen jaw but he waved her away.

He gestured toward Tess. "You know this guy?"

"Oh, yeah. I do."

"Ben." Nora's voice carefully measured to hide her terror. "If you don't get ice on that thing now, it's going to get worse." How she wished this intruder had been a burglar, a thief, a murderer, anyone except the person stepping in on them now.

Who would come looking for Tess here, except for Tansy's father? Nora would bet these words were rattling around in Ben's head, too. Words from the day Tess had come home and Nora had found the pregnancy test.

If you are pregnant, you know who the baby's father is, don't you? Ben had asked.

Tess's brown eyes had filled with irony. *What does that matter? I'm going to get rid of it. You know there'd be something wrong with it anyway, if it came.*

It matters, Tess, Nora ought to have shouted. It matters because a father has a right to a baby, too. It matters because someday, some month, some year, he might be standing in our living room and we wouldn't know what to do.

This boy was dressed in a puffy nylon jacket over a thin T-shirt worn so often that the neck had frayed. On the side of one jacket sleeve someone had stitched *VL* by hand. His dusty jeans hung in loose folds that made his legs look elephantine.

One side of his hollow face was striped with scratches and his curly dark hair hung wide around his face like the hood of a cobra.

A silver chain dangled from his belt loop to his pocket and he wore a gunmetal stud in each of his ears. When Nora met his red-rimmed blue eyes, they looked faded by life. Except for his hair, he was devoid of color. This boy reminded Nora of a ghost.

"You tell me why I shouldn't call Deputy Merrill Horn and get him over here right now," Ben repeated again.

"The car," Cootie said, as he looked pointedly at Tess and wagged his head.

"What about the car?" Ben asked. His jaw was pounding where the kid had belted him across the face. Another lost boy who got high to drown out the troubles of the world. Ben's anger hovered somewhere between sorrow and disgust.

Tess jumped in fast. "Cootie won't be any trouble."

"You may have to convince me of that. He attacked me in my own front yard."

"I attacked you because you were after me."

"I wanted to see who you were."

"You didn't give me a chance to tell you."

And Tess's thin voice, "You can put the gun down, Daddy. It's okay."

Ben lowered the Ruger by degrees.

"You might win a Scooby-Doo at a carnival with that, Mister." But Cootie still seemed a little concerned. "That's about all the damage you could do."

"It's okay, Daddy. You can put it down."

Ben held it a moment longer before he propped the thing against a chair, still within easy reach. The tension between Tess and Cootie seemed to flood out of the room the moment the gun touched the floor. It seemed to Nora that, at that moment, the two of them melded together, fell *into* each other. There might have been only two of them in this room.

"Thought I'd come see about you," Cootie said in a rush and Nora hated the pleasure she saw in Tess's face. Her daughter appeared so delighted to see this boy, so proud, so surprised, and there was an eager flush to her cheeks.

"Came to see if I could make you come back."

Ben had finally lowered himself into a kitchen chair and let Nora daub his wound. "You think you could have come to see my daughter at a decent hour?"

"There's something about you, Babe. You look different."

"There's been a lot that's happened. Do you want to see the—"

No, Tess. Stop. "Where do you live? How did you get here?" Nora interrupted sharply. *The baby.* Tess had been about to say, *Do you want to see the baby?*

"I drove." Then, "It's a long story. I just, I've been trying to get here for a long time."

He can't have Tansy, Nora was thinking. *I don't want him to touch her.*

It was five in the morning and Nora longed for sewing in her hands. She needed a needle to thread. A hem to stitch. A sleeve to gather. She needed the heavy reassurance of fabric draping her knees and her hands constructing a garment. Somewhere inside, Nora knew her perception was flawed but she couldn't change it. When she looked at Cootie, she did not see how far Tess had come. Instead she saw everything that Tess used to be.

Nora saw only a curling iron burning her arm and futile days with a Diversion officer in court. She thought of her Hamilton watch missing, money stolen from Ben's sock drawer, flakes of marijuana on the bathroom floor.

She remembered Tess's empty bedroom before it had become the guestroom, with the wrinkled note that read: IF YOU COME AFTER ME, YOU WON'T FIND ME. I CAN'T STAND LIVING WITH MOM ANYMORE. She saw Tess's last, most selfish act: *I'm not signing anything. I can't give her away.* Nora looked at Cootie and those things were all she could see.

Ben took the ice pack from his wife. "I'll do this myself. It's okay." This left her hands empty, and she needed something to occupy them, something to take her mind from the brilliance in Tess's eyes. With every ounce of her, Nora wanted to say to Cootie, *Go. Please just go. Don't take us back again.* She yanked the refrigerator open and brought out the egg carton, a can of Pillsbury biscuits, the pitcher of orange juice. "I've got bacon, too. You like bacon, don't you? How does breakfast sound?"

She didn't give him a chance to answer. How much of this was Scripture working in her heart? *If your enemy is hungry, give him food to eat; if he is thirsty, give him water to drink.* She would never know. As Nora broke eggshells and scrambled yolks in a bowl, as she laid the bacon in ribbons in the skillet and they began to sizzle, she never could have known that a mother hadn't cooked Cootie breakfast for ten years.

"Can't hang around," he said, shaking his head. "I've got to ditch—I mean, I've got to get back with the car."

Pale light had begun to filter in through the shades; Nora glanced at the clock as she poured eggs into the pan. Five minutes until five. "Sure, you've got time. It won't take long." The biscuits slid into the oven and the jar of jewel-red jelly came out of the fridge. Nora circled the table with plates, aligned forks, knives, and spoons, folded the napkins and placed them like little flags. Cootie gravitated to the table, so Tess gravitated, too. By the time Nora said, "Everybody come. It's ready," everyone was already there.

There was something sacred about it, something uncommon about the meal they shared. The tension didn't leave, but it was muted. They ate buttery biscuits and licked their greasy fingers. They moaned with delight when the hot bacon strips crumbled against their tongues. They drank milk so cold they could feel it when it reached their stomachs. Sparrows fluttered awake in the maple outside and began to sing.

When Cootie ate, he leaned forward into his food as if he was afraid it might disappear. He ate his breakfast in huge, eggy globs, using his fork as a shovel. The biscuit disappeared in two bites. He slowed once to wash everything down with orange juice before he reached for a third helping. Other than that, Cootie never rested his fork. Nora had the awful intuition as she saw Tess touch his jacket sleeve that he was starving for much more than a meal.

"Got this plan once, right after you left," he said around his biscuit to Tess, only all of them heard it. "Know what I was going to do?"

"No. What?"

"Kept thinking if I climbed to the top of the Magnolia Building and took a ride on that red horse, I could see all the way to you."

Tess laughed. "That would have been insane. Why would you do something like that?" But she diverted her eyes with shy pleasure. "All you had to do was drive a car and come find me."

"I know." Those faded blue eyes leveled on Tess. "But it wouldn't have been nearly so romantic."

Father, Nora thought. *It is not Your will that any should be lost.*

"They ran a story about that horse this month in *The Dallas Morning News.* Had to wait by the newspaper dispenser until somebody paid and I could grab the door before it latched and get a copy out."

Father, have You done all this so we could help this young man?

"When the horse first went up, it revolved 1.3 times per minute and it was built from 1,162 feet of red glass tubing. That's what the story said. On clear nights, pilots from all around can see it."

"You want more eggs?" Nora asked. When he nodded, she loaded more on his plate.

"Someday I'll get up there. Just for a chance to see all those glass tubes and wires and things."

As Nora handed him more bacon, too, she couldn't have known that sometimes Cootie dreamed he might find his mother there, at the top of the Magnolia Building. That she might be standing below those neon tubes, bent low to welcome him, her crocheted purse (oh yes, he'd always remember that purse) lying on the concrete beside her feet. Nora couldn't have known that he still dreamed his mother would say, "I'm sorry I let you go, Coot. My life would have been so different if I had you."

Father, what should I do?

"All you had to do," Tess said again, "was drive a car and come find me."

"All you had to do," Cootie said back, "was take care of everything the way you said you would and hitchhike back to Dallas."

Nora met Ben's eyes, their glance toward each other as sharp as broken glass. With foreboding Ben found the Ruger with his hand; he'd kept the gun propped close to his side. "Tess had other things she decided to do."

Nora felt connected with Ben in a way she hadn't felt in months, sharing this fear that seemed both well-founded and vague. Trying to figure out what to do next with him was like trying to drive through deep fog. All either of them knew to do was creep along toward the other side.

"Did you come here to find me?" Tess asked. "Did you want me to go back with you?" As if she were thinking, *Well, if you didn't come here with this on your mind, I can surely put it there!*

"I'm not leaving here without you, Babe, if that's what you —"

The first short bleat that came from the sewing room was almost indiscernible. If Nora hadn't gotten used to listening for this tender cry, she might not have even heard it. The sound might not have even registered until it was louder, or longer, or stronger. Nora bit her bottom lip and looked a terrified question at Ben. He began to rise. "I'll go."

Nora stood, too. "No, I can."

But they weren't the only ones who heard Tansy's cry. Tess had heard it, too. She beat them both. "That's the baby, Coot. Don't you want to see her?"

"What?"

"Weren't you coming to get me and the baby?"

Cootie's expression went flat and considering. "You promised you'd take care of that."

"Yeah. I know I did."

"There wasn't going to be any baby. I dunno what you're talking about."

"I changed my mind," Tess said. "That's what I'm talking about."

"Sure, I was coming to get you," Cootie said. But then, with all high shoulders and stiff back, "I wasn't coming to get any baby."

In the sewing room, Tansy began to bleat louder. The bruise on Ben's face had turned a vicious purple and had swollen to the shape of a pear. "You're no good for my daughter," Ben said. "You did this to her. You're the one who kept getting high with her. You don't take responsibility for your actions."

"Hey, man," Cootie said. "Your daughter's old enough to make her own choices."

While Cootie had talked, Nora had watched Ben's lips fold in on each other. There was nothing left except a tight dash of disapproval, like something drawn with a slash of a pen.

"That's what happened, Cootie," Tess said. "I made my own choice. Why did you think I didn't come back? Did you think it was because I didn't want to see you?"

Tansy's howls came from the crib, more strident now, those woeful, terse wails that could pull a person's heart out of itself. Nora couldn't stand it anymore. "She's hungry," she said. "I'm going after her."

"No, Mama. Sit down." Tess's eyes were moist almost to the point of tears but her jaw was set and hard. "I'll go."

Nora had in mind clearing the plates and rinsing them, but her legs felt twice their normal weight. She collapsed into the chair again, not believing she could feel this tired. Ben's voice wasn't quite even when he said, "She's a keeper, this little one. You wait and see."

Tess brought Tansy in all bundled in a blanket, helped her daughter balance her little head upright. Tansy's cheeks were flushed pink from wailing and her nose was blubbery and her eyes were the color of blueberries. Wisps of fine dark hair protruded from her head like dandelion fuzz. Dressed in a cherry-pink sleeper, she was too little to even do baby things. She didn't yet drool or tear up or smile. She just looked at Cootie, her blue eyes as big around as nickels, interested to see him. She was interested to see *all* of them.

It would have taken a fiend to look at that baby and be able to turn away.

Tansy did not protest when Tess placed her in Cootie's arms. Nora's body protested instead. Bands of panic encircled her throat. She wanted to snatch Tansy out of this young man's hands and send him packing. She wanted to grab Ben's gun herself and usher Cootie out the way he had come. Who cares if it wouldn't do more damage than winning a prize at a carnival. Aimed at the right area of his anatomy, that would be damage enough!

The boy held Tansy's compact little self away from his chest, his elbows as stiff as scissors.

"What do you think?" Tess asked. "Isn't she the prettiest thing?"

Nora's frustration came from so much more than Cootie's dangerous presence and Tess's calm pleasure. It came from deep inside her. It came because she had considered encouraging Tess to have an abortion. She was never going to let anything bad happen to this baby. *Never.*

Something came back to Nora, a memory fluttering like a moth, just out of her reach. The Christmas pageant—of course, that was it, one of many years that Creede Franklin had been Joseph, and a much-younger Frieda Storm had asked Tess to bring a doll. That's what Tess had said to Creede after she'd shoved her way to the manger. "What do you think?" she'd asked Creede, too, only she'd been talking about her doll, Pink Baby. "Isn't she the prettiest thing?"

Tess watched Cootie now, her face gone grave and pale and still. Give a little credit to Cootie, though; he *did* hesitate before he handed her away to Tess. "This isn't going to change my mind," he said.

Ben rose from his chair and clutched Tess by the shoulders, even then, as if he already knew he ought to hang onto her. "No one asked you to change your mind, buddy," Ben said. "No one asked you to come here and find them."

"It's okay he came here, Daddy. It's really okay. It's really all right." The deliberate way she ducked her father's grasp, the shy way she said those measured words, turned Nora's blood to ice. "If you want me to come with you, Cootie, I will. If you don't want me to bring the baby," she said, clutching Tansy against her, "I can leave her here."

Nora had reached for the tassel to pull open the shade. When Tess said those words, Nora lost her grip. The shade snapped itself and rolled up, *thwack-thwack-thwack*. Even that startling sound didn't make the others move.

Outside in the first morning light Nora could see a thick bank of clouds hovering toward the east. The sun had begun to rise beneath it, bleaching the sky to the same yellows and blues as a reflection on a clear stream. For long moments the low clouds blotted out all but that hint of light. Then suddenly, like the appearance of an angel's gilded wing, the sun topped the clouds. Every fluff beamed with gold.

"You can't go back with him," Nora said to the window. "We won't let you do that."

Ben jumped in, too, his voice a low growl. "Very significant events happen when you lose sight of where you're going."

Tess's eyes leveled on her mother in hostility and defiance. "I know where I'm going." For one split instant, everyone else faded; only Nora and Tess were in the room. They'd returned to the confrontation that, no matter how they tried to ignore, was never far away. "Cootie is one person who sees good things in me."

Tess might not be willing to give up her daughter for her daughter's sake. But she was willing to ditch it all for another violent payback to her mother? Something inside Ben snapped. When he rose and strode toward the telephone, he did not have to look anything up in the book. The sheriff's number hung on a little card Nora had thumbtacked to the side of the cabinet. GILFORD COUNTY EMERGENCY NUMBERS, the little card read, with a list including the clinic, the fire department, the city water office, and the number to the library's daily dial-a-story. Ben dialed it fast, 5-5-5-3-4-2-1, while Nora stood staring at her daughter and cried inside.

Lord? What is it about Tess and me that we crush each other's spirits? Why would she need to run this fast and this far?

"Sheriff's office. How I can help you?"

"I'm calling to report an intruder," Ben announced.

"You can't do that." Cootie shoved himself from the table and his chair landed on the floor. "Tess." He flung his hands at her and almost knocked the baby out of her arms. "Don't let your dad do that. I ripped off the car."

"Daddy." Tess wrestled for the receiver but it was too late. He'd already given their address to the dispatcher. "You have to stop."

"I'm not doing more time in jail."

"Tess." Nora took Tansy away from her. "You can't give this much up for him." When she didn't turn, "Tess, listen to me."

"This is my chance to have it, too, Mama. Didn't you see the look on Creede's face on his wedding day?"

"You aren't going to have anything the same as that. You'll get pulled back in," Nora said. "You'll end up getting high."

Oh, Father. You've got to change Tess. Nothing's any different now than it ever was.

Ben brandished the gun again. But this time, when he aimed the Ruger at Cootie, Cootie ignored it. He started for the door instead.

"Stop," Ben said, letting a shot fly at Cootie's feet. It sent up a meager fluff of carpet.

"I'm getting my stuff," Tess shouted.

Cootie said to Ben, "You aren't going to shoot me."

Tansy had started to fuss in Nora's arms. With a catch in her heart, Nora demanded this: "If you're going to go, you can do what's right for her, Tess. Let me call Janet Whitsitt. I can get those relinquishment papers to sign."

Only then did Nora see the glint of regret in Tess's eyes. "There isn't time. I should have done it the other day."

"You could do it now." But Nora and Ben felt like Tansy belonged to them, too. She was their granddaughter and, immediately, they had loved her. *Three days,* Nora thought, *and it would take everything I am to let this baby out of my sight.*

"This is who I am. I can't change that. This is who we are together."

The words seemed to come from the air around her, the trees outside, the sun that rose through the clouds. *Beloved, you pray for Me to change others. Pray for Me to change you.*

"Give us some address, some way to get a hold of you, *something.*"

"You'd only try to bring me back."

Let her go. Let Me work.

Tess shrugged into a jacket that was hanging by the door. "Bye, baby," Tess said, tears brimming in her eyes as she gave Tansy a light kiss. "Baby, baby, baby, baby."

"Tess," Nora whispered, broken, feeling as if her heart had fallen away and was lying limp somewhere. "He isn't worth this. Think of your daughter."

"I *am* thinking of her." And if Nora could have read Tess's mind, she would have seen everything she was thinking: *Maybe this is what I was waiting for, Mama. See, I do so many things wrong.* "I think it would be best if you have her."

Tansy's hand seemed to flutter up and touch the back of Nora's neck. Nora brushed a hand over her granddaughter's forehead. The delicate weight of the baby grew heavier as Tansy rooted against the warmth of Nora's arms.

CHAPTER SIXTEEN

---✒︎---

You are cordially invited to a BABY SHOWER

IN HONOR OF: *Tansy Aster Crabtree, new granddaughter of*
Nora and Ben Crabtree

DATE: *Saturday*

TIME: *7:00 p.m.*

PLACE: *579 Texoma Street, Fellowship Parlor*
Butlers Bend Baptist Church (SBC)

Light refreshments will be served

PLEASE R.S.V.P. TO: *Jane Ruckmann 555-4983*

The Crabtrees need all supplies, diapers, Desenex—beginning to
have problems with diaper rash—soft blankets and one-piece
rompers. If you have items you don't mind handing down, bring
them. Also, we are taking up a collection for a rocking chair (see
Sears catalog pg. 283). If you would like to go in with us on this,
let me know. It's a surprise, though, so please don't say anything!!

B en had to hand it to the ladies. You give a woman a good reason—even a *tragic* reason—and forty-eight hours, and someone will come up with a party. Scallops of pink streamers dangled from the ceiling. A slab of cake the size of Wisconsin sat in the middle of a Sunday school table; he was already waiting for one of those icing roses. Over in the corner beside the door, the stack of wrapped packages had become enormous.

"Oh, just look at this *baby*," Lavinia Simms said with a sideways glance at Ben. "Isn't she just the sweetest thing?"

"Have you seen what she does when you stick your thumb in her mouth?" he asked, acting the expert. "She latches on like a leech."

Ben didn't want anyone to see it, but he was lost. He often thought his granddaughter would stop crying if he could only make himself understand what she wanted. During the past forty-eight hours, he'd spent more time than he wanted anyone to know just lying on the bed with her, looking into her face, thinking, *What will we do with you?*

If this new child had seemed amazing and familiar in the hospital, she now seemed like someone he didn't know at all. Trying to put a diaper on this wrinkled and wise thing felt like trying to diaper Yoda from *Star Wars*. Ben felt as if he knew nothing when he gazed into her face, as if she were an old little woman as shrewd as the sea and he was just, well, *him*.

Although he wouldn't let it come to the surface, he felt responsible. Responsible for the maternity leave Nora had taken at Stitch 'N Time. (*Maternity* leave for a forty-six-year-old grandma, for heaven's sake.) Responsible for not making things right enough so Tess would stay. Responsible for the way Nora wouldn't turn the lights off in the baby's room at night. *("She won't know the difference between day and night,"* he'd disagreed with her. *"She'll never learn to sleep if you don't give her time alone in the dark." "I can't, Ben,"* Nora had told him. *"I won't leave her alone where she can't see.")*

Jane Ruckmann brought him back from his thoughts. "Can I, please?" she asked, touching his arm. "Can I hold her?" It took him a minute to figure out she wanted Tansy. "You could go get something to eat."

"Oh, yes." Ben gave the baby over, balancing her as if he were handing over something that might break into pieces. "Sure." And Jane scarcely had his granddaughter before three others were in line for a turn.

Where are you ladies in the middle of the night when we really need you?

Pastor Franklin gestured toward the gift corner with a plate that, Ben noted, held the piece of cake with the roses. "Lots of stuff there."

Nora sat at the head of the table and began tearing paper, slicing strips of tape with her nails. The pastor nodded in her direction, saluted with his fork. "Well, I had enough practice with presents at Creede and Candy's wedding. I'll help you load them in the car."

"Thanks."

"You want this cake? I certainly don't need it."

Ben nodded. "It's the rose I want. Let me have a bite."

If the two men hadn't been friends before, they bonded out of necessity here. It seemed impossible that baby paraphernalia could have changed so much over the past nineteen years. Where Tess had started in regular white Pampers sized Small, Tansy would begin life in mountains of newborn Swaddlers, with a notch cut out for the delicate umbilical cord area, pink penguins parading across the tapes, and a color-coded tab to indicate whether baby was wet. She would have her face shaded by two Baby Gap sailor hats, one white and one lilac. And that's as far as the two gentlemen could get without leaning forward in puzzlement, squinting across the room, relying on each other for technical information.

"What do you imagine that is?"

"What does it do?"

"You seen one of those before?"

They managed to figure their way through a headband with purple flowers, a rhino that laughed when you squeezed it, rattle shoes, coupons for free babysitting, a pacifier clip with a string *(And so, that attaches to something?)*, a tooth-and-gum cleanser with gum brush, a musical key ring *(Not the keys to the car already. By the time she's driving, maybe I'll be dead.)*, and a baby-view safety mirror that read on the box WHEN IT IS IMPORTANT TO SEE BEHIND YOU.

They didn't falter until Nora opened the Baby's-First-Year Cold-Care set and Pete saw the picture on the front of the carton. "Good heavens, you don't stick that thing up the nose do you?"

"Of course you do. I remember when Tess got the croup—"

Ben saw Nora shoot him a look of caution; oh, yes, he knew his wife's heart. He saw bitterness in her that he didn't understand, something dark that only seemed to grow over time. That look said, *Don't talk about Tess. I don't want to hear that girl's name.*

Well, he *did* remember. Remembered how Tess had tried to nurse with desperate, clogged little snorts. Remembered how Nora had asked him to time with his wristwatch while she counted Tess's breaths. The baby's breathing rough and choked, like something being strung through gravel every minute. Hot water steaming the bathroom and stars pricking the cold night sky. And when they'd gotten her to the hospital and put her inside a plastic tent with oxygen, all he'd wanted to do was climb inside with her. That had been the worst thing; being able to see Tess and yet not touch her. Looking at her, and feeling a thousand miles away.

Pete Franklin reached out to shake Ben's hand as they rose. Ben's fingers fit into many crevices, the way they would fit around crumpled paper. "You haven't come to me much, Ben, but I know these past years have been a challenge."

Ben surveyed the half-moon circles of his nails.

"There's not a person in this entire congregation who wouldn't help you take care of your new little girl."

"Thanks. We'll call on you, Pete, if we need to," Ben said.

"We could schedule a baby dedication if you'd like. It would signify a lot. Starting over again with this one, having a new chance."

"Nora and I will talk about that."

The minister took the cue and changed the subject. He picked up a box. "A baby-wipe warmer. Imagine that."

"Think I'll be able to do something useful with that?"

"Maybe keep bread warm? Or your shoes warm when it's cold?"

"Maybe."

"Put it on a timer so the pastries or the slippers would be hot in the morning?"

"Fine idea," Ben said, and they both laughed.

They had found something on which they agreed.

✎

"DOLORES?" Nora asked, peering inside the huge box. "Is this one from you? Do you want me to open this? What do I do?"

Until now, Dolores Kay Jones had been quiet. She settled into a seat beside Nora, her hands splayed across her polyester skirt like small doilies over a sofa arm, her eyes glistening like seed pearls. "You and Ben and Tess and the baby," she said. "You are such a special family. This is the best gift I could think of."

Dolores Jones's big box was full of smaller presents. Each one had been folded and twisted, taped and tied. Nora began to dig.

"Any order I ought to open these in?"

"No."

"This one, then?"

Dolores nodded.

First from the box came a beautiful silver-handled mirror, polished and glinting in the basement lights. On its handle, Dolores had tied a puffy homemade bow. Nora found a note tied there, which she opened and read.

HOLD THIS UP

"Okay." Nora did, and saw her face. "I see myself."

"Read the other side."

Nora turned the note card over. " 'If our faith is in ourselves, we are trusting in something that wavers.' "

She went rifling through the box again. The next gift she found was neat and crisp, with corners mitered, tucked under, Scotch-taped secure. She found a nick in the tape and peeled it back. She smoothed the paper flat in her lap.

Nora read these words scribbled across the top.

She lifted the lid and found a collection of coins inside. Pennies. Dimes. Nickels. Even a quarter or two. An entire collection of change. She poured the coins in her hand; a penny or two rolled away. The note was folded inside the small lid: "Jesus doesn't change."

"Oh. I get it," Caroline Rakes said, rocking back in her seat. "Jesus doesn't change. *Change*. Get it?"

Dolores picked up the coins that had dropped to the floor. "We think about Jesus two different ways." Dolores plunked one penny in Nora's palm. "We picture Jesus who came, the depths of a valley in His eyes, love pouring from His soul, following the call to the cross." She plunked down a second penny. "We picture Jesus who *will* come, eyes flashing, crushing the one who steals from Him, sustaining all things we know by His powerful word." One by one, Dolores dropped the other coins inside the box. *Plink. Plink. Plink.* "Only what happens in between?"

Someone had to organize these pennies, nickels, and dimes. This bothered Nora. When she got them to the house, she would go to the bank and ask for paper coin wrappers. Then she could keep them for Tansy, stacked in a bureau drawer, carefully heaped and counted.

"'The universe will wear away and be folded up like a garment, but you remain the same,' it says in Hebrews, 'and your years will never end.' Jesus is all love and all power and He will not *change*."

With each coin she placed back into the box, Nora thought, *It doesn't matter if Jesus doesn't change.* A dime. *It's the world that changes.* A nickel. *Every time it looks like He fixes something, something else falls apart.*

She would clean out the guest room where Tess had stayed. Tomorrow. She would take the sheets off the bed and wash them. Maybe she'd carry them to Cowboy Cleaners and have them steamed. No, better yet. She would iron them herself while the baby slept. She would wax the furniture, dust the blinds, wipe away every fleck of mascara that Tess left everywhere she went.

Everything would be clean and fresh.

She would trail her fabrics all over the floor and all over the bed and all over the chairs.

She would sew and crochet Tansy a baby blanket just like she'd wanted to, all along.

They started to complain about her taking so long to open each package. "Oh, sorry." She began to claw the paper, sending shreds flying, making everybody cheer. She uncovered a black-velvet hinged box with the words,

A Heart Encircled

"What's this?"

"Open it. Go ahead." Inside, on a small incline, laid a crystal heart on a slender cord.

"This is for Tansy, isn't it?"

"No," Dolores said. "It's for you."

Nora didn't know why, but she felt afraid.

"It's okay," Dolores said, as if she had known. "Turn it over and you'll see."

On the other side, she found the engraving, "Baby's First Christmas," and a tiny gold-etched circle where a picture would go.

"I don't—is there a note?"

"Yes. But the box was so small, I couldn't find a way to make it fit." Dolores pulled it from her skirt pocket and handed it over.

"'There isn't anyone alive who can heal a broken heart, no matter what they are willing to do. Healing a heart takes more than human love. It takes divine power. Hang this, and you'll remember to expect Jesus not to be greater than who He is, not to be different than who He is, but to be *who* He is. The powerful, loving healer of hearts.'"

I don't have a broken heart. Nora unthreaded the cord from the cardboard and held the faceted glass in her hand. She felt the cool, fine heaviness settle against the hollow of her hand, and liked it there.

"It's so pretty." Frieda Storm was gathering plates alongside Emma Franklin and carting them to the kitchen.

"Something you'll have forever," Lavinia crowed, slapping her knees.

And everything seemed fine until Caroline pronounced nicely, "She's going to come back someday, I hope you realize that. You're going to raise this baby, Nora, and then Tess will show up and break your heart all over again."

The room grew quiet all around her. Fifteen women, her pastor, and her husband waited to see how she would respond. They all heard the bitterness as Nora said, "I would never let that happen."

CHAPTER SEVENTEEN

———— ✦ ————

A nd that was how their lives began with Tansy Aster. For all the encouragement Nora and Ben had, all the well-wishes and all the advice, they moved through their grand-daughter's first years with numb acceptance.

This is how the days blur along. A family moves from supper to supper. From one day at work to the next. From one good sermon to another. The next visit to the chiropractor. The next Christmas. Switching from Bounty to Brawny. The next time *Doc* is on TV.

There were the sleepless nights, the first traumatic haircut of that dark brown hair so curly that it sprang from her head like corkweed, the day the paperwork was approved by the Department of Human Services and the state of Texas and they stood in the Gilford County courthouse to be pronounced Tansy's legal guardians.

There was the first stab at daycare. (*"I thought I'd found a lady who would take care of Tansy, only I can't do it,"* Nora told Lavinia. *"I went to inspect the house and there was a baby with a scab the size of a silver dollar on his forehead. I asked what happened and she said,*

'Oh, isn't it just awful? He rolled underneath the entertainment center and got stuck there.' Can you imagine leaving a baby to roll under the furniture? I couldn't get out of there fast enough.") There were the first inoculations, the first tooth to break through, the first smile, the first steps.

There were the dozens of baby blankets Nora sewed from flannel, the edges hemstitched and crocheted. Nora couldn't stop herself from making blankets. The frustration Jo Ellen Wort had evoked that day, bragging about Paige Lee having a baby, exploded out of Nora with her purchases of flannel yardages as soft as feathers. She started innocently enough, with a yard and a half, the same serene yellow as a canary's breast. After she carried the fabric home and laid it out, she reveled in the chatter of the needle, the ripples of shadow and light, the heavy way the flannel pooled across the chair. Nora scarcely finished scalloping the edges on the yellow one before she had her eye on sherbet green, and on a blue that made her think of traces of sky.

With each stitch Nora took, she journeyed further from her pain when Tess had said, *"I don't want you to make blankets. This is my baby, not your baby."* With each thread she snipped and each knot she tied, Nora cut herself away from her ache when Tess hadn't shared her baby moving. *"It's bad enough that I'm here. Just don't* watch *me all of the time."*

Sometimes at the sewing machine, Nora would hum and be satisfied. She would hum and think how she thanked God that she and Ben had this child to show for it. This jewel of a little girl. A new beginning.

Nora had noticed young mothers taking their children to the library, spreading out tablecloths and eating peanut butter crackers after story time. She decided to take Tansy to story time, too, and couldn't resist lazing on the grass beside the water trough on two of those infamous flannel blankets. She'd made so many of them, might as well put a few to good use. Once, she'd stood up, brushed off her pants and had taken a step away. She'd left Tansy in the grass alone, this child that had become so important to her. She wanted to know what this would feel like. She took another step. She counted the steps it took to walk away. And when she turned back, all she could see of Tansy were her fingers and her feet stirring the weeds. Like she was a growing thing in that lawn, as natural as the nut-grass. Then Nora had counted the ten steps back.

They went from tax season to tax season and claimed Tansy as a dependant. From one teeth cleaning to the next. From one Texas Aggie football game to another. This is how the days move along.

Nora did not count the times that she took a second glance at someone during those toddler years, wondering if it might be Tess. When she was least thinking about it, when she was heading into the grocery store or darting into the Shell station for gas, she would glimpse someone stepping off the curb, hear someone's fleeting call, see white-wheat hair glinting in the sun and she'd think, *That's Tess. There she is.* And she'd try to will her heart to stop galloping, the gooseflesh to stop forming on her arms. *She's left Cootie and come back to find us.*

On the day of Tansy's fourth birthday, Nora arranged the best party she could think of—a trip to Chuck E. Cheese's with Lavinia and Claude Simms, Fran Coover, Jane Ruck-mann, Dolores Kay Jones, Frieda Storm, Erin Hamm (Tansy's best friend), and a generous group of other acquaintances from Mockingbird Preschool. "I like this party!" Tansy had said, grabbing Ben's hands, jumping on his feet, swinging against him, until Ben had to say, "Hey, whoa there, girl! I'm not a punching bag."

"You're not a punching bag," she yelped back. "You're a grandpa!" Then she slid, as if she were boneless, all the way to the floor.

"Yes," Ben said. "A very *important* grandpa."

The table set at the foot of the stage had been reserved for eight four-year-old children. It was perfectly adorned with eight pointed birthday hats, eight noisemakers, eight Chuck E. Cheese's gift bags, and eight packs of free cotton candy. Nora had ordered pepperoni. The pizzas were waiting, ready to be placed in the oven on a rack. Tansy bounced on excited little feet while Nora straightened her velvet birthday dress. And Nora could not squelch her pride while the children ran amuck and the adults gathered at the table to chat.

It was amazing how they'd been able to start a new life during these past years. *I may not be the youngest woman on the snack calendar, but I do know how to pick the birthday spots!* Nora gave a little nod of her head along with the satisfying rush of pride.

Things began well enough, with the usual rush of adults at the counter ordering sodas. "And who's the birthday girl?" a waitress asked. Someone pointed to Tansy as she ran away, skipping off into the crowd with her little friends. Chuck E. Cheese (some poor employee in a fuzzy bear costume) jumped around the table singing *The Birthday Song*. The pizza order, which had been quadrupled at the request of the adult males, disappeared almost as fast as they set the pans out. The food gone, the children scattered in every direction.

The last time Nora saw Tansy, she was following the Simmses toward the prize counter. Between the two of them, Lavinia and Claude had accumulated enough tickets to trade in for some of the kitschy prizes displayed in the glass case. "I've got enough for one of those glow-in-the-dark neon bracelets," Lavinia had said after she'd finished counting.

"Do you have fifteen?" Claude had asked her. "I have 125. If we put them together, we'd have 140 tickets. We could afford the Dallas Cowboys alarm clock that shouts 'Hut One, Hut Two, Hut Three,' when it's time to wake up in the morning."

"I'd rather die than wake up that way, Claude."

"Something else then. If we put our tickets together, we could afford anything on the back row."

"I don't want to compile our tickets, Claude. I want to pick something out for myself."

When Tansy wanted to follow them, Nora held her hand a little longer than usual. "You stay right with them. There's so many people in here. It's hard for me whenever I lose sight of you."

Tansy raced off into the crowd and, when she grabbed Lavinia's sleeve at the counter and Lavinia started showing Tansy the bracelets she liked, Nora helped herself at the soda machine and turned back to visit with the adults.

Chuck E. Cheese himself delivered the birthday cake not ten minutes later. Erin had already climbed into the chair beside her mother. Tansy's guests converged from every direction. Nora's chest clenched. Tansy hadn't returned. Nora chided herself but, even so, she was worried. She stood on tiptoe and spied Lavinia and Claude weaving their way through a line of people at the salad bar. Tansy would be with them; of course she would be.

But at the same time, Nora caught a glance of someone headed toward the door. Her breath snagged in her throat. From the back, she could see shoulders in a puffy black jacket.

She couldn't see his sleeves, but Nora was almost certain one of them had a *VL* embroidered on it. Cootie was here. Cootie and Tess had decided they wanted Tansy back.

But here came Lavinia and Claude smiling. If anyone noticed she had gone pale, no one said anything. "Where's Tansy?" Nora asked before they got the chance to show off their prizes. "Isn't she with you?"

"Oh, goodness." Lavinia turned and looked behind her. "Where has she wandered off to? She was just here."

"I'm sorry," Nora said, pushing herself away from the table. "I'll be right back." She took ten paces, searching in every direction, before she began to call Tansy's name. Everywhere she turned there was a kaleidoscope of people, all of them strangers, children screeching, adults laughing, lights dazzling, video games clanking and ringing.

"Tansy?!"

Nobody answered. When Nora spun again, she caught another glimpse of the man headed toward the door. Her heart stopped, then started racing again. From this angle, he looked like he might be carrying something. His dark curly hair stood out like a briar thicket from his head.

"Tansy?"

Her chest clenched tight. "Excuse me." She began to sidle her way through the crowd. "Excuse me. I'm sorry. Excuse me. Excuse me."

Somewhere in the back of her head, Nora heard another commotion beginning. Or maybe it was only the others at her table, realizing she was worried about her child. In another world she heard the crying begin. It came from the sky tube in the play area.

The shoulders Nora had been watching belonged to a man who had elbowed his way out the door. Around her, everyone else had turned to watch the child stuck in the sky tube. Every parent in the place took a collective breath and wondered, *Is it mine?* A boy darted out one end. "Hey, there's a little girl up there. She's stuck."

Parents and children milled around the base. "She's stuck?" said one inexperienced father. "How can she be stuck? The sky tube is made for little kids to climb around in."

"Not this one. She isn't climbing around. She's sitting at the top screaming."

A throng of parents wandered around and tried to see up into the tube. There were peepholes ever so often, but all that was visible was a stream of kids pressing forward, moving along on hands and knees, shoving each other out of the way.

"Excuse me." Nora started to run toward the door. "Wait! Stop that man, please!" She nudged two more people sideways. "He just stepped out the door. He has my little girl!" She rushed past the security guard and went hurtling out the glass door, tripped over the threshold and almost fell to her knees. "*Stop him!*"

Someone got his attention. A woman who was walking behind him sped up, tapped him on the shoulder, and pointed back at her. Nora had a full view of the puffy black jacket. *Oh, I've got you now!*

But when he swung around to stare at her, she saw he had a wide face, not thin. His nose was broad, not sharp. He had green eyes, not blue. He was carrying a huge stuffed koala bear that must have cost three thousand tickets at the prize counter. It wasn't Cootie at all.

Her legs went limp with relief.

"Do you need something, lady?"

"No. I-I'm so sorry. I thought you were someone else."

181

He turned away, perturbed, and started on his way.

When Nora turned back, Jane Ruckmann had stuck her head out the door and was calling to her. "Nora? We think Tansy's stuck in the sky tube."

"Where?"

"In there." Jane pointed inside.

Although Nora was already breathless, by the time she was halfway there, she had begun to run. During the past five minutes, she had shoved at least a dozen people out of her way. A few more wouldn't matter now. She bypassed them all and crammed herself halfway into the sky tube even though the sign said you couldn't do it if you stood over four feet tall.

"Tansy Aster?!"

"I—it's m-me."

"Where are you?"

"I'm up h-here."

One of the younger, more petite mothers touched her on the shoulder. "Do you want me to crawl up there? I'm smaller than you are. Maybe I could fit."

"Thank you. But I'll do it."

There wasn't any way to stop the children from climbing in to the tube. Ben was there, too, for moral support, but Nora scarcely even saw him. She kept calling, "Tansy? Tansy, can you hear me? Are you okay?"

"I'm so s-sorry. I'm so *sorry*, Nana. Are you mad?"

"No, sweetie. I would never be mad at you. Not in a million zillion years."

Isn't it crazy, Tansy? I thought that man had you. I didn't even know where you were.

"There's s-stairs," said the teary voice. "I c-can't see where to put my *foot*."

"You can do it. Just go slow."

"Every time I try, somebody pushes me out of the *w-way*."

"Look, here I am. I'm going in the tunnel. I'm this far. Here's a corner. There! I think I see you. I'm stretching this far. What am I touching?"

"My feet."

"I can't go any farther."

"Please, Nana! Come get me. It's my *b-birthday*."

"You have to do this by yourself."

"N-no."

"Honey, if I come in any farther, they'll have to call a fire truck. They'll have to cut me out with a saw."

"Ple-e-ease!" And Tansy started howling again.

Nora's voice didn't waver. "If you're scared, you could go back the way that you came."

"I don't remember how to do it."

"Yes, you do. You did it without thinking before."

"I . . . well," still sniffing. "Maybe I *do* know."

"Just turn around. If somebody pushes you out of the way, then you push them out of the way, too."

"Okay."

"That's my girl."

It seemed to take forever, but Tansy began crawling in the opposite direction from the other swarming kids, sniffling all the way. Not until Tansy tumbled out into Nora's arms did she cradle the child against her chest and think what it had felt like, chasing a stranger, thinking someone had run away with her.

Maybe that man had looked like Cootie; Nora really couldn't remember anymore.

It had been so silly, hadn't it? Tansy had only been caught in the *sky tube*, for heaven's sake.

Nora knew better than to laugh. She didn't want Tansy to think she was laughing *at* her. But she *did* laugh a bit anyway, trying to cover up the question that rolled like a skee-ball through her head: *Why should I be afraid, why should I? Why do I keep waiting for the next thing that's going to be wrong?*

CHAPTER EIGHTEEN

―――― ∽ ――――

Anti-Abortion Sunday at Butlers Bend Baptist Church was marked by the placing of tiny white crosses all along the front walk of the church. Every other Sunday of the year, these crosses were hidden away inside boxes in the storage shed until church members met the day before services to decorate the churchyard.

Each of these crosses, painted white, sprinkled with glitter that glowed like fairy dust, was meant to act as memory and tribute to children who had died as a result of abortion in Gilford County.

On the bottom of each cross, Harold Ruckmann had attached tiny metal spikes to keep the yard ornaments upright in the ground. Most of Nora's friends showed up that day to help, starting on the north corner of the building, pushing the tiny stakes into the ground. Dolores Kay Jones, Jane and Harold Ruckmann, Emma and Pete Franklin, and Frieda Storm had volunteered to install them. On Sunday—the next day—during their after-church meal at Leslie's Chicken Shack, these people would talk about the emotional experience this had been.

Those who had forgotten to wear work gloves would compare their blisters; they would describe the sensation of planting the crosses for everyone to see. These volunteers would tell how, as they shoved the spikes into the ground, they could feel the giving way of the earth, the tearing of the grass, the separation of sod and roots. They would tell of particularly hard, rocky spots in the churchyard where they had used a hammer, how piercing the tough dirt crust felt like piercing someone's skin.

The first thing Nora had known about Anti-Abortion Sunday was the telephone call that had come on Wednesday, a few days earlier, from Frieda.

"I have an idea," she bellowed over the telephone without even saying hello. "I really have a very, very good idea. Thank you, Lord! I have an idea."

"Now, Frieda." Nora had to hold the telephone slightly away from her ear because Frieda was so excited. "You often have ideas. You ought not to treat it like such a miracle."

"Yes," Frieda managed in her elderly voice. "But this is a really *good* idea."

"What do you need, Frieda?" Because, for the past thirty years, whenever Frieda called about a good idea, it meant that she expected you to volunteer.

"Nora? Do you think you could convince Tansy to sing on Sunday?"

"What?"

"Do you think you could get her to stand at the front of the church and sing? Something simple. Something she already knows."

"Well . . . I don't know. Maybe in a week or so."

"This Sunday! It has to be this Sunday."

"I don't—"

"It would be perfect. We've all heard her in Sunday school. She winds up and chirps like a canary!"

"Yeah," Nora said, laughing. "I've heard her, too. Just the way she winds up in the Chuck E. Cheese's sky tube." Then, "But in front of people, everybody sitting in rows looking at her, I don't know."

"She sings *Jesus Loves Me*. Only she takes out 'me' and sings 'Tansy' instead. *'Jesus loves Tansy, this I know.'* You've got to talk to her and see if she'll do it. There won't be a dry eye in the house."

Nora tucked the phone beneath her chin and rummaged through the junk drawer. She'd been hunting for her tape measure when Frieda had called. Ben had borrowed it out of her sewing and he hadn't put it back. She said with a slight furrow on her forehead, "Couldn't somebody else do it? I don't understand."

"Oh, that's just the precious thing about you," Frieda said. "You haven't given yourself any credit. Look at the sacrifice you and Ben made."

"What do you mean by that?"

"Everybody in town talks about it, honey. We all know Tess Crabtree. We all know that she probably wanted to have an abortion and you wouldn't let her. Look at the way she ran back to Dallas the minute she could, leaving you with all the responsibility."

Nora thought, *Abortion. Abortion. Some people could really fling that word around.*

"She didn't even have the strength to sign that baby over for adoption."

"*That baby,*" Nora said defensively, "is Tansy. Please, Frieda. Don't criticize Tess or talk about her decisions to anyone."

"If not for you and Ben, Nora, Tansy Aster would be another statistic. Please think about this, Nora. Nothing need ever be said. But so many people just *know*."

Nora turned toward the wall. "I'll talk to Ben about it. I can't promise anything."

But when Nora hung up the phone and turned around again, Tansy was standing there with the tape measure in her hand. "I measured my doll's neck, Nana. It's five inches around."

"So *you're* the one who borrowed that."

"Yep."

"Come over here, little kid." Tansy came skipping to her immediately. Nora hugged her even as she said the words. "Let me . . . give you a . . . big . . . tight . . . hug."

Tansy hugged her back and asked, "What did Mrs. Storm want, Nana?"

"How do you know that was Mrs. Storm?"

"I heard you talking to her."

"Oh." This could be the most frightening thing of all about children. It seemed like they could figure everything out.

"Did she say something about me?"

"Yes."

The little girl's cheek, as soft as a rose petal, warm against Nora's neck. "Does she want me to do something?"

"Well, yes. She does."

"What, Nana? What?"

"You know how you love to sing *Jesus Loves Me*? Mrs. Storm wanted to know if you would sing for the service this week. The way you sing it in Sunday school, when you put your own name in. *Jesus Loves Tansy*." That cheek against Nora's skin felt so alive, so warm and soft and *real*. How had Nora ever gotten so lucky, that her life would seem this blessed, that she would have this second chance? "I told her you might not want to do it, though. It would be okay if you didn't."

The cheek pressed against Nora's neck was replaced by a cool, spidery little hand on Nora's face. With her small hand, Tansy turned Nora's head and made her nana look at her. "I *would* sing," the little girl said. "I'm big enough to sing. I would *like* to sing."

"You would?"

"Tell Mrs. Storm that, Nana."

Nora nodded, not knowing exactly what to say. She buried her lips in her granddaughter's hair.

ℐ

WHEN NORA PEEKED OUT of the master bathroom on Sunday morning, she saw Ben buttoning his one dress shirt clear up to his chin. She stood with her hip resting lightly against the bathroom sink, her mascara tube in the other hand, and watched while he tucked his shirt hem carefully around the circumference of his waist, tightened his belt a notch, and fumbled with his tie. Ben only dressed this way for the Texas Highway Department Christmas party, nothing else. And this was June.

Ben must have caught her reflection in the dresser mirror. His hands stopped wresting with his tie and he turned and winked at her. *Winked.* "Hey there," he said, grinning. "What do you think?"

"I think you might need a little help with that tie."

"You may be right," he agreed. "You know I've never been very good at this sort of thing." He dropped his arms to his sides and stood waiting for her like an eight-year-old.

When she crossed the room, she could smell the aftershave

on him. "Whew," she said, taking her hand and fanning her nostrils. "That's some powerful stuff."

"Don't you like it?"

"Well, of course I do."

When she loosened the knot and threaded the tie through its own loop, her knuckles brushed the underside of his chin. His skin was as smooth as Tansy's. He had *shaved*.

"What's the occasion, Ben? I don't understand."

"Well," he said, beaming down at her. "I thought I'd go to church with you this morning."

Her hands froze against his shirtfront.

"You remember, don't you?" he asked. "You've been inviting me for a while."

"Well," she said, running the tie up to the hollow of his throat with a slight smile. "I guess I *do* remember."

"I wouldn't want to miss the musical performance of the youngest Crabtree family member."

Twenty years. That's how long it had been. That's how long she'd been asking Ben to go with her and he'd been telling her no. *Twenty years.*

"I'd be happy to have you there with me, Ben."

From that moment on Nora's body started zinging like a live electrical wire. Nora was so excited, it took all of her concentration just to brush Tansy's curls and fasten her butterfly hairclips. It took extreme focus just to close the clasp on her Hamilton watch and to apply her lipstick between the lines. Ben was going to church with them!

Oh, Father. Help Ben to see You. Help Ben to feel everyone's love.

By the time Ben parked the Lumina at Milton Hubbs's Kick-A-Tire Trade-In's, Nora almost couldn't breathe. It seemed too much joy to carry, this thought of Ben sitting next to her in the pew at Butlers Bend Baptist. The thought of Tansy standing in front of the church singing.

Oh, Father. This is a miracle that he's here. And You've done it because of our little girl!

The Crabtree family walked toward the front door arm in arm, three abreast, Tansy's curls bouncing against the zipper of her dress, Ben's tie slightly askew, Nora's eyes as bright and shiny with anticipation. When Harold Ruckmann met them in the foyer with a church bulletin, he looked Ben all the way up and all the way down again. "Sure do like those shoes, Ben," he said, extending his arm for a vigorous handshake. "Can't say I've ever seen you wear those before."

"Let's sit over here," Nora said, directing him by the elbow to her favorite pew, the very spot she'd been sitting the day that the window over Pete Franklin's head had begun to glow.

While Tansy scooted over close to them, Nora opened the bulletin and explained it to Ben. She pointed out the places on the bulletin where they would stand up and the places where they would sit down. She pointed out the places where they would pray aloud and the places they would be silent. She pointed out the place where Tansy would sing.

Pete Franklin began announcements and Nora had a difficult time listening. When the visitor registry was passed down the row, Nora made certain Ben signed his name. When Pete read the Scripture aloud from Exodus, Nora propped her thick Bible on Ben's knee between them and trailed her finger along so Ben could follow every phrase. When the choir director gestured for the congregation to rise, Nora turned to Hymn #10, *How Great Thou Art,* and held the hymnal in front of Ben's nose so he could sing every word. Nora was so excited, she couldn't help herself.

Ever since the moment they had stepped out of the car and crossed the Kick-A-Tire parking lot, Nora had been so exhilarated by Ben's presence that she never even noticed the small glittering white crosses that encircled the flowerbeds and surrounded the trees and bordered the front walk.

Then Pete Franklin gestured and Tansy walked to the front of the sanctuary.

Frieda had planned the entire event, and Frieda was very good at organizing children's programs. Pete knelt on the altar steps and picked up his guitar. He sat, patted the step beside him for Tansy Aster to sit, too, and strummed an introductory chord on his Ibanez.

Tansy's voice rose, as clear and sharp as the glint of early sun on ice. It was so strong in its innocence that it could be heard over the rustlings of checkbooks and pens, over Fran Coover's nagging cough, and over the pencil-scribbling of Lance Buxton's youngest son. By the second time through, however, even those sounds had fallen away. No one moved except for the pastor strumming his guitar, and Ben.

Ben reached across the hymnal Nora kept propped on his knee and squeezed her hand.

His one motion, his fingers clasping hers, brought Nora back to herself. She cupped her other hand over his, leaned her head against his shoulder, feeling gratitude at the way her head fit beneath the crook of Ben's chin. Tansy finished her song to the sound of murmured appreciation and the nodding of heads. "I love Jesus!" she shouted, standing on tiptoe and waving at everyone. Pete Franklin shook her hand to thank her. When Nora surveyed Ben's face, she was staggered by the pride she saw there. Just seeing Ben's reaction, Scripture came to Nora's mind.

My frame was not hidden from you when I was made in the secret place. When I was woven together in the depths of the earth, your eyes saw my unformed body. All the days ordained for me were written in your book before one of them came to be.

Ben let go Nora's hand so he could bundle Tansy in his arms. "You did great," he whispered, planting a kiss on her nose.

"Thanks, Grandpa," she whispered back as Nora led her off to her class.

ᘒ

DURING HER JITTERY EXCITEMENT about Ben attending services today, Nora had stopped once or twice to wonder this: On which topic would Pete Franklin choose to preach?

She was certain that it would be something to move Ben deeply, something to stir his heart to ask Jesus Christ into his life, something he would find thought provoking.

But Pete had pursued the Scripture from Exodus 1:15-17, about how Pharaoh commanded Hebrew midwives to kill all male Hebrew babies. This entire subject made Nora squirm. Then Pete began talking about the white crosses in the yard. "I know all of you saw them as you walked in," he said.

Well, no, Nora thought. *Actually we didn't. Oh, Pete. Ben is here! Talk about something that will make him want to come back.*

"Each one of these crosses is a child who has been lost in Gilford County," Pete said. "This many in the past thirty years. Right here where we live."

For that one moment, the words Pete spoke, the crosses outside, did not seem to have anything personal to do with Nora. She decided that *anyone* who saw them lined up out there, like headstones in a cemetery, would be uncomfortable.

All the babies lost in Gilford County over the past thirty years.

The sermon dragged on as the joy that Nora had experienced at having Ben at her side withered away. Ben had just come to hear Tansy sing, anyway. After this, she doubted he would ever come again.

When they stepped out after the service with Tansy skipping and tugging on one arm and Ben checking her watch on the other, they encountered the expanse of small crosses. Nora tried not to stop and stare. But she did, anyway. How on earth had she missed these things?

And then, like an enemy stalking, the thought came.

I wonder which one is mine.

"Nana," Tansy was saying. "Can we go to Chicken Stack today?"

"No," she said absently. "Grandpa will want to go home."

"In fact," Ben added, "I'm going to run on out and turn the car on. Get the air conditioner running for our famous singer here. You two can catch up."

Leaving church on Sunday mornings, though, was not a catch-up situation. Especially when you were trying to get away with a very happy young lady who had performed the special music. "Good job, young lady!" everyone said, stopping them. "You have got to do that again sometime." "How did you get brave enough to do something like that? I could *never* do it."

And Tansy's small, clear-as-a-bell voice: "*Jesus* helped me. That's how."

When Nora searched to find Ben, she saw that Milton Hubbs had cornered him at their parking spot. She sighed. Years had gone by, and Milton was still after their Lumina. She watched as Ben shrugged noncommittally and directed Milton to the lever near the front grille. The engine was running and Ben had given him permission to peek under the hood.

Oh, Ben. No used-car salesmen today. Help me get out of here. Let's just go. Please.

"Well," Jane Ruckmann said beside her. "What do you think? I went into the church office and ordered a tape. That sermon was so good I wanted to listen to it again."

What do I think? I think the church shouldn't have these crosses here.

"I'm hoping Tansy's song got recorded, too. Did you know that it costs two dollars to purchase a tape? If you want to borrow mine when I get it, you can hear it again, too."

I think it isn't our place to display something that condemns this way.

"What's wrong?" Jane asked. "You aren't talking."

"I-I just—" Nora shrugged. "I don't know. My mind is somewhere else, I guess."

"Where is your mind?"

"I was thinking that, if I didn't know the Lord and I saw these crosses, if I had an abortion, I would think somebody was trying to make me feel guilty."

"These crosses are a *tribute,*" Jane explained. "Not something inflammatory. It isn't to make anybody feel bad. It's just *in memory.*"

"That's how you see it?"

"Yes."

Nora said carefully, "It doesn't feel like a tribute to me."

In the Kick-A-Tire lot, the only part of Ben and Milton Hubbs she could see was their hindquarters. With the hood up, they looked like two circus performers with their heads stuck inside the gaping jaws of a lion. She imagined them jiggling hoses, checking the carburetor.

What if a woman had an abortion and she didn't know about the forgiveness and love of the Lord? What if she chose this Sunday to visit our church? A woman like that wouldn't make it to the front door.

Frieda came running up to them. "Tansy, honey. You did so well singing today! Thank you! I hope you'll do this often."

What happens if those crosses chase her away? If she thinks those crosses are our way of pointing fingers at her?

Across the way, the two men had slammed the Lumina hood shut. Milton Hubbs had climbed into the front seat and Ben was leaning over his shoulder, pointing toward the odometer. You certainly couldn't tell by watching which man was the used-car salesman and which was the imposter. Nora wanted to yank up the next cross that she passed. It would be so satisfying, pulling that thing out like any shallow-rooted weed and then driving away. But, of course, she didn't dare.

Speaking of driving away, the Lumina was backing out! Good heavens, it looked like Ben was letting Milton Hubbs take it for a test drive.

"Ben," she cried. "Wait!" Then, to Jane, "We really have to go. I'm sorry." Then to Tansy. "Hurry. Grandpa's leaving without us."

As Nora scooped Tansy up in her arms (Ah, this girl was getting heavy!) and began to run, she told herself that she'd responded strongly to this because she was being righteous for someone else. She did not think that her response had anything to do with herself. She did not think: *What if that woman had been me?*

CHAPTER NINETEEN

———— ❧ ————

On most Sunday afternoons in July, the neighbors along Joplin and Meriweather Streets enjoyed their summer yards. At this very moment, an airplane was drawing a white-fluff contrail in a robin's-egg-blue sky. Sam Ellison was outdoors pruning his redbud tree next door and, on the other side, Judy Larson was laying out paving stones, matching edges like a jigsaw puzzle.

Ben Crabtree did not opt to spend his afternoon outside. Instead, Nora found him on his hands and knees in the corner of their bedroom, rifling through the bottom drawer of the file cabinet. "What are you looking for?" she asked.

He rocked back on his haunches. "You don't happen to remember where we put the title to the Lumina, do you?"

"Oh, gee. Let me think. I can probably remember."

"I thought I kept the car papers in this folder. But that one isn't here."

Then it hit her. "Why are you looking for the Lumina title, Ben?"

"Hm-mmm," he said offhandedly, as if he wasn't certain she would approve. "I'm thinking about trading it in."

"To Milton Hubbs?"

"Yes."

"Oh, Ben."

"That guy knows a good car when he sees one," Ben said. "He told me he's had his eye on it for a long time."

"He's had his eye on that car for *years,* Ben. But it's mine. Don't you think you ought to talk to me about this?"

"Okay," he said. "Here's the deal. That Lumina has 140,000 miles. If I wait too much longer, it isn't going to be worth nearly as much as it's worth today."

"Since the car is in my name, I think it's fair that I should be a part of the process."

"Hubbs has a Trailblazer I'd like you to look at. It's got low miles and he's offered me a good trade-in. Since we're driving children around with no end in sight, an SUV might be helpful."

Yes, an SUV *might* be helpful. But still, she didn't like being left out of the decision.

Under Nora's supervision, Tansy and Erin had been making mud pies in the backyard. Nora had left the hose dribbling in the flowerbed. She'd better not leave the girls alone much longer; they would look like mud pies themselves if she didn't watch.

So without thinking too much about it she said, "I keep the Lumina title in the cedar chest. When you open the lid, you'll see your grandmother's quilt on the left side. Dig under there and you'll find my papers."

"Glad I asked," he said, shaking his head. "I never would have found it there."

When Nora hurried outside, she found Tansy smudging mud under Erin's eyes. "Look, Nana. I'm making her a football player."

"You girls have about five more minutes before I turn this hose on you." Nora turned the water up and made a broad spray with her thumb. She flicked water along the row of hedges. "Tansy, don't get any dirt in her eyes, honey. Be very careful."

Nora loved the sounds of water. It beat a clump of periwinkles, pooling in dark leaves, plastering stems and blue-pink petals to the dirt. Crickets leapt to higher ground. Petunias lolled sideways under the bombardment. Then she sprinkled water over the girls, too, as they danced in circles through the grass and shrieked. All three of them were laughing when Ben slid open the patio door and called to Nora.

"Honey?" he called. "Will you come here a minute?"

"I'm wet," she answered. "Did you find the car title?"

"I did."

"Good. Okay, girls. Into the laundry room this minute." She tickled them each in the ribs to get them headed in the right direction and they shrieked again. "Erin, I'll bring you an extra pair of Tansy's pajamas. We've got to do laundry before I can send you home."

But Ben was still standing on the patio with his brow furrowed. "I found some other things of interest, too."

"You did?" She craned her neck to see what he had in his hand. There was a stack of folded papers, a clothbound journal, and two or three steno notebooks in which she'd jotted poems and recipes and birthdays that she wanted to remember.

Goodness, Nora thought, suddenly worried. *Had Ben taken the time to look through any of that stuff?* That clothbound book had been her journal from high school. She ticked off subjects she might have mentioned during her senior year and decided that, other than mention of her old boyfriend and one anecdote about a water fight in which she'd broken her toe, there would be nothing to make Ben do anything more than laugh himself silly.

But the journal wasn't what Ben was holding up to show her.

"I was curious about this," he said, holding up a slip of paper with yellowed edges.

"What?"

"Come look at it. It's odd."

She stepped onto the patio and took it from him. When she unfolded it and looked, the sight froze her blood.

The receipt was for doctor's services at a clinic in Dallas, generically titled Care-of-the-Metroplex Women's Center. Like any physician's receipt, portions of it were illegible. Even though the words couldn't be read, Nora knew what they were. *Vacuum aspiration and curettage.*

"What is this place? Why would this be in here, Nora? Do you know what this is?"

Dumbly, she shook her head. "I don't," she lied.

"It's from twenty-seven years ago. We were dating each other then. Did you have surgery or something that I didn't know about?"

"I—I don't *think* so," she hedged.

Care-of-the-Metroplex Women's Center had been an abortion clinic. It might even still be in service there; Nora didn't know. At the bottom of the receipt, the cost of her abortion procedure had been tallied. $217. Beside that, the red ink stamp: PAID IN FULL.

Nora had saved it because it was a medical paper. She'd been trying to act grown up and grown-ups were supposed to save things like that. After all these many years, she had even forgotten it was there.

It was almost ninety degrees out here, so there wasn't any reason for her to be shivering with cold. If Ben questioned her, she would explain it away. Her clothes had gotten wet with the hose.

"Nana!" Tansy called from the laundry-room door. "Me and Erin are in here! We're waiting for pa-*jam*-as."

"I just don't remember what that is," she lied. She looked at it again and shrugged. "You know what they say, Ben. If you can't remember something, it must not have been important."

"Are you sure?"

"Here, let me have that thing." She took the slip and crumpled it up in her hand, her heart pounding. She couldn't believe it was so easy to lie to him. "I'll take care of this and throw it away."

⁓

TANSY CAME IN one afternoon carrying a dilapidated cardboard box from her closet. "Can I play with this?"

"Oh," Nora said, putting her own hands beneath the box, too, just in case it wanted to topple. "I had forgotten all about those."

Tansy plopped the box on the carpet and pried open the lid. "Nana, what are they?"

"Pieces to a tea set."

Tansy picked up one wad of newspaper with her little hands. A tiny teacup, made from eggshell porcelain, rolled out onto the floor.

Nora continued. "It's to have tea parties with."

"Whose is it? Is it yours?"

"Oh, well. Just . . . be careful, sweetie. It breaks."

"Why is it wrapped in newspaper?"

"I did that."

"But why?"

"When something's very breakable, you want to protect it."

As her granddaughter pulled out yet another newsprint-wrapped object, Nora realized she would have to sit down this minute and show Tansy how to handle teacups. Either that or she ran the risk of having something chipped or cracked.

"Here." Nora knelt beside her granddaughter. One by one, Nora unfolded pages torn from the *Butlers Bend Echo-Bulletin,* dated long ago. Dated the day that Nora had sorted through Tess's belongings and put them away.

"Look," she said to Tansy and revealed a platter no larger than a sand dollar. "Here. Do you want to hold it? Set it down carefully on the floor. *Carefully.*" The melancholy she felt upon seeing this tiny plate was something Nora hadn't expected. In this one vulnerable moment, Nora ached for her missing daughter with a sharp pain that felt physical. An invisible hand seemed to grab her heart and squeeze.

She and Ben had been through the entire Dallas phone book on more than one occasion, searching for a Cootie Banks. Ben had confessed that he'd driven through several dicey neighborhoods when he'd been in Dallas for an asphalt conference, hoping to catch a glimpse of someone familiar. "I was afraid I was going to get *shot,*" he'd told her later.

"Here's the little teapot," Nora said. "And here's the lid. It fits like this." She set it on top with a gentle *clink.* "See? You can do this one. You get to put the lid on the sugar bowl."

"Does real sugar go in here?"

"It can."

Once Nora had gained confidence in Tansy's cautious hands, they spread the entire ensemble before them between their knees—the sugar and creamer, cups and saucers, the teapot with its spout curved like a ballerina's arm.

"Why is this here, Nana? Did you buy it for me?"

"No."

"Why do you have it then? Who does it belong to?"

Silence. In that pause, Nora muttered up another of her quiet prayers before she spoke. "It belonged to your mother, that's who it belonged to."

"Oh." Tansy sat still for a time. Then, "Do you think she would like me to play with it?"

"Yes, I think she would like it."

"Can we have a tea party right now?"

"Hm-m-mm." Nora didn't have to think about that very long. "I don't see why not." And as Nora filled the tiny teapot with warm chai, she cradled it in her fingers for a moment and felt the heat against her palm. She poured two-percent milk inside the miniature creamer. She dug deep inside a drawer and found a box of sugar cubes. Ben had gone through the cookies—such a sweet tooth he had!—so she covered the diminutive platter with a stack of crackers and butter.

They'd settled into their chairs accompanied by a teddy bear and two dolls and had begun to smear butter on crackers when Tansy asked, "Nana?"

Nora had finished the cracker and took a tiny sip of tea, just the way a lady of breeding is supposed to sip tea, with her pinkie finger extended. "Yes?"

"How many babies did you have in your tummy?"

The teacup paused in midair. Nora stared at her.

"Well, I—"

She couldn't swallow as her heart began to ramrod in her throat.

Why would Tansy ask a question like that?

Tansy shoved a cracker in her mouth. There were crumbs all over her lips. "I think, maybe, *two.*"

"Tansy, honey," Nora's voice wavering. "What are you asking me about that for? Why would you want to know?"

"Was my mommy in your tummy?"

"Yes."

She kept chewing. Nora ought to tell her not to talk with her mouth full, only she couldn't. Her blood had turned to ice.

"Then, was I in your tummy?"

Oh.

Oh.

Just a child's question. As insignificant as the questions on the doctor's form that asked every time she went in for her annual exam, *How many pregnancies? How many live births?*

"No, *you* were in your mama's tummy. Your *mama* was in *my* tummy."

"Where is she now, Nana?"

"Who?"

"My mama."

Those other questions, Nora hadn't expected. This one, she had known eventually would come. She took a deep breath before she spoke.

"We don't know, little one."

"Why did she leave me with you, Nana?"

And now here Nora was, left fumbling for words. "She had hard things in her life. She left because she thought we could take better care of you then she could."

"Did she tell you that?"

"No. But it's what I think."

"Do you ever look for her?"

"We used to, Tansy, but not anymore. Don't let your tea get cold. You'd better sip some."

"Didn't she want me, Nana?" Tansy, turning a sugar cube over and over, each granule sparkling as it caught the light.

"Oh, yes. She wanted you; don't ever doubt that." Nora had been practicing these words for a long time. "Only, you have to understand this one thing. We wanted you more."

CHAPTER TWENTY

B en had Tansy out inspecting the highway next in line for resurfacing, Project 290-04, when he heard the Grumman G154 Ag-Cat overhead.

That's the way it always happened with Creede Franklin. Boy could be gone forever and all you'd hear above would be the buzzing of bees. But let him come home on leave from the United States Air Force and, within hours, the sky would be full of him again.

"Hey, Mr. Crabtree!" The biplane came at him so low Ben fought the urge to protect his head with his arms. He couldn't do that. He used his hands to cover Tansy's ears instead.

The plane rose over the highway, banked sharply to the left, and aimed right toward him. Ben straddled the middle of the road and stood still. Here it came. Straight on. The plane yawed to the right at the last possible second.

The old duster bounced three times when Creede set it down in the pasture. Baxton Lance would have something to say about that. Just like that kid, taking it upon himself to use Baxton's alfalfa field for a landing strip. He landed wherever he wanted, like the whole of Gilford County belonged to him.

The propeller chopped and slowed. Creede unfolded himself, climbed out. "Heard you were back in town, young man," Ben shouted. "How's the United States Air Force treating you? How's Candice?"

For all the times he'd used the word *kid* and *boy* and *young man,* Ben would never see Creede Franklin as anything else. "Howard Ruckmann told me you knocked a piece of stem crystal over in Jane's china cabinet this morning, buzzing their place."

Creede, whistling *Jungle Boogie* through his teeth, came sauntering through the grass. He reached out to pump Ben's hand with palms as big around as baseball mitts. "Guess I'd better give Missus Ruckmann a call and apologize. They don't have stem crystal in Iraq. At least not where I fly."

"Well now, son." Not meaning to sound stern, but it came out that way anyway. "You'd best realize where you're flying now. You're not in Saddam's backyard. You're in mine."

But Creede wasn't looking at him. His whole demeanor had changed. He was staring at Tansy instead.

"Don't tell me this is who I think it is!"

Tansy poked out her belly. Her mouth twisted like a candy wrapper.

"This is our Tansy. Tansy, this is Cr—Mr. Franklin."

Creede glanced at Ben again. "She doesn't look a thing like—" He clawed his hair with his huge hands. "Well, no, she *does.*"

That was what everyone thought. No one said it aloud in front of her, but they all whispered the same words. *She doesn't look a thing like her mother.* Then they realized they were wrong.

Tansy was the spitting image of Tess. Except for all that hair. All those curls, all the wrong color.

"Gosh, you're growing up." Creede bent to her level. "Last time I saw you, you were only about"—he indicated with his hands—"yay long."

"Thought she'd be a good one to help me inspect this road." Ben peered past his elbow and lovingly jostled her arm. "Project 290-04, Gilford County. Wexler Paving starts resurfacing this road on Monday."

They all three stared at the road for a moment.

"Looks like a fine highway to me. You ought to see what passes for roads in—"

He stopped when Tansy let go of her grandfather's hand. She picked up a chipped stone and rolled it between her fingers. She looked it all over before she offered it to Creede.

"Thank you."

She hid her hands behind her back.

"It's a very pretty rock."

She spoke. "It's granite."

Creede turned it inside his fingers, too. "Mind if I keep it?"

"It's a present," she said. "You're always supposed to keep a present."

"Well, thank you!" Then, "I tell you, Mr. Crabtree. This Ag-Cat is a queen among planes. Sure, I fly F-16s. But no matter the technology, no matter the newest thing, there's always something about the first plane you fly."

"Is there?"

"Same way there's always something about the first girl you love—"

That comment hung between them. *He's talking about Tess,*

Ben thought. When he saw the melancholy in Creede's eyes, he knew he was right.

"I feel like I've lost my closest friend sometimes," Creede said. "Do you?"

"I feel like I've lost her over and over again."

"We all do."

Neither of them had ever said her name. As though to counter the presence of Tess between them, Creede said, "You asked me about Candice. She's doing okay. But it's tough on her. We don't have a lot of time together right now."

"It's tough on any girl, being married to a flyboy."

"Sometimes I think I ought to give it up and stay closer to home. She doesn't like Eielson very much."

There was a moment of cautious silence.

"Say." That same old grin stretched the width of Creede's face. "What would you think if I took you up?"

Well now, Ben thought. *Nora would never approve of me letting Tansy do something dangerous like that.*

"Notice anything different about the old girl?"

Ben eyed the green-and-yellow biplane with suspicion.

"Dad took the hopper out. Once I left for the force, he figured I wouldn't make money dusting crops. He converted her."

Ben knelt to brush dirt off Tansy's hand, buying himself time. "Afraid we'd better take a rain check, Creede. Nora might not like— Well, she keeps a pretty close eye on this little one. Doesn't want anything to happen to her."

"Converted her so she's got two passenger seats. Got a seat belt in there for both of you. Cockpit's totally gone, did you notice that? Aren't many people get to fly open air above Texas, smell all that fine dirt. Oil. Cow. I-75 roadkill. *Skunk.*"

"I don't think we should," Ben insisted.

Creede pitched Tansy's rock up and caught it in his fist. "It'll be something she can tell her grandchildren about. Her first time up, with an honest-to-goodness lieutenant. Whaddaya say, kid? Up and down." He winked. "Just ten minutes flying. Want to go?"

Ben could have killed him for making it sound like a carnival ride. "I don't think Nora would—" Even though she was way too heavy, he spun Tansy up into his arms, gripped the hem of her shirt with an anxious fist.

"Grandpa," she pleaded in the tiny voice that he would probably never learn to say no to. "I want to."

"It wouldn't hurt anything," Creede whispered.

Tansy Aster was big and heavy already. But still, she could feel so small to Ben sometimes. She lay with her cheek and the heavy weight of her head pressed against the ridge of his jaw.

"The open-air flying, it's a guy thing. Women don't understand the thrill," Creede said. "I wouldn't force you—"

But suddenly Ben wanted to go up in that plane worse than anything. He wanted to make a decision about Tansy for once! Nora drove him crazy sometimes, always looking for danger. "You'd bring me back to my car? Right here? Resurfacing Project 290-04?"

"I'll set you both down right here."

"You promise?"

"Yes." The men's eyes met. "I do."

Tansy's face still lay against his, her skin as cool as an apple peel. She touched his cheeks with her hands; one of her littlest fingers, which wasn't that little anymore, jabbed him in the nostril. "Grandpa, let's *go.*"

But this isn't danger, he reminded himself. *This is Creede.* "Yes," Ben echoed his granddaughter. "Let's go."

❧

BUTLERS BEND from the air was very different from anything Ben had seen from a city airport. Packs of industrial complexes and traffic in line like fire ants. Every roof the same, cul-de-sacs in perfect circles, in-ground swimming pools like blue buttons. But below him here, oh, he'd never known! This place of his life, like a giant's bedspread beneath him with wrinkles and folds, continuously mussed by people he liked and could see.

The wind rushed beside his ears. Ben felt exhilarated and free. He knew his heart had lifted off from the ground at the same time the airplane did. Living with Nora and Tess and now Tansy had bound his insides into knots. In this hour, on this day, the Grumman Ag-Cat gave Ben this: his mental strain was soothed. He thought, *Can it be this way? That a person doesn't know what he's living with until he leaves it behind?*

"See down there?" Ben pointed toward the courthouse cupola that stood like a fancy cake in the center of town. "And look at that!" The Butlers Bend water tower became an enormous egg on a stand.

The first person he saw was Roy Frakes, shoving at least a dozen grocery carts snaked together across the Food Basket parking lot. Then here was Dolores Jones stepping through the double doors of the bank. Jane Ruckmann and Howard, sharing a bite at What-A-Burger's outdoor table.

It now occurred to Ben, as people pointed up at them and waved, that Nora would hear of his whereabouts before he ever had the chance to get home.

The heaviness settled on his heart again. For years, he had walked on eggshells around her. If he made one wrong move, he had decided somewhere along the line, she would blame him for all of it. *Well, I don't care!* Ben thought. *Let people tell her. I deserve a little fun now and then.*

Tansy's head fit just below his jaw as he pointed everything out to her. He loved the way her hair tickled his chin. She waved at everyone who looked her way. Since everyone seemed to be glad Creede had come home for some of his leave, and since Creede was doing a fair amount of barnstorming, that added up to just about the census count of Gilford County. In the pilot's seat behind them Creede bellowed into the sky, "There's nothing better. There is nothing *better.*"

Ben clasped Tansy tight against him and nestled his face in all her crazy curly hair. Up, up they soared, past the steeple of the church and the baseball field with its steel trumpets of lights and the only bend in the road for at least thirty miles. Butlers Bend.

"Hey, Creede," Ben shouted over his shoulder. "Know why the road makes a turn like that?" And that's when the engine stopped.

Eerie, deathly quiet. Suddenly they could hear the birds.

Tansy flagged her hands up over her face and screamed with joy. "Eeeeeeeee."

Ben shoved her hands down by her sides and held them there. He pivoted in his seat to have a view of U.S. Air Force Lieutenant Creede Franklin. "Creede?" he asked with a hopeful little smile.

Nothing but silence. And a breeze. A tiny, lilting breeze.

Don't ask, Creede motioned, shaking his head.

"Grandpa. I can't . . . can't even *breathe.*"

"Doesn't matter. I'm going to hold you." He turned to the pilot behind him again. "Tell me, Creede," he said, "that you cut the engine on purpose."

Creede shook his head.

Ben knew there were precious few readouts and control dials in this thing. Nothing much to fiddle with. They'd gone from a power plane into a glider. What had Creede said he knew how to fly?

Ben felt Creede pull the nose up. The propeller windmilled in front of them. Creede tried to start the engine. It growled like something angry, died away.

"We're . . . gonna have to . . . ride this thing . . . to the ground."

"What can I—?"

"Just sit tight."

"You said you'd get us back—"

"Number one rule of flying," Creede announced through gritted teeth. "When the engine goes out, all promises are off."

Below them sprawled the members of the Mighty Fighting Armadillo High School Marching Band, which must have assembled for summer camp. Such a great view from up here of their lopsided double-wheel formation. Ben recognized strains of *The Theme from Spiderman* just before saxophones tilted awry, trombones fell to the ground, and snare drummers took off running.

The Ag-Cat cleared the rim of Armadillo Stadium. "Made it," Ben said, his voice cracking. But up ahead was Frank Stoneman in his massive tiller, breaking up his black field, leaving acres of corduroy-textured dirt. Rough terrain.

"Hang on to Tansy," Creede barked.

For seconds, Ben didn't recognize the warm, metallic taste in his mouth. He licked it, and the sharp pain gave him a hint. His lower lip was bleeding.

Pecans showered as the plane clipped the tops of trees. Mockingbirds and jays rose, complaining. All Ben could see were shadows, furrows, the propeller blades slicing ahead. What a dumb way to get them killed.

"Here we—"

The wheels hit once and tore up the dirt. Hit again, and the plane went toppling. Ben remembered this sensation of flipping from the time he'd lost his balance running through the revolving barrel in the funhouse at the Texas State Fair. He could see nothing, yet he noticed every shadow in the dirt clods, every tendon in his arms. He noticed Tansy's dark curls springing in every direction from her head.

∽

EVERY TIME he saw Creede Franklin for the rest of his life, he knew he would think: "That's just great. You got new seats put in but forgot to put in the new engine."

Creede, behind him, was laughing. *Laughing.* "Gear got stuck in a hole or something. Must of tore off."

So there they were, their mouths full of North Central Lowland, their three seatbelts fastened tight, all three of them hanging upside down.

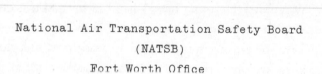

CHAPTER TWENTY-ONE

National Air Transportation Safety Board
(NATSB)
Fort Worth Office

OFFICIAL ACCIDENT REPORT

Date: August 10
Vehicle: Grumman G154 Ag-Cat
Owner: Pete, Sr., and Creede Franklin
Cause of Accident: Engine lost power.
     Engine Assembly Failure Cylinder, Total.
     Original cylinder cracking caused by
     fatigue.

How could you?" Nora stood directly in front of him on the porch. He couldn't get into their house without walking past her. "How *could* you?"

Ben could guess. Caroline Rakes had phoned the minute Jonathan had come barreling in with his convoy of grocery carts. And Jane Ruckmann had been unable to resist using her new cell phone to say, "I'm sitting outside at the What-A-Burger and guess who just zipped by overhead!" Nora had heard from someone how they buzzed the courthouse, from someone else how they spooked Baxton Lance's entire herd of white-faced Hereford cows.

Then, on her own, she must have heard the sirens.

"It sounded like fun," he said now.

He saw Nora's legs give way beneath her. She sat down right on the brick stoop, staring at the Band-Aid on Tansy's cheek.

"Why?" she asked again.

"Why not?" He took Tansy's hand in his and tried to lead her past her very angry grandmother. "Why not?"

There she sat, her spine braced against the world, hugging her knees with her arms. "That old airplane, Ben. Of all things, why did it have to be that old, dangerous airplane?"

"Oh, sorry. Why not the Marsalis Zoo where a tiger could have gotten her? Why not at the church playground where you won't let her swing too high because she might fall out?"

"You know how I hate flying. You know how it terrifies me, Ben."

"She's just a little girl, Nora. You can't protect her from the world. You can't keep regular things from happening to her."

This time of evening even birds stopped singing. He and Tansy's two-headed shadow fell across the brick in a smudge.

"Nana, we had a really good time up there. We had a *really* good time coming down. We crashed."

"I'm aware of that." Nora shook her head at the sky.

Ben finally opened the front door. When it swung wide, though, he didn't go inside. He gave Tansy a loving pat on the bottom and said, "I have to talk to your nana about something."

"Can I have a snack? Can me and Nana have a tea party again?" Tansy asked.

"No. Not right now." Another little tap on the backside. "Go find your Little Leap and play with that, okay, sweetie?"

"We'll be inside in a little while," Nora added.

"Okay, Nana." Tansy's fingers curled around the knob and she pulled it. The last thing they saw before the door latched was Tansy's eye, still peering with curiosity through the crack.

"You're making her into a substitute for Tess. You're substituting Tansy for our real daughter," Ben said, turning on her.

Tess, who was so far away from them.

Tess with her broken soul.

"I'm not doing that."

"Well, the way you're acting, the way you won't let her breathe without you worrying about her. You're making her into a substitute for *something*."

"You think that's wrong?"

Ben hadn't realized what they were doing until he'd gotten up in that airplane. He'd only thought they were plodding along, doing what they had to do to survive. But, no. "We've gone rushing ahead, built our lives again on Tansy, not what came before."

"Why not, Ben? How can that be wrong? Why can't we cover up the bad with the good?"

"I think it makes us hold on too hard."

"You think *I'm* holding on too hard. That's what you said, didn't you?"

"I'm talking about myself, Nora. I'm talking about both of us together."

Ben remembered coming out of the bathroom one day years ago, drying off his jaw. He nicked himself almost every time he shaved. There at his bureau, as he stuck tissue against the spot he'd nicked, he found a piece of construction paper propped there—a drawing of a house.

On Top Of My Hart,
That's Where You Stand.
Love, Tess.

Tess, the daughter who had broken their hearts.

Tess, as she'd begun to grow, her angular pale face, her hair straight down in her eyes when the other girls styled theirs and pulled it back. Tess, with Creede Franklin as her first love, who had seemed a different person dressed in cornflower-blue satin the night they'd gone to the eighth-grade dance.

Tess, who had stood on top of his feet and had grabbed his hands and had said, "Teach me to waltz, Daddy! Will you teach me to twirl like the prince did with Cinderella?"

Nora spun around to him, tears sparkling like jewels in her eyes. "Isn't Tansy good for us? Why can't we just take what's here and enjoy it? Why do you have to punish me for that?"

Ben said, "Because I want my wife, Nora. I don't understand everything. The more you're holding onto Tansy, the more there is something of you that isn't there."

"I thought you said you were talking about yourself, too."

"Well, I—"

"You always find something wrong with what I'm doing, Ben. Do you know that? No matter how hard I try, you dig deep and find something to criticize."

"Nora."

With a sharp, gasping cry, "Don't you know that *I* miss her, too?"

"You never talk about her, Nora. You never do."

"What if having Tansy was the gift God wanted us to have all along? What if you're so busy trying to make me do the right thing that you make me miss the blessing?" Nora asked.

"You never think about Tess. You never talk about her."

"What good would it do, Ben? Prolong the misery?"

"You don't ever want her to come back."

Her words came sharp and hard. "No, I don't." Then, "I would never let that girl get ahold of this child."

"Listen to yourself. You don't want your own daughter."

"I did once. Don't you think I did?" Nora squinted up at him. All he could see of her were straight angles, a mouth stretched taut like a rubber band. "Don't you think I did?"

"I never see you doing anything except going forward, Nora."

She fended him off with her arm, holding it square over her chest so he couldn't touch her. "Leave me alone, Ben. Just leave me alone. There is more to this than you will ever know."

CHAPTER TWENTY-TWO

⸺ ❧ ⸺

The dirty sheets that came in at Bunyan Dry Cleaning that day were sorted by the dozen, eleven of them piled inside the twelfth, which was knotted at the corners into a huge sling. Just before two in the afternoon, Tess left the front counter at Bunyan Dry Cleaning. The other girls could handle the rush. More dry cleaning came in on Monday than on any other day. The phone rang more often, too. Bunyan Dry Cleaning did the sheets for three downtown Dallas hotels. Hotels used plenty of sheets on the weekends.

Tess dumped the two mountainous piles of sheets onto the floor and began to recount, marking the receipt that had come in with the hotel trucks. The soft-press machine was already steaming. After only a few minutes of working on it, her hair frizzed and her cheeks were wet and she never thought she'd be anyplace cool again. As she worked, she swabbed sweat from her face with one wrist.

One statement that she'd made to her mother all those years ago had proven true. She had said, *If I have a baby, a person related to me would exist somewhere. Someone I would have to wonder about. Someone I would have to think of.*

Sometimes at Bunyan Dry Cleaning, a frilly bedspread would come through, or a little woolen coat, or a pair of jeans with pink embroidery. When they did, Tess would catch herself thinking, *Maybe Tansy wore a coat like this.* Or, *Maybe Tansy had something like this in her room.* Or, *I wonder if she knows what I look like.*

Tess did not know if she would recognize her daughter's face anymore. She tried to recall the details of her eyes and nose and tiny mouth but she couldn't do it. *I wonder if she knows that Cootie didn't want her.*

When Tess arrived at the house in the evenings, she was not in the mood to wade through Cootie's friends. He bragged about it, how this place had become a virtual command post, peopled by high school kids mostly, who admired Cootie and wanted to be like him. Some nights, she felt like she was cooking hot dogs for a hundred people. That's all they ever had to eat. Hot dogs, eaten by boys who had given themselves new names because they saw Cootie as a hero.

Tess thought most about these things when the nights grew quiet and she was alone. After darkness fell, the boys would disperse. When they returned, they played their rap and spoke in hushed tones. Were they in fights? She didn't know. Were they hurting other people? Tess tried not to care. But while they were gone, even the house would seem to whisper of these things. In every creak of the floor and every sigh of the roof, Tess would remind herself that it was Cootie who mattered, not the suspicions she had begun to have about him.

One night as she sat reading beneath the small circle of light from the floor lamp, she glanced out the window to see a car cruising slowly up the street, its high beams reflecting off the pavement.

Tess pushed herself up with one hand and her book fell to the floor. She wanted to hide. In that moment, alone and afraid, she knew the lamp illuminated her through the frayed curtains. She shoved the sofa out from the wall so she'd have crawlspace behind it.

She kicked something with her toe. At her feet, hidden in the space between the furniture and the wall, was a pile of guns. The barrels gleamed at her in the dull light. She knew, from the things Cootie had told her, that he'd put hands on a few people. Tess didn't know Cootie had guns.

Shoving the armament aside with her feet, she dove behind the sofa at the same time she heard the door bust open. There she crouched, wedged between the wall and the couch, her breath coming in sharp, horrified gasps. The kitchen floor creaked.

"Tess?" came Jimmy Ray's voice. "Where are you?"

Thankfulness poured over her. It was only Jimmy Ray.

"Tess?"

"I'm here."

When he walked into the room, he caught her climbing out from behind the furniture. With a discreet toe, she nudged the gun barrels back under the couch.

"Something scare you?"

"I heard the car," she said. "You were driving slow."

"I was looking out for people who knew me," he told her. "Didn't want anybody squealing to Cootie that I came back here."

"Why'd you come?"

"I don't much like the idea of him leaving you here alone all the time."

"Nothing's going to happen to me."

"That why you were hiding behind the sofa?"

"You caught me." She grinned back. "Right."

The couch was old enough to have fleas. Together they pushed it back against the wall. If Jimmy Ray knew what she had found, he didn't say a word about it.

So she asked instead, "Jimmy Ray? Why's everybody worried this time? Has Cootie hurt somebody?"

Jimmy Ray hesitated. "Coot don't talk to you about that stuff?"

"No." She followed Jimmy Ray into the bathroom where he ran a comb under the faucet and attempted to flatten his hair. "He's got plenty of other people to talk to besides me."

The comb left runnels in Jimmy's hair like plow furrows in a field. He didn't speak.

"I think I ought to know."

He tapped the comb on the edge of the sink and laid it on the cabinet. "He has to be the one to tell you. I won't."

"I don't like it, if he does."

"Why do you think those kids follow him the way they do? He doesn't have a choice, Tess. He's going to keep the reputation, he's got to keep people scared."

Tess had tried so many times to make this place look like a home since she'd come back. On the table in the family room, she'd placed a bowl of broken glass she'd picked up along the curb and washed. She'd "borrowed" a candle from a table in the deli next door to where she worked and placed it in the bowl. Now she picked up a match and struck it.

"You ever think about going back to your family, Jimmy Ray?"

"Hey, no. Why should I? There's nothing good for me there."

She touched the match to the wick and, after the candle flamed, she shook out the match. "I wanted to be Cootie's family. When I came back here, he told me that I would be enough."

Jimmy Ray stared at the flickering candle as if he didn't want to answer. "Nobody's willing to do anything that makes us look weak."

∽

SEPTEMBER NIGHTS in Texas could be just as hot and breathless as the days. Tess laid awake waiting for Cootie to return that night and by three, when she heard him pound open the door, the sheets were knotted and damp around her. She unwrapped them, padded into the kitchen, and squinted into the bright light. "Coot?"

He slammed a kitchen drawer. "Hey, babe. You're awake."

"Yeah, I am. What did you do tonight?"

His hand stayed on the drawer pull. "I did good stuff tonight. Real good stuff."

"Cootie, I found something—"

But he cut her off. "Did Jimmy Ray come here?"

"Yeah." There wasn't any reason to feel guilty, but she did. "Why?"

There wasn't any reason to lie, either, but Tess did anyway. "I don't know."

He eyed her for a moment.

"Cootie, I found—"

He grabbed her arm and pulled her against him. "Don't go

to work tomorrow. What do you have to say about that? Just stay here with me."

"I have to work. If I don't work, we don't eat anything."

"Call in sick. I made a little money tonight. Let's celebrate tomorrow."

"Do you mean, just the two of us celebrate?"

"Well, I was thinking we ought to have everybody over. We could cook out on the grill in the middle of the day."

"I'd do it if it was just the two of us. I miss you, Cootie."

He ignored her. "We could sit on the front steps drinking from cans and soaking up the sun."

"We don't have any grill."

"We'll go buy one. What would you say to that? What would you say to grilling steaks for everybody instead of hot dogs? What would you say if I told you that I made enough money to do that?"

"Cootie, what *happened* tonight?"

He kissed her hard, and didn't answer her question. "I just keep gaining ground."

"Oh."

"We'll do something just the two of us soon. I promise. You're my whole life, babe. I don't know what I'd do without you."

"Do you really think that, Cootie? Do you *really?* Because I need to know."

He took her face in his hands and held her so close that she could see gold specks in his irises. "Look at me, would you? Look at me. You are the best thing that's ever happened to me. Bad things go on sometimes, but you're *good.* I'm hanging on to the *good,* babe."

The confidence swelled in her chest. Tess would be willing to do anything if he kept saying those things to her. How she needed to hear that she was loved. Her heart drank it up and, still feeling dry, needed more.

✑

COOTIE MADE GOOD HIS PROMISE to buy everyone steaks. The front yard filled with people before noon. The oily smell of charcoal permeated Bunyan Street for at least five or six houses in every direction.

It surprised Tess but, in the kitchen, the boys scrambled to help. One volunteered to salt and pepper the meat. One splashed steaks (and the kitchen cabinets) with Worchester sauce. They didn't have many ingredients for a salad, but Tess managed to make do with a head of lettuce and grated carrots and mayonnaise.

Outside, the sky above them was a great vault of blue. The sun shone so bright that it made Tess's head throb. Someone had a car stereo blaring, the hip-hop rhythm hammering, the fun of being together amping in their chests.

Cootie had deemed himself the master of steaks. When he laid them over the hot coals on the little hibachi grill, they hissed. In the dusty side yard, Jimmy Ray had inserted spikes and someone had come up with horseshoes. Cootie grabbed Tess and held her hip against his ear while he used his other arm to skewer and flip sirloins. She laid her hand against his threadbare T-shirt, felt the wrinkles beneath her fingers and the warmth of his skin beneath.

"You going to be cooking meat all day if that's the only grill you got," Jimmy Ray told him. "Going to take three hours to feed everybody on that thing."

Cootie shrugged and Tess felt his muscles move beneath her fingers. "Guess I don't have much else to do."

"Tess." Jimmy Ray gestured for her to come. "Come play horseshoes with us. You're always the one who works. You ought to have a little fun."

"I'll bring out the salad. You wait for me." She bent over and kissed Cootie on the top of his head, satisfied with everything he'd told her. After she retrieved the salad, she toted it outside to the cardboard box that they'd turned into a table, her mind happily engaged with a dozen challenges of entertaining. After she set it out, she wandered to Jimmy Ray's side.

He handed her a rusty horseshoe and she balanced it against her chin, measuring the distance to the metal spike with squinted eyes. When she threw, the horseshoe missed. It hit the ground with a metal thud. She tossed it again. No better the second time.

Jimmy Ray jumped into the back of Cootie's pickup and started mouthing the hip-hop words as if he was on a music video.

In this mind-state, set in an underground way, if you listen to the sound, it has to pay . . .

"Get that punk down," Cootie shouted. "Nobody wants to hear that."

"Hey," someone called from the makeshift table where a line of people had begun dishing lettuce onto paper plates. "Where's the beans? Cootie said he bought beans."

Tess handed the horseshoes to Jimmy Ray. "I'll get them." She'd forgotten she had those beans heating on the stove. When she went inside, she spent a minute digging in a low cabinet for a large serving bowl. She dumped a huge glob of pinto beans into it. Before she carried this out, too, Tess stood in the doorway for a moment, fixing her eyes on each of them, measuring her life.

Someone had turned the music off. A sparrow flew low across the yard, its flight path straight and downward, like the slash of a knife. Cootie dropped a steak on an upheld plate. He rose, sauntered to Jimmy Ray, and held his hand out to try his hand at horseshoes.

"I love you," she mouthed to him. He smiled back. In spite of her worry, she enjoyed being Cootie's female; his position made her feel exalted. With no effort at all, he threw three horse-shoes in a row and rung them all. The clamor of metal upon metal lingered between them in the silence, as she thought of her hand against his shirt, the warmth of his skin beneath. She loved the danger of him, the way he hung onto her when she was walking away.

"Hey," he asked everyone in the yard, lifting his fist in victory over those horseshoes. "Where's my guitar? I'm in the mood to write a song, something with a mean riff. I want to write a song for Tess."

For the first time in her life, she felt shy in front of these boys. She cast her eyes to the concrete steps.

"Where's my guitar?"

"I have it," Jimmy Ray told Cootie. "I was fooling around with it last night in my room."

"Get it now."

Later, Tess would try to remember the last words Cootie spoke aloud to her. It wasn't *I want to write a song for Tess*. He hadn't spoken that to her. He'd said that to everyone in the yard.

Tess had forgotten a serving spoon. She turned around to go inside. Jimmy Ray walked in the house behind her. She set the beans down, opened the cabinet door again, and stooped low. They'd used all the silverware in the drawer, but Tess remembered tossing a wooden spoon in here. In the other room, she could hear Jimmy Ray strumming Cootie's guitar, probably making sure he'd left it in tune. Tess leaned her forehead against the cabinet for a moment, getting her bearings back. She felt cared for, and the warm happiness unfolded in her like a bloom.

She reached for the spoon just as gunfire erupted outside.

The shots were so rhythmic that, at first, she thought she might be wrong. But maybe she had expected something like this. Maybe she had lived for *years* expecting something like this. Windows shattered. Bullets sprayed the house in a pattern from left to right, *pah! pah! pah pah pah pah!* When she heard Cootie's sharp cry of pain, she knew. She jumped to her feet; she had to get to him. But Jimmy Ray hit her hard and took her to the floor again.

"Don't get up, Tess. You can't."

She let out a grunt, a lock-jawed note of distress that wasn't so different from the moans she'd made in childbirth with Tansy. *Hnnnh. Hnnnh.*

When Tess lifted her face to look, sun streamed like lasers through the holes in the front wall. "Cootie!" she shrieked. Something whined past her face; she heard it *zing* like a rubber-band breaking. Ammo pelted the vehicles outside, rattling like hail.

"Stay *down,* Tess. Please, stay *down.*"

"They've shot him."

"I know they've shot him."

"Jimmy Ray." She struggled beneath him. "I've got to get out there."

"They'll make another pass."

"They'll kill him."

"If you go out there, they'll kill you, too."

Later when her nightmares would come, Tess would see this over and over again. She would know that the most horrifying part hadn't been the second round of shots or the screams outside or the pinto beans showering their heads when a bullet shattered the bowl.

The most horrifying part was this sickening fear of being helpless. She kept staring at her trembling hand covered with bean juice, knowing she couldn't go to him. She hid her face in the crook of one arm and whimpered.

When Jimmy Ray finally let her up, Tess almost flew out the door. The steaks had been dumped in the dirt. The smell of cordite hung in the air. One boy lay face down on the ground, lettuce scattered around him like fallen moths. Another sat in the dust staring numbly at the horseshoes, a red rusty stain spreading over his pants leg. The horseshoes were all three still ringing the spike, just the way Cootie had thrown them.

When Jimmy Ray ran out behind her, he'd dug out a 12-gauge shotgun. "Put that *away*," she screamed at him, certain he was going to make it start all over again. But when the passenger in the silver Cadillac that was easing toward them again saw it, they heard him shout, *"Floor it. Floor it. Floor it."* The tires squealed as the car made a U-turn and Jimmy Ray brought his hands together over the trigger as the car accelerated away. He aimed, but didn't shoot.

Tess sat beside Cootie in the dust and cradled his head in her lap. His face was slippery with blood. "Shhh," she whispered to him the same way she had once whispered to a sleeping baby in a hospital room. "Shhh." She didn't think he even knew she was there.

"We have to get out of here, Tess," Jimmy Ray said. "When the police come, they're going to find coke in the basement and a stockpile of guns. They'll take us in for that."

"I'm not leaving him, Jimmy Ray."

"What difference does it make? He doesn't even know."

"We've got to call an ambulance or something. Everybody needs help."

"We can't stay."

At last Cootie responded. He tried to grasp her arm but his fingers fell away, leaving bloody tracks. "Sh-h-hhh," she whispered again. Somewhere, in another world, she was crying. And she knew, just as certainly as she knew that Cootie was dying, the last words that she longed for him to say.

I'm sorry, Tess. I'm sorry I didn't want you to have our baby.

There was spit on his mouth as she held him. She pulled up the tail of her shirt and wiped his face. "Cootie, can you hear me?" But he never answered. Instead, as she held him in her arms, she felt the muscle go out of him for good.

"Tess," Jimmy Ray urged her as the sound of sirens rose in the distance. "We have to *go*."

She stared up at Jimmy Ray blankly. She stared at the yard again. And Tess saw everything that she'd thought she was, everything that she thought had given her merit, lying shattered and broken and dead in the dust.

PART THREE

Nora

CHAPTER TWENTY-THREE

The late-afternoon storm swept across Butlers Bend in gusts of breeze, and the clattering of wind chimes and a wall of dark cloud coming toward them from the distance. A bank of black sky approached at unrelenting speed from the west. As Nora watched, flat bursts of lightning illuminated the clouds in sheets from within. Thunder rumbled, echoed deep in her soul.

Later, when Nora would remember it, she would think how odd this had been: As she waited for Ben that day, she did not think of Tansy missing with panic. This didn't feel like the time when their granddaughter had disappeared in the sky tube at Chuck E. Cheese's or the time Caroline Rakes had phoned from the Bargain Food Basket and shrieked, "Creede Franklin's got Ben and Tansy up in that deathtrap of a plane. The engine's sputtering and they just buzzed the parking lot so low I'm surprised Roy has any hair left on his head."

How odd, all those times of worry, and now, in this instance, to start by feeling calm.

"We can't find her, Ben," she said as he rolled down the window of his yellow truck. "Tansy's gone."

He checked his watch. "She's playing at Erin's, isn't she?"

"No," Nora told him. "I've already phoned."

Ben, too, must have felt unworried. "You might call the bus barn. If Carl Campbell drove, he'll know if she was on the bus or not. He'll know which direction she headed after she got off."

Nora nodded dumbly. She couldn't think straight and her fingers had begun to tingle. She couldn't think how to find the bus-barn number in the phone book. "I don't—" But she shook herself out of that one. She wouldn't tell Ben she didn't have the wherewithal to find one phone number. He had enough to think about without her losing it.

"Nora." He winked at her. "It's going to be okay. Think of all the times you've been afraid and there hasn't been anything wrong."

"I hope you're right," she said.

"Of course I am." And he was grinning. "Hey, on second thought, I've got to park the truck at the house. I'll call the bus barn, okay?"

Nora drew her strength from her husband. Now that Ben was here, they would certainly find their granddaughter. Tansy and her grandpa together; everything would be all right.

When the rain began, it smelled so sweet and the parched land needed it so badly, the drops pelting her, sliding down her neck and her arms, felt almost pleasant. She turned her face into it, water rolling across her cheeks and her eyelids. There she stood in precious oblivion until Ben came to join her in the street.

"What did the bus barn say?" she asked him. And her heart stopped when she saw his grim face.

"She was in class. Nothing unusual. Mrs. Cedarholm said she gave her report on deep-sea creatures. And then—"

"She's here? You found her?"

"—she rode the bus. She was on it, Nora."

That horrible rushing in her ears again, and she had a difficult time hearing anything past it.

"She got off—?" Nora started.

And Ben finished it, "—at her regular stop."

The rain didn't seem so friendly anymore. Another play of lightning backlit the clouds and the thunder wasn't nearly so distant. "He's sure of that?"

"Yes."

She stared at him. It was the concern in her husband's eyes that was her undoing. "Which direction did she go?"

"He isn't sure."

"Did she start toward the house?"

"He says he thinks so, honey."

"He doesn't remember?"

"He says he didn't really see."

"He didn't *see?* I thought a bus driver was supposed to make sure everyone was safe."

"He would have noticed anything unusual, Nora. He said that to me. He said, 'If she had gone the opposite direction than she was supposed to, I would have noticed.'"

Ragged breath burned in her chest. At last Nora sank to the curb. She couldn't keep herself upright any longer.

Ben said, "We have to get the sheriff."

In spite of Nora's unease, an odd sense of purpose filled her. "Maybe if we wait." She didn't know why she even spoke it. Ben's suggestion had such an ominous finality to it; it was this she wanted to fight. "Maybe if we just . . ."

Tansy had gone missing an hour and twenty minutes ago. "Every minute counts in a situation like this. That's what they say." Nora felt Ben's hand, cool against her arm as the rain began to plaster her blouse against her skin.

∽

THE TRAFFIC SOUNDS, horns and bells and snippets of music, wove around the voices in her home. As if she observed someone else's life, Nora watched numerous squad cars slide into place against both curbsides, their tires hissing on the wet pavement, fitting one behind another along the street.

In a larger town, this ordeal would have been peopled with strangers. In Butlers Bend it was Bill Mott and Gene Hansen in uniform. Donnie Crider and Merrill Horn. Why, Nora had taken a fistful of black-eyed Susans and a potato salad to Merrill's mother only last Saturday when Tabitha Horn had broken her ankle.

"Don't worry," Donnie said now, kneeling beside Nora's chair with a gallant smile. "I've been doing this for two years. There's no way anybody can get away from us. We always find the kid."

Gene Hansen asked questions about Tansy—her age, her size, any distinguishing marks they should know, if she had any idea where Tansy might hide if she got angry or wanted to tease them. He asked these questions even though Gene had known Tansy since she'd first appeared in the Butlers Bend Christmas pageant.

"Can't somebody be out there looking?" Ben asked.

Ben wasn't nearly as cool anymore about this as he had been when he'd started. He paced the width of the three front windows, back and forth, over and over again.

"Anybody report any suspicious vehicles in the neighborhood? We can't go out with an AMBER Alert unless we've got a make/model and a color."

"Claude might have seen something. You know how he's always out after those birds."

"We'll start with that."

"I know this is tedious, Nora." Gene held up his pen, spoke with a tone of true apology. "But we've all gathered here. Even if she walks in the door this second, I've got to file some report."

"She has a small scar in the middle of her left eyebrow."

And suddenly Nora began to babble on and on. It was either that or give in to her stomach, which was threatening nausea.

"She was running in her nightgown one morning; I don't know what happened. Maybe she'd been in the bathroom and the floor was wet. Anyway, she hit the molding in the corner when she fell. Seven stitches. They put a square of white paper over her face in the emergency room so she couldn't see the needle."

"Pierced ears? Does she have pierced ears?"

"Yes."

"Was she wearing earrings?"

"Yes." Nora pictured them. "Little blue stars."

"Anything else? Her birthday—?"

"She's seven." And it poured out, everything she could think to say about Tansy, everything she could force herself to remember about this morning. "Her hair was braided, one long braid down the back. She wanted her favorite purple hair ribbon this morning. I remember that. A white T-shirt with a number on it—number 34 in light blue. Pink-and-white tennis shoes. No brand name. Those you get at Payless with pictures of flowers on the sides. And a Rangers hat." This stopped her, finally. She thought about that. It terrified her that she couldn't remember. "I don't know if she wore her hat."

They say there are times a broken heart can be felt, coming on as physical pain. Thinking of that hat, those crumpled seams and folded brim, Nora's heart knotted and burned.

Oh, Father. I'll do anything. Anything. Why are You doing this? If there's something You want me to sacrifice, please let me see.

Two hours later, they still had no vehicle description. The police had a command post set up, and a case number ten digits long.

"Case type?"

And here it seemed like every officer stopped and held his breath, watching them.

"Are we talking a family abduction, Ben? Do you think it could be that?" Bill Mott gave Nora a reassuring squeeze on the hand.

"We don't know." Ben started pacing again. "We think it could be. We *hope* it could be. There is a slight possibility that her mother might have come to take her back. Or maybe not. We don't know."

"Non-family abduction?"

Everyone waited for Gene.

"Well, do we know it was an abduction?"

Nora stood, her voice firm. "We don't know anything, Gene."

Gene scrawled in the blank: *Lost, Injured, Missing,* then braided his fingers in a tight knot on his desk. "Ben, you could help us with this if you could give us any other leads about your daughter."

"Look. You've got to understand," Nora said. "She walked out of our house and left us responsible for her newborn."

"And now?"

"Tess has no claim."

"You're the legal guardians?"

Nora nodded. Ben said, "We took care of that just as soon as we could."

∽

THERE IS NO NIGHT darker than the night of a missing child. The phone had stopped ringing hours before. The last person to bring food and sit with them had departed just before midnight.

As Nora stood in Tansy's room, breathless in its emptiness, she remembered that it had been Tess who taught her the enormity of that. A place full of someone's belongings is much emptier than a place full of nothing at all.

The yellow coverlet on the bed hung like a ruffled skirt. A tube of Little Kitty lip gloss lay open where it had rolled the last time Tansy had played dress-up. The porcelain tea set, much treasured since Tansy knew it had been her mother's, was set out as if for a party.

With Tansy missing all these hours, Nora couldn't function enough to even keep things in her hands. Money got misplaced. Keys couldn't be found. A jar of Lavinia's fig preserves dashed to the ground and the Ball jar shattered into pieces.

With Tansy gone, Nora had to stop and think where the coffee belonged in the pantry. When Nora went to the Internet and tried to look up any AMBER Alert information, she struck the wrong letters when she tried to type in Tansy's name.

Now, as she stood in Tansy's room, the fan throbbed. Mimosa branches swept the window. For a moment Nora imagined she had heard something. Her chin lifted. Even her heart seemed to wait. She shoved aside the curtains.

"Tansy?"

She could see nothing out the window, only the reflection of her own nose.

Back outside again just to make sure. How many times would this happen? Hearing a sound, stopping, letting herself look and be disappointed?

Out in the yard, limbs rustled like water. The whole world moved, wheeling out of control.

CHAPTER TWENTY-FOUR

—⟳—

Jimmy Ray had gone outside to smoke.

Tess could see him beyond the smeared window of the café, standing with his shoulders hunched, one hand shoved inside his pocket, the other clinging to the Marlboro.

She imagined she could hear the soft pop when he pulled the cigarette away from his lips. He followed with an impressive puff of smoke, streaming from his nose.

This world had so many different ways of hurting people.

Each time the waitress walked by, her tennis shoe snapped. She wore a nametag that said she was "Laneer." She kept flirting with the man in the booth across the aisle. "Well, you've been here for a long time, haven't you?" the customer asked.

"Nine years."

"What you need is a boyfriend. Somebody to get you out of this place."

A flip of her ponytail. "Nope. I got too many kids for that."

Too many kids. Tess tightened her grip on Tansy's arm and felt a pleasant kind of sorrow soaking into her. *I've got a kid, too. And I almost gave mine away.*

"I don't like my hair short." Tansy kept scraping it aside to get it out of her eyes. "Now I can never have a braid."

"But I saved your braid. It's in the car on the floor."

"I didn't want it in the car on the floor. I wanted it on my head."

Tess sighed. "It'll grow back."

"You don't know that," Tansy pouted. "You haven't ever watched my hair grow." She stared at the luncheon plate of fish sticks and mashed potatoes.

"Don't you have to eat something? What's going to happen to you if you don't eat something?"

"I'll shrivel up and die."

"What if I ordered you a cinnamon bun? What about that?" Silence.

"We'll try that. I'll see if they've got one."

Soon, Tansy was staring down at a sugary pastry as big around as a stewpot lid. Tess sighed. This after Tansy had been in the women's room so long that she'd had to knock on the door three times and ask, *What's taking so long? Did you fall in?*

"Come on, baby. Just eat a little bit, okay? Do it for Mama."

"I don't *want* to do it for you. I don't think I *like* you."

"Well, you could try."

"I want Nana."

After a good while, the sugar *did* win out. Tansy unwound the outermost layer of gooey roll and started shoveling it in. Tess couldn't stop staring at Tansy's short, full curls and remembering Cootie's hair, how it had looked laying across her lap. She closed her eyes and tried to make the sight go away.

Jimmy Ray had come back inside and was staring at the television blaring from a high corner beside the cash register. He stood there for a long time watching, shoving his sleeves up and down. When he slid into the booth next to Tess he said, "It's all over the news."

"What? That we've taken her?"

"Oh, no. Not that. Not yet."

"What is?"

"Everything that happened at the house. Everything about Cootie dying."

It was the first time Tess had heard Cootie's name out loud in the past day. Her shoulders lifted and fell. When Tess lifted her eyes to his, tears started to stream although she didn't make a sound.

"Hey," Tansy interruped. That's all Tansy would call her. "Hey, I need to go to the bathroom." "Hey, I can't go to sleep." "Hey, I'm full." "Hey," she said now. "I don't want any more of this cinnamon roll."

"We'll wrap it up and you can eat it later."

Jimmy Ray pulled at his shirt pocket, poking around for a cigarette. He didn't have another.

Tess's eyes met Jimmy Ray's, strong in both her conviction and grief. "Cootie is gone. I don't have anywhere to go home to anymore."

"Maybe this isn't the time," he said, "but we could go off together. Set ourselves up somewhere faraway from what's happened. We could start over."

"No, Jimmy Ray." The heaviness in her heart was a mixture of hopelessness and mourning. "No more starting over for me. It never does any good."

"What other choice do you have?"

She scrubbed her face fast, furious with herself that she showed how badly she was hurting. "There's a certain path I have to take. I want to show her a part of her father before it's too late."

⌒

ON THURSDAY, Nora bought new fabric. Ben was always scolding her. "You spend more money at The Stitch than you make working there." But Nora never could resist. The day before Tansy had disappeared, she had found an entire McCall's pattern section of mother/daughter dresses—pages of capri pants and camp shirts.

She had laying out and cutting to be done. She lined up each selvage, making each thread straight. That done, she arranged the pattern pieces with difficulty. It would never do for the thick green lines and the thin blue ones not to come together at every seam.

She could not see herself as she worked. If she could have, she would have seen a woman who looked older than she ought to, her mouth bristling with pins. She would have seen someone with her eyes surrounded by anxious lines, a worried frown, as faint and tightly knit as the seams she made with her Singer machine.

Nora did not allow herself to think as her scissors bit into the fabric. She would cut out two patterns today, one large and one small.

One mother (grandmother) camp shirt.

One daughter camp shirt.

These would be ready, she kept herself sane by thinking, *when Tansy came home.*

Later that afternoon, while Ben was sorting through bank statements and utility bills that needed to be paid, Nora marched into the room with a stack of Tansy's handmade baby blankets, folded neatly and stacked in her arms.

Ben put down the letter that read PAYMENTS MADE AFTER 30TH WILL BE SHOWN ON NEXT BILL and narrowed his eyes at her. "What is that?"

"I'm taking these blankets down to Dr. Strouth's office. I'm going to donate them there."

"Donate them? What would a doctor's office want with baby blankets?"

"I've already gotten permission from him on the phone. The nurses will give these blankets out to girls like Tess, who decide to have babies under difficult circumstances. If the babies are adopted, the blankets can go with them."

"Well." He shook his head at her. "You made about two dozen. That ought to last Butlers Bend about twelve years."

"There's nothing better than a soft flannel blanket that's been made by a grandma," Nora said pointedly. "These may scarcely be enough. I may need to make more when these run out. Maybe I can get others from the Stitch to help me."

Ben stared down at the pile of windowed envelopes and statements of accounts that littered his desktop, looking weary and jostled, as if he'd been on a difficult journey.

If Nora had thought about it, she would have anticipated these things. She would have understood that the household numbers were swimming in front of his eyes. She might have known he'd been adding columns twice, three times, making sure that he'd figured right before he dared scribble another check and attach a stamp to the envelope. But she saw only her own pain, and could not escape from it.

"You could wait to do trivial things like this, Nora. Tansy is missing. I don't know how you can focus on anything else."

"We are two different individuals, Ben. I have to deal with this on my own terms."

"I don't understand your terms, Nora." When he said it, Nora knew exactly what he meant. *My grief is more important than yours! Mine is worse than yours. I love Tansy more!*

She was too exhausted and frustrated to check her words. "You don't care more about Tansy and Tess than I do! I know you think you do, Ben, but you *don't.*"

"What do you mean by that?"

"I think you know what I mean, Ben."

At her answer, he rose from his chair and took the blankets away from her. He set the stack on top of his desk, and lofted one of them. The blanket caught air and unfolded of its own accord, sailing down.

"Stop it," she said. "Please, Ben. Don't."

"Why does this bother you so much?" He lofted another one. And another. And another. "Why did you ever sew all these things? Why did you disapprove of everything our daughter ever did? *Why did you chase Tess away?"*

Nora suddenly felt like she was smothering. The walls seemed to collapse in around her. She hit the door hard, desperate for air.

She plunged down the steps of the house and scarcely gave a glance toward Donnie Crider, who was taking his shift watching their house. Nora was aware only of the hum in her ears and the motion of her feet; she focused on the sight of one foot after the other appearing in front of her.

Lord, You died so I could be forgiven for what I did, so why do I keep thinking about it?

She walked the length of Joplin Street, gasping for breath, and turned the corner beside Lavinia and Claude's house, her heart pinching when she passed the spot where Lavinia had found Tansy's backpack in the yard.

She walked faster, not noticing the pebbles skittering away from her feet on the sidewalk or the pill bugs that were scurrying out of her way. She passed Meriweather Street and knew, from the conversations she'd had with Erin Hamm, that the two girls had been together until Tansy had walked past this intersection. She strode past the bus stop where, ridiculously, the bus still stopped and children still poured out and bounded without much thought toward their homes.

She hadn't known Ben was following her. When he caught up with her, he wrenched her wrists and turned her around. "Nora, come here. You mustn't run away."

"I *can't*," she gasped against his chest. "I can't do anything *except* run away."

"From what?" He grabbed her shoulders but she wrestled away. "What are you trying to run away from? Is it me?"

A tiny lizard, probably an anole or a chameleon, scurried on tiny, thin legs up the trunk of a tree. Even as Nora watched it, it began to change color, from green to a muted green to grey. A blue jay swooped from the roof and chided her with its sharp, insistent call.

I had my abortion while I professed to be a Christian. And I forgave myself. And You forgave me, Lord. Why is there a problem now?

If You don't look at it anymore, Lord, why do You make me still look at it?

She let her husband pull her against his chest. And the answer to her question, when it came, seemed to come from the blue jay's call and the knowing eyes of the lizard and the breeze rustling the leaves in the trees.

Beloved, you can say you are healed and stay broken, or you can look at it again and bring it to My cross.

She leaned her head against her husband's chest. *I don't know how to do that,* she cried to God. *I don't know how to do that.*

"I don't know how to tell you what I have to tell you," she said to Ben.

I am with you, Nora. You are never alone.

"What is it?" Ben asked. "What do you have to tell me?"

She had been nineteen when it happened. The very same age that Tess had been when Nora had wanted to encourage her daughter to do it, too.

"Nora. Look at me." Ben lifted her face with her hands. "What's wrong, honey? You look sick." Nora gazed into her husband's eyes and the memory played out in her head.

❦

"I don't know whether this is good news or bad news," the university physician had told her after he'd checked her into the college infirmary because she couldn't even keep fluids down. "You have the flu and you also have something else. You're going to have a baby."

The next morning, free to go to her classes, terrified to say anything to the boy she was dating, Ben Crabtree, Nora headed to the college counseling office instead. When she told them what she needed at the front door, they offered to set an appointment for her so she could talk to someone, and they handed her a green slip of paper with names and addresses of women's clinics, places she could take care of her problem.

No one was pressuring her to make this decision. No one knew. Her parents couldn't have accepted this; they wouldn't forgive her. Her grandparents wouldn't understand. She saw everything and she saw it clearly.

This was legal, so what was there to feel guilty about?

Nora didn't feel a need to listen to any counseling. Her mind was made up; this was the solution. To handle this any other way would mean the end of the world.

That morning, Nora just wanted to get it over with. She had been throwing up for days and she didn't want to be sick anymore. Although she was scared it would hurt, her college suitemate had told her it wouldn't be too bad. She ate Twinkies for breakfast, and those made her throw up, too.

When they directed her to a dressing room, she found a folded, crisp hospital gown and a miniscule pink pill. The pill made Nora think everything was funny. In the corner of this second waiting room, a television blared Bugs Bunny cartoons.

When they called her name this time, she took her place on the examining table. A picture of the mountains hung on the wall and, ridiculously, she repeated Scripture: "I will lift up mine eyes to the hills from whence cometh my help." A red-and-white striped canister waited at the foot of the table and she thought, It's decorated like a child's peppermint stick.

Even to this day, she did not remember a doctor's face. She only remembered the mountain photo on the wall and the red stripes and the incorrigible tugging inside her stomach that went on forever. Not until loneliness gripped her did she realize that, as long as she'd been pregnant, she'd felt as if there had been another person with her; for those three weeks, she hadn't noticed it until it was gone, she'd felt like two people instead of one.

⁂

Nora had none of the symptoms everyone talked about. She had bled for a while and then it was finished. She didn't freak out when she saw the shape of Tess's little body on an ultrasound. She didn't cry when she heard Tess's heartbeat for the first time. Indeed, she had watched carefully for those things, and they hadn't bothered her at all.

"Oh, Jesus," she whispered. "Help me." And at long last, tears of remorse and grief began to spill over. *I don't completely understand my heart. Help me see this through Your eyes so that I might be broken in spirit before You.* She cried now because she had lost a child so many years ago. She had never known this baby and it was the first time she had wept for it in three decades. *Show me the truth in Your name.*

"What is it, Nora? Why are you crying? You look awful. Honey, what is this?"

I can't go back, can I, Lord? But I can go forward.

And so she said it to him very quietly.

"I had an abortion, Ben."

He stared at her.

She held her ground and stared back.

"What? I'm sorry. I—"

"You heard me. You heard what I said."

That was the moment that Ben's eyes turned to ice. He dropped his arms and stared at her. "I don't think I heard you right."

"Yes," she told him. "You did."

As if his expression could become any icier than it had already been.

"When?"

She didn't answer that.

"When did it happen, Nora? Tell me."

"Is there a right way to regret something, Ben?"

And he asked, his voice like stone, "Was the baby mine?"

She nodded, wordless.

"Before Tess?"

But she couldn't speak anymore. She had said all that she could say. Even so, he kept asking.

"Were we dating? Was it while we were in college?

"Would it have been a boy?"

"Didn't you think I had a right to know?"

Nora stood with her eyes closed in front of him. He'd followed her. He'd asked. She'd given everything to him that she could give.

She knew it when he turned away from her and headed back to the house. And she felt like a part of Ben stayed attached to her, as slender as a thread, when he walked away, unraveling her.

CHAPTER TWENTY-FIVE

M errill Horn sat at his desk, the digital photographs squared off in a pile in his hand. Ever so often he still reached for his morning coffee, that brewed-in-the-back-room, been-sitting-since-yesterday, clear-as-mud, would-probably-dissolve-a-spoon-if-you-tried-to-stir-it-with-one elixir.

Every time he reached and found it not there, he chewed himself out. He kept forgetting he'd finished the cup thirty minutes ago.

Ben Crabtree threw open the door and rushed in, his wife behind him. "What did you find? Why did you call us here?"

Merrill reached for the coffee cup that wasn't there again. Donnie Crider said, "We don't have good news, I'm afraid." Merrill handed over the photographs without saying another word.

"What is this?"

"That"—A low-key nod—"is where your daughter's been living, Mr. Crabtree."

Ben sat down hard. "I don't understand."

Relations were strained between husband and wife. Merrill could tell by watching the two of them, how they sat in the folding chairs, their legs crossed against each other, their spines stiff, their shoulders as square as kitchen cupboards. Yes, this could take a toll on a marriage, Merrill knew it. He watched as Ben handed the photograph to Nora and saw Ben make certain that their fingers didn't touch. Merrill watched Nora's red-rimmed eyes as she cast them at her lap, as if she didn't feel worthy of looking at her husband. Instead, she took in the buckling sidewalk in the picture, the chain-length fence that ballooned and gaped like a torn net, the bullet-ridden front wall.

"As far as we can tell, this house was hit because of a gang rivalry. It's all about body count, Ben, when two groups decide to have it out. If you've been watching the news, they've covered this extensively on the Dallas channels."

Well, yes. Ben and Nora had been monitoring the news, of course. They'd kept the sound turned low so it wouldn't disturb the visitors who came and went, who spoke in murmuring sympathetic voices. As long as the pictures on screen were about Iraq or the economy or gang wars or traffic problems, they didn't pay attention. If a story had appeared about a missing child, Ben would have turned it up and made everybody listen.

The most appalling detail in the photo, or so Merrill thought, was the geographic pattern of the bullet holes as they swept across the house. Bullets had cut and curled the skin of a black Ford like a tin can. Glass jutted like fingers from a shattered window and, inside, Merrill could see a freshly painted white wall.

In spite of the desperate neighborhood, someone had been struggling to make this place a home.

When Merrill had interviewed the Dallas authorities late last night, they'd told him that a young woman of Tess's description had been around for years. She'd been quiet, as far as Merrill could tell. No one had known much about her. No one seemed to care.

"There's a gang rivalry in that part of South Dallas. They found coke and a stash of firearms when they searched the house. They also found bodies, Ben."

"What are you trying to tell us, Merrill?" Ben asked.

"I'm giving you background. This is what we know."

"But the bodies—"

"Tess didn't show up in jail. She didn't show up in any hospital. Neither did Tansy."

"Did they show up in the morgue, Merrill?" Nora asked. "Is that what you're trying to say?"

They waited for the worst. Merrill plowed in. "Both of them are still at large."

"I want to go there," Ben insisted, rising up out of his chair. "I want to talk to the neighbors."

"I'd save yourselves the despair if I were you. Everything the neighbors had to say is in those Dallas police reports. I brought copies of everything for you."

"There might be something else, though. Something no one else has thought of."

Merrill picked up the coffee cup again and, finding it empty, shifted it from one hand to the other. "They've gone through everything with a fine-toothed comb. I made sure of that."

"Any sign of a little girl? Could someone in the house have been hiding her?"

Another slight frown. "Oh, no. No sign of her. You see—"

"No, we don't see," Ben interrupted.

"—this happened a few hours before Tansy went missing." After a long pause, Merrill Horn made certain they both understood what he was trying to tell them. With a careful nod he leveled his eyes on them. "This may have something to do with your granddaughter's disappearance, though. This happened in the morning. Two days ago."

✍

WHEN THE AG-CAT BIPLANE buzzed overhead, upsetting the dachshund collector's plate at Dolores Kay Jones's house and flinging the plastic communion cups to the floor at the church, everyone knew that Creede Franklin had come home. He was stationed at Barksdale, in Louisiana, these days and his last assignment had been flying F-16 fighter planes into Baghdad.

When Creede had first started flying, he'd been exhilarated and frustrated by the biplane when other pilots discussed their newer models. But he'd done a stint in a C-5, too, and after flying a plane large enough to transport a football team and their entire turf, too, the Ag-Cat felt buoyant and responsive. He flew at home now and felt like he lilted over the earth without any strings attached.

Without any strings attached.

That went a long way toward describing his life these days. Candice's decision had been tough enough to handle when he'd gotten home to Travis after a few weeks. But he'd always had another assignment, another rush of adrenaline, another mission to fly supplies to the boys in the field.

But this week, spending a few quiet weeks of leave with his parents, the truth was beginning to sink in.

Candice didn't want a military husband. When she'd taken a vow to love and cherish him "until death do us part," she must not have factored in Baghdad. When it had ended a year-and-a-half ago, they didn't even have children to show for their time together.

Then, when Creede had landed the Ag-Cat in Buxton Lance's field, Claude Simms happened to be out scoping mockingbirds and had told him about Tansy Crabtree being missing. *A long time ago,* he thought when Claude told him, *I knew Tess better than anyone else. There was a time in my life when I might have been able to figure out where she'd taken her daughter.*

As he helped his father clean out the garage and drove to the gas station to fill up his dad's car, something hit him. He stood staring at the logo on the gas pump. *People think you're a hero, Franklin,* he lectured himself. *But you know you've never been a hero to Tess.*

Creede made a call to Barksdale Air Force Base on his cell phone as the gasoline gurgled into the tank, and that clenched it. He found his father still working in the garage when he arrived home.

Pete was hanging the fertilizer spreader on the wall.

"Dad?"

Pete lowered his arms and winked at his son. "You got here just in time to help carry Mom's boxes upstairs."

"I'll carry the boxes, Dad. But I need to talk to you first."

The relationship between father and son had changed since Creede joined the Air Force. Creede knew that although his father still saw him as a son, he saw him as a man as well. There they stood with their shoulders squared, their dusty sneakers toe to toe. "I want to talk to you about Tess."

"Tess?" Pete's chin lifted. "Why do you want to talk about her?"

"Claude Simms told me that the police have found where

she's been. Since the house is cordoned off and she's hiding, I think I know where she might be."

"You going to tell anybody about it down at the sheriff's office?"

"No. I owe Tess something. I want to do this myself."

"What?"

"You think that old crop duster can clear Reunion Tower?"

For only a slight beat their equal stature broke. The father asked, "You're taking the Grumman over the city?"

And the son answered, with a devilish little salute, "Won't require more duress there than she was under in these fields in Gilford County. *Sir.*"

"Oh, really?"

"I phoned my superiors at Barksdale and they have conversed with our Texas congressmen. I've been approved to fuel at Addison Airport."

Pete stared at his son.

"When the Dallas officials are notified, I believe they'll bend their protocol. I believe they'll give clearance for a full flight. We'll find out."

They looked with admiration at each other. As Creede moved to go, Pete said, "There was something else I wanted to talk to you about, Creede."

Creede was already far off, mentally preparing for a flight, examining the sky when Pete said, "I know about that tattoo, son."

Creede stopped short.

"I knew about it the week you did it, back when it was puffy and red."

Creede glanced back over his shoulder. Their eyes met again. "Were you mad?"

Pete thought about that, shook his head. "Not mad. Not ever mad. But worried. She wasn't the sort of girl I wanted you to end up with."

"Yes, Dad," Creede said, knowing life was always waiting to throw kinks into plans and that the heavenly Father was bigger than all of it. "And Candice was."

"Sometimes God's plan is different than we imagine."

"I listened to you."

"I know. You took my guidance often. It meant a lot to me."

"Thank you for acknowledging that."

"Maybe sometimes that guidance was wrong."

"You did it because you loved me."

Pete narrowed his eyes. "Yes, and I still do."

"I've cared about Tess ever since I can remember, Dad. We were kids. We ran all over these farm fields together. That doesn't go away."

"No," Pete agreed. "I suppose it doesn't."

With that, Creede's cell phone rang.

He glanced and saw the number was from his base. He answered, "Captain Franklin here," and flashed a thumbs-up sign to his father.

৶

WHEN CREEDE TOOK off from his grandfather's cattle field and banked his plane toward the southwest, he wondered how soon he might be able to see the glow of the object he was seeking. Flying over Plano, following familiar highways and buildings, he marveled at how vibrant and different these Texas colors seemed compared to the shades of brown in Iraq. Below him, cars strung along the length of Central Expressway like rosary beads. His radio crackled and the control tower at Addison gave him an altitude change.

As Creede pulled up, the Dallas skyline came into view. He banked and enjoyed the sensation of the entire world tipping beneath him. The Trinity River arced to the west like a moat, its flat water glinting like gunmetal. The tall buildings, as clustered as they were, canted beneath him like turrets and keeps and spires of a castle.

Other landmarks in the skyline dwarfed the old building. From Creede's view, everything around it stood streamlined and sharp and tall. The Magnolia Building looked like an old squatter in the middle of the towers around it.

Lord, thank You for giving me this hunch. Thank You that she talked to me when she was home.

At the corner of Commerce and Ervay, he dropped three hundred feet. He'd have to fly a tightrope act to get a decent view. But Creede had flown tightrope acts before, including one this past month over Karbala.

With a confidence born of experience, he banked the Grumman again, his circle smooth and broad. He had only one shot, two minutes at the most, before he would have to pull up again.

The roof appeared below him. Looking down on the attic, he saw hipped rows of green Spanish tile. And there, on its top, stood the forty-foot red Pegasus that had marked the heart of Dallas since midway through the Great Depression, its legs in full gallop, its wings outspread.

The red neon figure was larger than Creede had imagined. Even in the dusky light it seemed to singe the sky. One leg crooked as if it might be pawing the ground. Its wings, hundreds of feet of gleaming red glass, rose from its neon withers.

But maybe he was wrong. He couldn't see anything there.

He'd missed his chance. Creede pulled the stick and gained altitude. That was all the time he had, making the pass this fast.

He ached with frustration. Once he'd cleared the taller buildings, he radioed Addison again. As the control tower cleared another pass, Creede's words in answer sounded calm, but his skin felt clammy and the knot in his abdomen grew tighter. As he made a broad sweeping circle over the city, he replayed what he'd seen on the roof of the Magnolia Building. If they were hiding up there, where would he look to find a clue of them? A late-afternoon shadow. A corner, maybe. Or beneath the steel fretwork that crisscrossed and sheltered the center.

When he made the next pass, he had to remind himself to breathe deeply. He descended and trimmed his airspeed, hoping to give himself a few more precious seconds in which to search. He flew by instinct now, by feeling the drag on the wings, knowing if he let too much speed go, the plane would stall. And here, in downtown, it wouldn't be as easy to get out of a fix as it had been in the fields near Butlers Bend.

He aimed the Ag-Cat directly at the monstrous red horse, coming in lower this time. If he was going to see anything, he'd have to skim the top of the building. As he neared the green tile, he relied on his instincts.

One second. Two seconds. And Creede caught a glimpse of motion. In one corner beneath a large limestone embellishment, something moved in the shadows. He saw a cardboard box set up as a table. There might have been a sleeping bag, but he couldn't be sure. One thing, above all others, let him know that he could be certain. A stuffed bunny lay in tangles on the roof.

That was all the time he had again. He pulled up within yards of another skyscraper. He radioed Addison and let them know he would be returning north.

❧

BEN UNFOLDED A CHAIR in the police station and sat down. He leaned across Bill Mott's desk and tried to recall any names he might have heard Tess mention during those months she had stayed with them. But seven years gone by can make for a fuzzy memory. The list was brutally short. Going over it made Ben realize how little of herself Tess had shared with them during the short period she'd been back again.

Finally, Ben gave up trying to think of more names or information. He picked up his jacket and started for the door when he noticed a picture of Bill's daughter propped in a gold frame atop the officer's desk. The girl was dressed in a red satin gown, dangling earrings, and a wrist corsage. Beside her stood a boy looking like he'd be more comfortable wearing a paper bag than the black tuxedo jacket.

Ben swallowed, made a gesture. "Nice picture of Jess. Cute."

"Ah, yes. Before the prom last spring, all dressed up for her fancy evening."

"She's beautiful."

"She's so grown up."

"I can see that."

"It hasn't been long since she thought boys had cooties."

Ben laughed, only the laugh wasn't wholehearted. He couldn't shake the feeling of something nagging at him.

. . . *since she thought boys had cooties.*

Cooties.

Cootie. That boy's name had been Cootie.

No. Realization hit Ben. *Connor.*

The boy had first introduced himself as *Connor.*

"Bill," Ben said, leaning forward against the desk. "I think I might have another name."

Bill yanked out a piece of paper and a stub of a pencil. "Let me have it."

"All this time we've been looking for a Cootie. He said it to us once when he came to the house. *Connor.* He called himself Cootie but his name was *Connor.*"

"Connor . . . Connor Banks? Is that who we are looking for?"

"I believe so."

"I'll run it through the system," Bill said. "See what comes up."

∽

NORA WAS AT HOME alone when the knock sounded on the Crabtrees's front door. When Nora answered it and recognized her pastor, she froze with fear. "Pete? What is it?"

He reached a hand to her. "Don't be scared, Nora. It's—"

"Why are you here?"

"I've come because of Creede. He's asked me to do this."

"Pete?" She touched his arm, her fingers trembling.

"Creede landed at Addison Airport a few minutes ago and phoned me. He's taken a tour in the crop duster. He thinks he's found them."

Creede. Nora backed away, holding the door open so Pete could follow her. The moment her legs touched the edge of the sofa, she sank onto it. "Ben isn't here. He's at the sheriff's office. If Creede's found her, does he know if she's safe?"

"We'll drive to the courthouse and get Ben, Nora. If you'll come with me, I'll explain on the way."

CHAPTER TWENTY-SIX

The helicopter rotors pulsed in the air, sending off a vibration that throbbed against Nora's eardrums. As it lifted off and left her and Ben standing on a landing pad two blocks away from the Magnolia Hotel, Nora felt as if she wasn't standing in this odd place, that someone else was moving her, and touching her heart, and making her breathe. The helicopter pilot had given them directions during the flight. They knew which streets to cross to find their way.

When they stepped into the elevator lobby of the Magnolia Hotel, the gold-leaf and plaster ceiling seemed surreal. For long absurd moments, she considered their surroundings and thought, *Tess has brought Tansy Aster to a palace!* She'd read about it once in *Texas Monthly,* how this old oil building had been transformed into an upscale downtown hotel.

Ben spoke briefly to the concierge at the front door and, within moments, an armed security guard appeared, prepared to go with them. Once the elevator doors slid shut, Nora saw they were etched with the outline of a flying horse.

This strategy had been laid out quickly. If Nora's conversation with her daughter did not go well, a Dallas SWAT team would move in. Nora saw the security guard check the status of his pistol and he said, "We can only hope that they aren't armed."

Ben said nothing. Even in his fear for their granddaughter, he had not reached out to his wife since she had made her confession. He carried his own strain alone as Nora stared at the floor numbers as the elevator proceeded skyward. As the numbers climbed, a green light moved across the panel. "How did they get here?" Nora asked the uniformed officer. "Surely someone would have caught them trying to sneak onto the roof. How are they going up and down?"

"The laundry department," the security guard said, scowling. "Apparently, she's been doing the hotel laundry for quite some time. The people who know your daughter *do* care about her, Mrs. Crabtree. Of course we'll have an in-house investigation. When she told them why she wanted time up here, the van driver in the laundry department helped them."

The doors slid open on the twenty-fourth floor. The top five floors, the sign explained, were serviced only by a secure elevator for guests with passes to the penthouses. "We'll have to get to the fire escape." The guard led them down the hallway. "Here."

For four floors, as they banged up enclosed stairs, Nora could barely see where they were going. They came to a final grey door with metal webbing. Nora shoved it open, and caught herself, swaying. Nothing stood between her and the pavement four-hundred feet below except for a narrow iron grate, barely wide enough for one person. Above her head rose a tapering stairway with open metal steps, one slim rail on either side.

The rickety collection of iron stairs disappeared over a ledge of limestone. The height made her reel. "Don't follow me," she said to Ben, to the guard, both of whom looked like they wanted to overrule her. "It doesn't look like these will support all of us."

"I should do this, Nora," Ben rebuked her. "Tess trusts me."

"No, Ben." She didn't look at the ground below. She didn't look at the sky above. Nora clung to the rails and focused where her next step would be. Only one step. "It has to be me."

It isn't my purpose to change the situation, beloved. It is my purpose to change you.

"Tansy?" she called over the wind. "Tansy, can you hear me?" Only the silence answered her.

She stepped up on the first rung, felt herself begin to totter. She stepped up to the next rung anyway.

What if I stopped trusting what I think I deserve, and started trusting You, Father?

When she climbed over the ledge, no one was there. "Tess?" The security guard below her had drawn his gun.

Nothing.

Oh, Father. Please.

"Tess, honey," she called again. "Are you here?"

City sounds from below seemed to tumble away with her voice. The wind soughed over the ledges of the building. Overhead, the neon lights buzzed and crackled. Everything around Nora seemed to sway.

"We know what happened, Tess. We know what happened to Cootie."

Taxis honked and, below them on the street, headlights were twinkling on. The legs of the neon horse above them illuminated the silhouette of its steel oil-derrick base with red.

Nora could tell that Ben had made his way up behind her. Even without looking, even in this place where they needed each other, she could sense his injured dissatisfaction with her. Down in the lobby, a SWAT team was waiting. They could be summoned with nothing more than a radio signal from the security guard waiting on those tapering steps.

"Tess," she called again. "We're sorry about what happened to Cootie."

When she glanced back at Ben, his face was grim. He had grown more distant every day. He evaded her eyes even though she cast them imploringly in his direction.

The wind seemed to have stopped in some sort of weird, anticipatory stillness. Nora moved across the roof, each step with caution, and fraught with uncertainty. She had grown so used to the silence that, when the sound began, it caused her to start.

From the opposite side of the roof a little voice began to sing out to her Nana, strong and clear. *Jesus loves Tansy, this I know, for the Bible tells me so . . .*

"Tansy!" Ben called behind her.

. . . little ones to him belong . . .

The child only sang three measures before someone shushed her. But she was here! She was safe! Nora took another step forward, feeling braver.

"The only reason you're here," came Tess's stiff voice, stopping her, "is because you want Tansy back. You never would have come looking for me."

Another long period of silence in which none of them spoke or moved. In the evening sky, an airplane contrail gleamed as brightly as the moon. A gull landed on the ledge and then rose again on its wings.

Tess stepped out from the shadow toward her mother. Tess, holding Tansy's hand beside an ornamented chimney stack. Tansy's hair had been cut in short, snipped curls all over her head. Tess must have taken the scissors to it.

Nora could tell by the look on Tess's face that the girl was fully expecting to be stabbed by her mother's anger. But when Nora spoke, "Baby, baby," the gentleness in her own voice surprised her. "Why are you here?"

"Don't come any farther. I don't want you to."

Lord Jesus, Nora prayed. *Show me what to do.*

"Do you see me, Tess? I'm not coming toward you."

Tess began to gasp. Tears began to choke her. "It's . . . He . . . he said it to me once, Mama. His mother went away when he was a little boy and she told him to look up here, you know? He said it to me when he came to find me, did you know that? He said he kept thinking if he climbed to the top of the Magnolia Building he could see all the way to her. That he could see all the way to *me.*"

"Baby."

"He never *did* come up here."

"Tess."

"I always thought she would m-meet her dad, you know? I wanted to bring her up here to help say good-bye. I always thought . . . well, some day . . . I thought she would get to know him, but she n-never d-did."

Oh, Father. Help me to know what to say.

"H-he loved this horse. That's all he ever had, just a memory of his mom. I brought Tansy up here so she could s-*see.*"

One step toward them. "Tess, I'm so sorry," Nora said.

"Don't come any closer."

But Tansy broke free. She ran across the roof and lunged toward Ben. He scooped her up, practically from mid-air. "Is she really my mom, Grandpa? Is she the one? She says she is."

Ben nodded. "Yes, Tansy. She is your mama. You okay?" He kissed her hard on her face and clenched her against him. She kissed him right back.

"Are you up here alone?" Nora asked Tess.

"No. Jimmy Ray's here, too."

"Baby," she said, reaching for Tess. And when she did, Tess backed away and let out a ragged sob.

Beloved, here's what I wanted you to see.

Watch what she's doing, backing away from you.

Think of all the times you've backed away from Me.

This fleeting thought came to Nora's head like the swoop of a bird. Suddenly, there came a knowledge so full and certain within her that it couldn't have come from anywhere except heaven.

It goes so much further than my confession, doesn't it, Lord? It's about me understanding the depth of what I've done.

It is knowing that You care for me the same way that You care for the baby I aborted.

It is about You supernaturally showing me where I am hiding my grief.

And she saw it—she saw what was happening inside herself, saw what she had done to her daughter. And why. And this amazed her. *Thank You, Lord. Oh, thank You.* And seeing this part of herself, her own unreleased grief affecting everything, her heart was able to change.

"I need to tell you something, Tess."

He always wanted me to see the brokenness that was keeping me from Him.

"There isn't anything more we have to say to each other, is there, Mother?"

"Listen to me." Nora held up a hand. "When you were little, when I told you that you were doing things wrong, you weren't wrong at all."

Tess stared at her.

"I was putting my shame on you. I was the one who had done something wrong."

Tess narrowed her eyes at her. Nora could only imagine how difficult it must be to soak in the words she was saying.

"Every time I saw you, honey, you reminded me of something else."

"What?" Tess demanded. "What did I remind you of?"

"A long time ago, I did something I wasn't proud of. Something that bothered me deep inside. Only I didn't know it bothered me."

"You have to tell me."

"We'll talk about it soon, I promise."

"Mother—"

"—but from the moment you were born, every time I saw you, you were a reminder of that to me."

All the earth seemed to spin around them. "Did you look at me and think I was a mistake, Mama?"

"No. Oh, *no*." And when Nora took this deep breath, more words of truth came from the very core of her heart. And she meant this, *oh yes,* how she meant it. "You are the best thing that could have ever happened to me."

Tears began to roll unchecked down Tess's cheeks. Her hands unclenched at her sides. Jimmy Ray appeared from behind Tess and held her shoulders. "I think she needs you, Mrs. Crabtree."

And Nora began to cry, too. "All those times, if you felt like you did things wrong, if that's what made you leave, it wasn't you. It was me."

"From the beginning, I couldn't do anything good enough for you."

"No, Tess. It wasn't *you*."

Their eyes fixed on each other. This was going to take a while to sink in. For both of them.

This awareness shifted everything in their relationship.

"I started it. Until you started rebelling against what I was doing to you, honey, it was always me."

The daughter took a step toward the mother.

The mother took another step toward the daughter.

"We can't start at the beginning again, Tess. I'd like to find some other place for us to begin."

"Sometimes I think I deserted Tansy because it was all I knew how to do," Tess said. "I need you to help me try again with her, too."

This would be another road to travel, another place to pray, another challenge on dangerous ground, something else that felt impossible. But, when that time would come, Nora would rely on her firsthand knowledge of Jesus, who had said, *With man this is impossible, but with God all things are possible.*

"It can take a long time to understand about ourselves, why we do what we do."

Tess said, very quietly, "Mama, I don't have anywhere else to go. Can I come home?"

Nora nodded. And said, "Bring Jimmy Ray with you." She smiled at the haggard boy who must be hurting as much as Tess was hurting. "You both look like you could use a bath and a hot meal."

❧

EVEN AS BEN STAYED ANGRY at Nora during these days, he also realized this one important thing.

For so long, there had been a heaviness in their lives that he hadn't been able to understand.

Now, even with Jimmy Ray keeping the fountain clean at the library while he looked for a place of his own, even with Tess seeing a counselor twice a week, even with Creede calling from Barksdale Air Force Base to talk to Tess, even with Tansy and Erin singing karaoke at the top of their lungs, that heaviness—the feeling that had always been there just beneath the surface—seemed to have dissipated.

Oh, yes. He still acted stiff-necked toward his wife. He tried to fathom the idea that they might have had another child; Nora had told him they *did* have another child in heaven. But that thought was too big to grasp and he sometimes let it drift away.

When his wife would slip past him to water the ivies these days, she was always humming a worship song. When she lightheartedly snipped yellow stalks with her scissors, he would see her spinning the plant around when she was finished, running her fingers through the healthy leaves, taking pleasure in the verdant, solid green.

He caught her drying pans in the kitchen after another big meal, and he realized she wasn't hurrying to finish the chore. She was polishing the cookware to a fine sheen, her hand moving extravagantly slow, as she stared out the window with a dreamy expression on her face, as if she were thinking of someone who loved her. But when Ben found her at the sewing machine again, her head bent over plaid fabric and a McCall's pattern, he felt certain that this marked the end of Nora's serenity. Whenever she pulled out her straight pins, her tape measure, and her collection of threads, he'd always thought, *Now we're in for it. This is what she does whenever she wants to avoid something.*

But he found his wife humming at her sewing table, a smile on her lips as she constructed two matching shirts, as he peeked inside the door.

Good grief, no matter what the case, it was hard to stay mad at someone who was just so *happy.*

That night, he couldn't keep his eyes off of her as he watched her towel dry Tansy's hair after bathtime. "Look," she said, tousling all those short little curls on Tansy's head the same way she would toss a salad. "I saw a picture in the magazine and the model had her hair short like yours. If you put a hair clip right here, look what it does, Tansy! We can even use gel on it. You look like a princess." And the two of them spent a long time examining themselves in the mirror together, one with dark curly hair and one with straight blonde-gray hair, their eyes and their foreheads and their graceful necks, one large and one small, coming from the same mold.

He watched her sit beside Jimmy Ray Garcia at the kitchen table and offer advice to him while he circled apartment rentals in the *Echo-Bulletin.* "That one is in a complex and it has a balcony." Or "That one is in the basement of Frieda Storm's house. It doesn't have much light but, if you work long hours, Frieda sometimes offers to cook for her tenant. I think you'd like that." Or "That unit is right beside the Texas and Pacific tracks. It's cheap, but the noise might drive you crazy."

Jimmy Ray gave her a proud smile. "I've never had anyone help me like this before. Thank you."

Ben had already donned his pajamas when he heard Nora

sewing again. He climbed into bed and puffed his pillows beneath his head, certain that he would fall asleep without her beside him, the way he'd done for months. But he didn't understand why his heart kept pounding.

Presently, he heard the sewing machine stop. He heard the snap of the plastic box when she put her belongings away. He heard the music of Tess's voice intermingled with her mother's.

"What are you doing up so late, Mama?"

"Finishing something I've made for you."

"What."

"This. I hope it fits you."

"Oh," a surprised exclamation. "Thanks." Then, "Oh, there's *two* of them. They match."

"They're mother-daughter shirts. One for you and one for your daughter. What do you think?"

Ben heard his daughter. "B-but I thought these would have been for *you* and Tansy."

"I'm not her mother, honey. *You* are. *You* get the mother-daughter shirt."

"How can you trust me that much after what I did? Taking her away from you like that?"

The rustling silence that followed must have been an embrace. "Because it's a part of healing for us, to be able to trust each other. Good night, sweet Tess. I'll see you in the morning."

It's a part of healing for us, to be able to trust each other.

In their bedroom a few minutes later, Ben felt the mattress sag. He felt her crawling in beside him. He lay with his hip-bone pressed into the foam and his backbone as stiff as a blade. She touched his nose and scooted toward him.

The next thing he knew, her head was on his shoulder. Her ear lay on his chest right against his clattering heart.

"Ben," she whispered. "Are you awake?"

"Yes."

He'd always wanted to have a boy.

He'd always wondered what it would be like to have more children. That's what he would argue; Nora had taken that chance away.

They laid there in the same position for a long time, his heart pounding, her temple resting against the pulse in his throat. They laid there some more, her knees bent to fit against him, his knees locked and his legs as unyielding and straight as planks of lumber. But when he felt the wet of her tears against his chest, he came undone.

Ben rolled toward her and swept her hair away from her wet face with his hand. She whispered through muffled sobs, "Oh, Ben. I'm so sorry. I'm so *sorry.*"

He wouldn't say, *It's okay.* Because it wasn't okay. He remained wordless, letting his fingers brushing her wet cheeks and her sodden hair and her sniffy nose communicate for him.

Whatever else happened, for better or for worse, they were in this together.

Ben waited for a long time, wondering what he should say. He had feelings about this, oh yes, he did. Important feelings. They had only been dating in college, but he felt like she had taken a part of him and stolen it away.

"Something's happened to you these past days, hasn't it?"

He felt her hair crumple as she nodded against him.

"You're peaceful."

She nodded again. "Yes."

Then, "If you had only *asked* me, Nora. If you had only given me a *chance* to be responsible for this. If we could have made the decision *together.*"

"I know."

"I've been so distracted, thinking of what you took from me."

Her entire body wilted. His conscience battered him. *But what if you had never married her. You might never even have known.*

Ben couldn't understand it but, even as he blamed her, he yearned for this new serenity that his wife had shown. He felt blank with exhaustion. He thought, *God, if this is something You've given her then I want it, too.*

She rolled over to the other side of the bed, pulling three-quarters of the blanket with her.

What if you hadn't spent your life with her? What would it have been like?

He couldn't answer that question. He couldn't even imagine these past years without her. And when that thought came, the sensation of losing her left him bereft.

"Nora," he whispered into the darkness. "I'm sorry, too."

She didn't move.

He remembered his college dorm at UT with its posters of ABBA and The Eagles and Iggy Pop, the friends who crowded onto the floor to watch the Dallas Cowboys on the tiny television he'd brought from home. He remembered the way he'd worn his hair feathered over his ears and his boat shoes untied and his Izod shirt collars neatly folded.

And he thought: *I'm not so sure of who I was then.*

I only know who I am now. And I love my wife.

"Nora," he whispered.

Silence.

"I don't know what I would have done when I was nineteen. Sure, it's easy for me to judge you now. When I'm honest with myself, I don't know how I would have reacted to it then."

Outside the window, he heard one of Claude Simm's favorite mockingbirds making catcalls in their maple tree. The moon glistened like an opal in the sky outside. In the distance, the train tracks began to rattle as the 1:00 A.M. Texas and Pacific whistled its approach into town.

"It wasn't my only choice," she said, "but I thought it was. I was so sure it would be the end of the world."

Suddenly, halfway between dark and moonlight, she was there. For a moment, they found themselves entangled in bed-sheets and pajamas. He felt her touch him on the cheek, and the weight of her head found his chest again.

"We'll never know what I would have done, I guess," he said. "I can handle that, I think."

"I can handle it, Ben, if you'll hold me."

And so he did. When they finally drifted away, intertwined with each other, they sank peacefully into sleep like stones sinking through deep water.

EPILOGUE

———⁂———

B utlers Bend Baptist Church had never looked prettier than it did this Saturday morning as Nora Crabtree was ushered up the aisle and seated as the mother of the bride. Creede Franklin stepped toward the altar with his father at his side. Two dozen candles flickered and danced in the room.

This wasn't an ornate wedding ceremony at all. Only the very closest friends and family had been invited to attend. After all the time and struggle for both bride and groom, this was too poignant a celebration to share with many others.

Afternoon sun shone pure and luminous through every window and the heavily polished pews smelled of hickory and Murphy's Oil.

As the music changed to *Minuet in G* and the families turned to watch the processional, one small girl pranced proudly up the walkway. She wore black patent-leather shoes, a dress with a black velvet bodice and a skirt with rows and rows of ruffled lace. Her dark curly hair, which she loved wearing short and tousled now, was crowned with a wreath of baby's breath. In her hand she clutched a bouquet of tiny purple tansy asters, which her mother had picked from Buxton Lance's cow pasture this morning especially for her to carry.

Although Tansy Aster Crabtree was still the right size to be a flower girl, her mother had asked her to be her bridesmaid instead. She was the *only* bridesmaid. And she was the groomsman, too, Creede had told her, because they would all three become a family of their own. Her mama and Creede wanted the three of them to stand in front of the pastor while the bride and groom took vows. It was going to take her a while to get used to her new last name. Franklin. Well, nobody had better call her Crab-Apple Tree at school any more!

When Tansy reached the bottom step and Creede winked down at her, Dolores Kay Jones struck up the *Wedding March* on the church's breathy organ. The small group of well-wishers turned, expectantly waiting for the bride.

Ben lifted his chin in pride and touched his daughter's arm. Yep, she was a little scared. He saw her hands shaking. "You ready?" he mouthed to her.

Tess's violet eyes met her father's, and he ached when he saw the deep happiness there. She looked so beautiful to him, with her hair back to her natural blonde, her eyes rimmed with just a tad of lacy mascara, her cheeks flushed with a healthy glow. "Thank you, Daddy," she mouthed back to him as she wrapped her slender fingers around the crook of his elbow. She gave a slight nod. "Yes, I'm ready."

"I'm so proud of my daughter," he whispered and, this time, his words were loud enough for people to hear.

"I love you so much," she mouthed back. And with that, he stepped forward to escort her toward Creede and Tansy.

Once her daughter had reached the front of the sanctuary and the onlookers had been seated, Nora glanced up at the stained-glass window positioned directly over Pete Franklin's head. For one quiet minute, she observed the glass that had not been destroyed in the tornado and that had glowed with mysterious light that one Sunday years ago. It didn't appear unusual or mysterious or miraculous now. It remained, each pane of color as true as a jewel, the sunshine rich and even and true behind it.

As Tess and Ben had come up the aisle, Nora's Bible sat open across her knees. Oh, how she loved this book now! Even the weight of it in her hands felt delicious. All morning, the morning of Tess's wedding day, one word had been pouring into her soul. *Light.*

Light.

Earlier, she had looked in the concordance for all the verses in the Bible that contained the word *light*. There were so many to pick from, it might have taken a month to read them all. But she had found this one in Ephesians almost immediately. Here was her verse, right in front of her on this day, the pages spread and balanced against her knee.

She hadn't brought her reading glasses. Who wanted to carry glasses in the little evening purse she'd bought for Tess's wedding?! But if she kept the words at a distance, she could read them.

"For you were once darkness, but now you are light in the Lord . . . find out what pleases the Lord . . . everything exposed by the light becomes visible. This is why it is said: Wake up, O sleeper, rise from the dead, and Christ will shine on you."

She read it twice, three times. *Oh, Father. Thank You for my new life with my daughter. Thank You for all that You've given us.*

As Nora embraced the joy that God wanted to give her, there was a sense of discovery in her heart that felt almost sacred with intensity.

Thank You for shining on us.

At the front of the church, Tess Crabtree extended her left hand to Creede Franklin. Pete Franklin dug in his pocket and handed his son a gold wedding band. Creede reached toward the little girl who stood beside their knees and looked a question at her. She nodded her head, *yes.* And all the dark curls on her head bobbed. Only then did Creede slide the ring on Tess's finger. He lifted the veil and her eyes rose to meet his. And for that second, that moment before they kissed, the expectancy on Tess's face was visible to everyone.

There she stood amidst everyone she loved, confident and beautiful and assured. Nora caught her breath at this amazing sight of her child, blessed, welcomed. How she rejoiced in miracles. And outside the stained-glass window, to the south in the city of Dallas, the neon Pegasus might have bloomed into movement and life and winged its way heavenward amid the sound of angel song.

Author's Note

———— ✥ ————

S o many of the books I have written have been based on true stories and true struggles in a Christian woman's life. *A Rose By The Door, A Morning Like This,* and *When You Believe* were all written, researched, and documented through the struggles of friends and family.

If I Had You is my own story.

Last year in church, a woman stood up and began inviting anyone who had had an abortion to a Bible study called "Healing Hearts." I had listened to this invitation many times before. My reasons for ignoring it had always been the same: "I'm already there. I know Christ died to wipe away my sin. Of course, I'm forgiven."

But on this day, Jesus wouldn't let me turn away.

The room grew huge. The one woman speaking became a tiny speck in a sea of heads. Light poured into the windows behind her and her silhouette was like a pinprick against it. I couldn't see her face. I could only feel my own heart growing so heavy that I couldn't breathe. Minutes later, I realized that my face was wet, and that I had been crying.

When I whispered to Jack, my husband, that I was thinking

about doing the study, he said, "Maybe you ought to leave that well behind you."

"I know," I answered. "I was thinking that, too."

It is easy to keep things like this quiet, even to ourselves. We come to a point where we convince ourselves that it happened in another life, and that it doesn't affect who we are today. But in a confidential group with five precious Christian sisters, we began to examine the Father's view of the choices we'd made in our lives, and the Father's view of us.

To look at the depth of what you have done, to see the detestable for what it is, is to stare face-to-face into the presence of a Holy God. When Isaiah cried out, "I am a man of unclean lips living among a people of unclean lips," he was faced with the same thing. I had lived with that part of my life locked away in pride. I had rationalized and justified. Over and over again I had put my reputation, my relationships, and my fear ahead of the Father's heart.

In my own life, living forgiven in Christ, I thought I had come through my abortion unscathed, that God had healed me, and that I had forgiven myself. When I asked Him to show me anything in my life that I hadn't seen, He began to reveal an entire list.

While my fictional character, Nora, channeled her feelings into deep shame when she saw her daughter, my feelings came out in other places altogether. Some mornings when I would drive my children to school, I felt so depressed that it seemed like a camera-filter of darkness covered the sky and my children's faces and the neighborhood around me.

When I was in high school, I loved to fly. But something happened while I was in college. By the time I married Jack, my nightmares about planes crashing made it difficult to sleep, never mind traveling. Throught the next twenty-five years, talking to friends and counselors in our church, no one could explain why these dreams haunted me. Last winter, I prayed the same prayer that Nora prays in this book. *Lord, help me. I don't completely understand my heart. Help me see this through Your eyes so that I might be broken in spirit before you. Show me the truth about my abortion in Your name.*

Within minutes of praying, my Father began to show me. I kept trying to grasp God's forgiveness and mercy. But my human heart couldn't quite get there. Every time I set foot on a plane, something hidden, something that I didn't even know was there, whispered that I deserved to die.

Although it wasn't required in the Bible study, I felt the Lord asking me to be honest with both of my teenaged children about my abortion. Avery, my fourteen-year-old daughter, was gentle in her forgiveness. Eighteen-year-old Jeff grew quiet and asked me more questions than I had ever allowed myself to ask. Did I know whether it was a boy or girl? How far along was I? Did I have any idea what it had looked like, the color of its hair?

We held onto each other and cried.

Jesus wanted every part of me, even the part I was hiding from myself.

We think sometimes that the longer we wrestle with something that we're somehow helping God in a process. But repentance isn't about emotion, it's about a decision. We can't go back to innocence, but we can go to the cross. That's the only way we can walk away clean before God.

If current trends continue, statistics show that 43 percent of women will have had an abortion in their lifetimes.* Sue

*Study conducted by *U.S. News and World Report*

Liljenberg of Healing Hearts Ministries believes that number could go higher. I share with you this story from the depths of the Father's love and forgiveness, not to jump on the bandwagon with a hot issue, but to tell you of the mercy and grace and healing that the Father poured out on me at a time in my life when I didn't know I needed it. When I lift my hands to my Father in praise, I lift them to a God who has plucked me out of the depths. Understanding His love for you can change your dry paint-by-numbers Christianity into a masterpiece. I have learned that the deeper a woman is able to go in her honesty to her heavenly Father, the more realistically she is able to view her own humanity, that's when she can begin to understand what Jesus did for her on the cross, and rejoice. I dance before Him in joy, and you can, too. How powerful and how gentle is our loving, seeking, healing, passionate God!

Your heavenly Father wants to have you completely. It is my prayer that, like Nora, you will ask the Father to show you the truths in your heart regarding your abortion, that He would enable you to see this through His eyes. If you cry out to him, His love will overpower you and show you where He still wants to heal you.

The Master's mercy knows no end. It dawns fresh and new and strong, every morning.

Deborah Bedford
August 2004

I love hearing from my readers:
P.O. Box 9175
Jackson Hole, Wyoming 83001

HEALING HEARTS MINISTRIES

IF YOU OR SOMEONE YOU KNOW has been touched by post-abortion trauma, the Father can use a Bible study support group such as this one to break through in your life.

Healing Hearts offers intimate ten-week-long studies in your community, led by trained Christians who have experienced abortion themselves. If you are a man touched by abortion, there is a study for you, too. If you can't find a group meeting close by, you can take the study on-line with a one-on-one counselor.

For more information, visit www.healinghearts.org, e-mail info@healinghearts.org, write P.O. Box 7890, Bonney Lake, WA 98390-0966, or phone 1-888-792-8282.

Directions for making
Nora Crabtree's baby blankets

BEGIN WITH ONE YARD of 45" cotton flannel of your choice.
If the fabric is not already prewashed and preshrunk, launder
and press it.

Turn the flannel under 1/8" on all sides and hemstitch.

Select a cotton crochet thread #10, in a color that accents or
blends with the flannel. A variegated color is fun!

Using a #5 steel crochet hook, finish off the edges of the
blanket with a large shell trim, chain 3, skip one loop, double
crochet, chain two, repeat. Do this along all four edges.

༺༅༃

THE FLANNEL RECEIVING BLANKETS used in this story were first
sewn for my babies by my mother-in-law, Mollie Lou Bedford.
How excited she would be to know that I have used her idea as
a part of this book! During the writing of this story, our family
has lost our precious Mollie. In honor of her, I have included
her instructions for those of you who enjoy crocheting. I hope
you will make many blankets for babies you love. You could
even make these your ministry to a crisis pregnancy center or a
hospital that serves young or at-risk pregnant women in your
area.

READING GUIDE

1) The author starts this book with Scripture from 1 Kings 3: 22–27. Why do you think she chose to introduce this story with this particular passage?

2) In Chapter 3 Nora Crabtree is in church and the light shining through Jesus' cloak turns the floor and her pastor's head red. It seems impossible, but Nora sees her hands glowing red, too. Why do you think this is significant?

3) Do you think the situation in the book when Nora argues with herself about Tess—about not wanting her to have a baby—is realistic? Why or why not? Do you think there are women around you, even yourself, who might have the same thoughts?

4) In Chapter 5 the author uses a story of a long-ago Christmas pageant to describe the beginnings of the relationship between Tess Crabtree and Creede Franklin. What symbolism can you find in this scene? Do you think there is a deeper meaning when Paige Lee Wort says, "Sheep aren't supposed to come this close" during the pageant? Why do you think the author wrote a scene depicting one of the main characters trying to get close to the baby in the manger? Given the theme of *If I Had You,* why do you think it is important that Tess was trying to get close to something that belonged to her?

5) In Chapter 8 Cootie tells Jimmy Ray that Tess confided in him about her mother. She told him, "Every time I catch my mother looking at me, I see *guilt* in my mother's face."

Do you think Tess is the cause of that guilt? Why or why not? Cootie's next statement is this: "You know how it is. People see that you expect the worst out of them and, eventually, they'll give it to you." Do you think Cootie's statement is true about how humans see things? How is the heavenly Father's view of us different from Tess and Cootie's?

6) In Chapter 14 Nora remembers the story from Luke 7:11–16 about Jesus meeting a woman at the town gate of Nain. Nora knows that when the Lord meets us in our sorrow and confusion, he doesn't condemn us for our mourning. Instead, he feels deep compassion for us. Can you find the verse in this Scripture that tells her this? Why do you think it is significant/symbolic that this incident happened at the town gate?

7) In Chapter 18 Nora Crabtree becomes angry when she finds out her church is celebrating Anti-Abortion Sunday by filling the churchyard with small white crosses. Why do you suppose she responds the way she does? Do you agree with her response? Why? If you were to do something different, what would it be?

8) In Chapter 20 Ben Crabtree thinks, *Can it be this way? That a person doesn't know what he's living with until he leaves it behind?* He has this thought because he's felt his heart lightened by flying with Creede. Do you think this thought is significant to any other part of the story? Why or why not?

9) By the end of the book, Nora comes to understand that her fears and her relationships with others include symptoms of post-abortion trauma. Can you name what those symptoms are with Tansy? With Tess? With Ben?

10) *If I Had You* is an unusual title for a book about mother/child relationships and abortion. Why do you suppose the author chose to name this story with this title? Name the characters' lives that might have been different if they'd "had" each other.